For the women who are isolated by fear
and thought this could never happen to them.

TABLE OF CONTENTS

ACKNOWLEDGEMENTS

Thank you to my wonderful support network, the women (and men) who created the net that caught me when I was falling.

Thank you, Jess and Michael, for the countless phone calls and pep-talks. Thank you for reminding what was real when I lost hold of reality. Thank you for being my tether to shore when I was almost lost at sea. Jess, I want to be you in my next life. Your kindness and gentleness, and perseverance seem to have no end. I don't know how any heart could be asbig as yours, but I'm grateful that you keep space in it for me. Michael, you are the best of men. I wish there were more of you in the world. Thank you for keeping me grounded over and over again.

Thank you to my book club, my first readers and constant cheerleaders in the writing process. Thank you for accepting my mess and keeping me for your own. I don't know how anyone lives without friends like you. You have been my shelter.
Thank you, Rob, for providing a place for me to hide without judgments and conditions. I might still be trying to leave if it weren't for you.

Gary and Char, thank you for adopting me, providing me with housing, a shoulder for crying, and plenty of wine. I could not ask for better parents. I love you both so much.

Thank you to the ex-pat girls: Rasika, Sharita, and Julia. You helped me find my wildness and were my first teachers on how to have the life I always wanted. Thank you for your support. Wherever you are in the world, I hope it is everything you dreamed.

To Jess, mi alma gemela. You are the ocean to my shore. And everyone else who held my hand, hugged me, smiled at me and made a joke when I was sad. The world is a beautiful place and you reminded me this was true. I hope this book brings you perspective and hope. Thank you for taking me in, in all of the small and big ways.

He's attracted to independent women.
"He's like an exotic bird collector," she said.
"He only wants a woman who is free because
his dream is to put her in a cage."

-Trevor Noah, Born a Crime

PROLOGUE

"Babe?" He says as I climb awkwardly up between his legs to a ledge where I can finally reach to clip my personal anchor system into the bolted hanging station about a 200 feet above the ground.

"In your dreams..." I sass back.

We laugh as I awkwardly pull myself into a position where we can switch sides of the rope to begin his belay for the next pitch.

I love rock climbing. I've been doing it now for several years and I moved to this small town in Central Oregon to be closer to my favorite crag. In Portland, I used to run a business, but I realized a few months ago that wherever you start a business you stay. I wanted to be somewhere closer to these rocks, so I closed up shop and moved out here to start over.

I discovered rock climbing after graduate school, three years ago in 2013. Since then, it has entirely consumed my spare time. When I closed my business, I decided to see if I could change my lifestyle and make outdoor recreation a full-time job. It's not that I don't love being a therapist, I do. It's just that the mountains are always calling. I have always done things "the right way." Go to college, then graduate school, then start a business. Now, I'm ready to discover a wilder lifestyle; be more free. What could life be like if I didn't follow all of the rules?

I was recently hired at the local rock gym (as their oldest employee) teaching climbing. Now I spend all day, every day, around the activity that I love.

That's where I met Ben, my climbing partner on this trip. We have become good friends through a few climbing adventures gone awry. He's quick to lighten any awkward moment with a well-timed joke.

I have been wanting to do this particular climb for a long time, but I am neither strong enough, or brave enough to lead it. Leading is where the climber moves without protection from a fall until his first bolt. Once he clips the first bolt, he then climbs above the rope, clipping each subsequent bolt as he proceeds. This protects his fall from the ground, but is still the most dangerous part of climbing. When you fall above your clip, you will pendulum swing the distance of the rope from the bolt, eventually, and hopefully softly, coming in contact with the rock below. Managing the fear of this fall and trusting your belayer (the person on the other side of the rope below) to create that soft landing is the terrifying. Many climbers can perform several grades above their leading abilities when they have the rope secured above them (on top rope.) I have always found it fascinating how much fear can prevent a person from performing at their actual physical limits. Many climbers do not even consider top-roping to be "real climbing."

Fortunately, Ben is both stronger and braver than I am, so I have the opportunity to experience more routes with him as a partner.

This particular day is perfect. The sun is not too hot, the rock is not too cold. Ben is feeling strong and we are both in good spirits. He sends each pitch of the route with the confidence and strength of practice and honed skill. I follow behind breathlessly admiring the view of the mountains from this crag and the beauty of this vertical dance.

The last pitch starts with a beautiful flake horizontal to the ground. The protection is sketchy at best and there is no way to protect his fall without some risk, but he never once looks down and sends it flawlessly. When it's my turn I indulge the impulse to look down just once. I can afford the extra fear because I'm on top rope and the hard part is over.

I swallow the fear with a breath and then let it out slowly. I love to flirt with my limits. I can feel the soles of my feet ache and my hands start to sweat as I stare at the 300 ft drop below us.

I have always prided myself in my emotional control. I can lead at almost the same level that I top rope. It's something I've worked hard to achieve. It required me to become very familiar and even comfortable with my own fear. I have learned how to sooth myself and how to manage my body's physical fear response. I am confident that in any situation I can remain calm and make the choices necessary to be safe, even when my body is screaming.

I take in another breath and turn back to my climb. At the top, we take some photos; all smiles and laughs. We exchange congratulations and feel rather proud of ourselves. After we safely repel from the top, we head to the pub for a burger and a beer, the perfect end to the perfect adventure.

PART ONE

LEAVING

October 30, 2019

I am standing in the living room turning in circles. Time is doing that
strange thing, where it slows down and speeds up at the same time.
My mind bounces around the room noticing each thing that I own,
everything that matters to me. I have no idea what to put in bags first. I
know that I will need clothes and toiletries, because I will need to go back
to work in a few days. I am practical enough to know what things I will
need to get through tomorrow as if today had never happened, but I do
not know what I will miss, if you deny me entry when I return.

My heart pounds when I think of you coming home to find me like this,
when I think of your retaliation. I have to leave now, quickly, before
you get here. My brain feels like mush, unable to focus on what needs to
be done. I am wading through a marsh, moving in slow motion. I can't
make decisions because there are too many thoughts crowding for entry,
demanding my focus. Focus. I need to focus.

Should I grab my essentials or my sentimentals? I don't even know when
you will be home. Do I have 10 minutes or 10 hours? Instead of focusing
on the present my mind keeps bouncing to what might happen if you
walk through the gate; Images of you yelling and breaking things, or
maybe you'll try to convince me to stay. My resolve is a balancing act,
barely teetering towards action. I might make it if I don't have to leave in

front of you. I have to move! Quickly, pick something up, anything! Put it in the basket.

I text Rob, to see if his invitation for housing still stands. He tells me where he hides his house key because he's out of town. I'm relieved. I don't want anyone to see me like this, not even such a good friend. Then, I walk to the closet and carry an armful of clothing to my car out front.

▲

I gave up trying to sleep around 5AM the next morning. I text you to ask if it would be alright for me to come by and pick up more of my things. It's 6AM now and you respond with an affirmation. When I arrive to the house 15 minutes later, you are still sleeping in your bed. This creates the ominous awareness that you are still drunk and have no knowledge of the messages we just exchanged. I have no doubt you believed I would come home and crawl back into our bed as I had allowed you to do so many times before.

I begin to realize that you aren't even aware that I have left you. It is possible that all my anxiety about leaving last night has not saved me from the scene that will ensue today once you wake up to find me packing. I go to the kitchen to begin packing glassware. I am trying to work quietly because I want to delay any interaction with you. The anxiety of what you will say when you wake up is creeping in on me, but my resolve is more solid today.

I open and close cupboard doors noiselessly. I find and open tote bins in silence. I begin to parcel out what is mine and what is yours, an activity I have done many times over the last three years in my mind during our arguments, like Psyche, cursed to spend her dreams separating impossible piles of mixed grains on the kitchen floor.

When you finally wake up, my fears are confirmed. After a brief moment of disorientation, you understand what is happening. Your voice raises cursing me for the unreasonableness of the hour. Then you are following me throwing things into my boxes, shattering picture frames. I can hear myself pleading and throwing things out of the boxes on to the floor. You get so close to me that I can taste your wrath, raising your hands to me as if you would grab me and throw me from the house. At this gesture, I stare into your eyes unmovable like a stone, because I know you don't dare touch me. It's the only line I can hold and I think you might be just a little afraid of me too right now.

You want me to leave the house so that you can lock me out as I move to the bathroom with a bin. You are crowding me, posturing, yelling, using all of your 6' 2" frame to intimidate me. It's working and I can hear my voice reaching a higher pitch and my pleas become more desperate. You still smell like stale beer and I wonder when you got home. Maybe I should have returned and finished all my packing then.

I call the police from the bathroom floor, crying and pleading with you to stop while collecting my shampoo. The dispatcher on the phone says, "You don't have to respond to him when he's speaking ma'am." I know he is right, but I can't stop. I can't stop pleading with you to stop screaming, stop saying all those terrible things, stop calling me those names, just stop. I just need it all to stop and I am lost in a wave of tears. There is no hope of finding the ground under my feet when I am this far out to sea. I just want to hear the silence for a moment, maybe then I could find the ground.

When the police arrive, I am in the front yard carrying a basket out of the house. I hope the neighbors can't see. The police explain to you that as long as I have property in the house, I am entitled entry. You curse at them and at me, and I finish putting things in the car. When they leave you curse me for calling them. To you, this is the deepest betrayal.

I drive away to the silence and a moment inside my own mind, but I can't stay there long It is more frightening than all your sounds. Besides, there is too much to do. I need to find somewhere to store the airstream. I need to unpack and repack myself to fit in my new, tiny, upstairs bedroom. Doing anything is better than being alone with myself right now.

"Oh no. My papers." I think, remembering my packet of important papers in the gun safe. I need the title for the airstream to reserve a place for it.

My car title, my birth certificate, my passport, and all of my other legal
documents are still in there. I wonder, if maybe, I can sneak in the back
gate and collect this envelope without you noticing.

I open and close the gate as noiselessly as possible and your dog doesn't
even bark. He just walks to me with tail wagging and head low. Just like
me, he is frightened. You stumble out of the back door with a nearly
empty bottle of leftover wedding wine in your hand and I make a mental
note to take the case with me on my next trip. In the meantime, the blood
drains from my face and I take a deep breath.

You can't hardly stand, but you can yell. Leaning on the door frame, you
demand that I pay for my car. You are screaming that you bought it for
me and now I owe you! I know that if I don't comply, you will attack the
things that I left in the house, but I am a terrible liar. I always have been.

You see through my promises and disappear into the garage, suddenly
able to move again quite quickly. You emerge with an ax and begin to
beat the block from underneath the airstream, threatening to collapse it. I
float away from myself. Somehow from outside of myself, I can see that I
am standing in between you and the Airstream. I am screaming now too.
I am calling the police again. I am pleading with dispatch to send them
faster. "Where are they?" I demand, right before they pull into the back
driveway.

I am crying again, washed out to sea and confused. It is as if I don't even
realize that I can leave now with my papers in my hand. I am rooted
to the gravel covering the beautiful little space we designed for our
Airstream AirBnB just a year and a half ago. The weeds that crept into the
yard over the last year of neglect have wrapped themselves around my
ankles and I can't walk out of the gate.
This time there are four officers. The same two from this morning and
two more. It must be shift change, my far away brain notices. I suppose
it is about that time of day. I run out of the gate as they explain to you,
yet again, about my rights. This time you are too drunk to veil your
bile towards them. They are unimpressed with both of us, for different
reasons.
As I stand next to my car hiccupping with sobs, trying to hide my face,

the youngest officer walks towards me with his back to you. He asks softly
if you have ever hit me. "Has he ever caused you physical harm ma'am?
Ever, at all?" Hinting that they would love an excuse to arrest you. Your
behavior is appalling even to strangers. I shake my head, because, again,
I cannot lie. You will get at me in any way you can, except the ones that
might have real consequences. You know how to get as close to the line
as possible without crossing it. Punching things next to me, but never
me. Throwing objects around, but never at me. Threatening to grab me,
hovering your hands just over my shoulders, neck, or arms, but never
taking hold. Shaking with rage, you proved time and time again that you
have more control than you want me to believe.

The officers from this morning ask me why I am here again and why I
haven't left yet. I studder out, "Because he told me I had to stay" growing
smaller with each word. I am ashamed of how pathetic my words sound
as they fall out of my mouth. It's as if I did not realize that I still had a
choice about where I place my body in the world. I climb into my car, my
face hot from tears and shame, and drive away to the new place that is not
my home.

THE MOST BEAUTIFUL

March 2017

The first time I saw you, I was a bartender at a brewery where you were contracting. I was moving kegs from the storage fridge in the back to the front of house for my morning shift. I would walk through the brewery with my dolly empty, squat down and rotate the keg onto the platform, then push it back through the brewhouse to the bar. There I would roll it up into the kegerators setting up the taps for the day. I might make this trip twenty times before we opened making sure that the next shift, which was busier, would be well stocked.

I was friendly with the brewing staff. Honestly, what brewing staff isn't friendly with their cute lady bar-tenders? We would smile and wave and I'd let them watch me walk through, because it was good for my self-esteem while I was so very single.

Then one day, there you were. Tall and baby-faced with brewing boots and a hoody. You wore a flat-billed hat over your brown wavy hair and had a distinctly 90's skater punk style with an attitude to match. Your smile was cynical, if it was on your lips at all. It made an appearance when you were looking at me and I wanted you the moment I saw you.

You were in the cooler room separated from the brewery by a large glass pane. I saw your face and your long, defined arms, strong from lifting kegs under your wet t-shirt. You were sloppy from your work but I didn't mind it. You seemed to defy the very air you were breathing, almost arrogant. I couldn't look directly at you; I was too shy. Your eyes were intense, so I let my hair fall between us, hiding my face, as I shuffled past to finish my chore.

You came out of the fridge to watch me walk back, later saying, "I had to make sure the front was as good as the back." When you told this story, you would recall that you were surprised by my face, saying "It wasn't what I expected to see". You could never describe what you had expected to find, but I was not it. "You were the most beautiful woman I had ever seen" was all you could say about that day.

I felt my stomach in my throat any time you walked into the bar in those days. You were the first man to have that effect on me in years. You came in for a beer every afternoon when you finished your shift, but I was so shy around you that we hardly spoke. You later accused me of being cold. We would laugh at how out of character this was for me.

I asked the other girls about you, "Oh yeah, everyone likes Hank." They would say with a roll of their eyes. You were so pretty, everyone wanted you. I didn't think I would ever have your attention.

▲

You left for Costa Rica shortly after that and it would be months before I saw you again. I would ask around about you to learn that you had recently broken-up with your long-time partner and were struggling to move on. It helped explain why you lingered, but never made an effort to connect with me.

After you came back from the jungle, you started to spend more time in the bar on your lunch breaks. You found little reasons to come up front and ask me for things during work. One day, you left me your card, asking me to text you when a certain shipment of grain arrived. I held that shiny piece of cardstock in my hand, your full name scrawled across the top, underlined by your title, Head Brewer. I debated the meaning of this gesture. Did it mean you liked me too? Did it mean you wanted my number? "No," I told myself. "I am sure he is just trying to make sure the grain doesn't get wet from the rain." I put it down, convincing myself of your disinterest.

The other brewers arrived later that day and confirmed the shipment with you. I asked them about it and they looked at me from the side. Of course, they had contacted you. There was no need to send you a message anymore and I did not want to make a fool of myself. So, I tossed your card in the trash to keep myself from using it for unprofessional reasons. Even then, I did not trust myself. I sighed with disappointment and went back to bar to find something to clean on my suddenly, empty morning shift.

A few days later, you came in for beers after your shift as usual. You sat at the edge of the bar with your IPA and talked with the other regulars. I withdrew from the usual crowd to the other side, growing shy as I always did around you.

When you stood to leave, you announced across the bar, ending the various conversations of the group, "You didn't text me the other day about the grain."

"Oh. Yeah. The other brewers showed up and told me they had communicated with you and so I figured you didn't need me to," I replied.

"That's definitely the only reason I gave you my card." You said coyly, picking up your coat and walking out the door.

I died a little in that moment, standing there stunned in front of everyone, all pretending not to listen. I had been not so secretly pining for you for months and you finally made a pass at me and I missed it.
"What an idiot!" I swore at myself internally. Then I pouted my way back to the regulars and invited them to give an opinion.

They were not impressed. "If he's interested in you, he can ask you for your number like a grown ass man!" They demanded. Like a group of fathers, they were all invested in my happiness and well-being.

Despite their advice, I sulked for the rest of the day and plotted how to be more direct the next time I saw you.

▲

A few weeks later your best friend's band was playing at the bar on a Friday night. I was working the evening shift as the first to be cut, meaning that I might have time to join you once I was off. I knew you would be there and I planned how I would approach you over and over again in preparation for that night.

I saw you walk in and breathed a sigh of relief, a new chance. After my shift ended, I went out to the crowd to linger close by, and I was not disappointed. We danced and laughed. I teased you about your attempt to get my number without asking and told you to put on your big boy pants and ask me out like a grown up. Then you turned to face me directly, almost a little startled, pulled your phone out of your pocket, and extended it in your hands as if they were a silver platter asking me to input my number. I blushed and you noticed how I did not capitalize my name. I never do. Then, we danced and laughed the rest of the night until I decided I had better head home.

I slipped away from the party to collect my things from behind the bar and exit out the back, but you noticed and followed me. "Where are you going?" You asked, pouting a little.

"I have to go home to my dog." I smiled at you. "Would you like to walk me out?"

You scrambled to close your tab and followed me to my car. When I turned to say good-bye you slowly and gently placed your hand on my waist and pulled me into a kiss. A perfect, sweet, delicious kiss. A kiss that lasted hours and was still too short. Gently you leaned into me pressing me up against my car, pulling me tighter with your strong arms, and I lost myself in your mouth. The best first kiss ever.

When you finally pulled away, I offered you a ride home, because I knew

how many beers I had served you that evening. You declined thinking
I was trying to go to bed with you. I wouldn't have ruined the romance
of that kiss for any one-night stand, but I didn't expect you to know that
about me yet. I held my breath as you walked away.

▲

Three weeks later, I had not seen or heard from you. I was floored. I
asked everyone. Where were you? You knew my schedule. You were here
with me every day before that party. What happened? Why hadn't you
called?

I had all but given up when you came into work that day. You were
clearly avoiding me, but I would not have it any longer.

I corner you outside the brewery at the end of my shift, "Why haven't
you called me? It's OK if you're not interested in me. I'm just confused,
because sometimes it seems like you do."

" I don't have your number." You said innocently.

"What?! Yes, you do!" I grab your phone from your hand and show you
my number in your own contacts list. Were you being coy or did you
really forget that I gave you my number? I can't tell.

"Oh. Fine! Ok then! You want to go on a date? I'll take you on a date!"
You practically throw your hand ups in resignation.

"Well, that's exactly how every girl wants to be asked out." I reply with
my eyebrows practically in my hairline.

You make some half-hearted attempts at smoothing it over and we settle
on a date in a few days and a nice restaurant not far from here. I walk
back inside practically floating and already planning my outfit. The girls
at the bar are impressed by your restaurant choice but I am too new to
town to know what a date at this place indicates. All I know is that I have
been waiting for this for 6 months and the anticipation is driving me mad.

Two days later I am so nervous I don't think I'll be able to eat anything. The butterflies have turned in to birds of prey and I'm afraid I won't be able to contain them. I am two minutes late after looking for parking and the first thing you say to me when I walk in is, "You're punctual." I can't tell if you are being facetious or not, but I set aside my hesitancy and order a glass of wine.

The waitress is asking if we want another round when I finally confess that I'm so nervous I don't think I can eat. You order us a Mezza Platter and another round laughing at me. I pick at a carrot as I work my way through my second glass of wine and the thousands of questions you are throwing at me. This is not how I had imagined this going. You are so intense and your questions are everything you should never ask on a first date. You started with religion and politics and then graduated to values and family.

I am used to defensive and combative people, so I put on my best therapist skills and answer your questions thoughtfully and openly, but my own first date anxiety only grows. I had thought we would laugh and flirt and maybe talk about these things sometime over the next few dates. Now, I'm not sure if there will be any more dates. I can tell that you like my answers, but I'm not having fun and we are not laughing. I have been waiting for this date so long, that I consider giving you a second one just to be sure that you are not any fun and that this is not just your anxiety talking.

When we leave the restaurant, you seem to be in increasingly good spirits. You even ask me if I would like to get a cocktail next door. I say yes because you are still the most beautiful man I have ever been on a date with and the sexual tension between us is palpable. I have been waiting for your attention for months and now that I have it, I won't be that quick to dismiss you. At this place, we begin to laugh a little. You seem to know everyone in town and this place is no exception. I am nervous about being seen with you in public on a first date, but you do not seem shy. Perhaps you're even showing off a little.

After one more cocktail, you are walking me to my car again, and this time when we get there you land one gentle kiss on my mouth before

turning and walking away. I am confounded and on my drive home,
I try to pull apart my feelings about you, analyzing each as if up for
negotiation. Would I like to do that again? It was an intense experience
and I generally prefer more laughter and playfulness, but I am not even in
my driveway before my phone notifies me that you would like to see me
again. I stop asking myself questions and confirm with you that I'd also
like that.

▲

The following weekend you are supposed to be on a ski hut trip and out
of cell service. I don't expect to hear from you until sometime next week.
So, when you stumble into my bar on Sunday with your roommate's
girlfriend, Rebecca, I am surprised to see you.

You start to tell me how the batch of beer you brewed last week
unexpectedly crashed over the weekend, something about the glycol unit
and temperatures and you might have to dump the entire thing. You are
clearly distressed and this is why you didn't go on your ski trip. I bring
you a beer on the house and you excuse yourself to the bathroom.

Rebecca leans in and I like her immediately. She says, "You know he
really likes you right?"

"Oh! Really? I wasn't sure." I reply, flattered and relieved.

"Yeah, he just has difficulty saying these kinds of things." She qualifies for
you.

When you return, you finish your beer and head home, to my
disappointment. I was hoping you would close the bar down with me on
this slow Sunday night, but instead, you invite me to come over when my
shift ends.

I close the bar at record speed that evening and drive to your house
discovering that it is only a few blocks away. You have two roommates,
Buck and Bo. Buck is dating Rebecca who I have already met. When I

arrive tonight, Bo, opens the door and invites me inside. He tells me that you are in your room, pointing through the house to the door off the kitchen. When I knock, there is no answer. So, I knock again and wait. Finally, I push it open a crack and whisper your name into the partially lit room. The room is tiny and it doesn't take long to identify your unconscious body face pressed sideways into the pillow. You are sleeping, and so damn cute.

I push the door open and step inside, hesitating for moment. Should I wake you or just leave now? The choice leaves me feeling awkward and uncomfortable. Who invites you over and passes out before you arrive? I decide that I should at least nudge you. I sit on the side of the bed and gently brush your arm until you begin to stir. I am in love with you already, like a choice I didn't make. Like gravity, I can feel it pulling me. It is too late. I can't fight it anyway, and now I am not even trying.

▲

We spend that night in bed, first yours and then mine, well into the next day. We don't have sex, you just touch me like you are exploring a woman's body with the curiosity of first time, but without the clumsiness of inexperienced hands. You are memorizing me.

All night we wake up, touching until I am almost mad, then falling back to sleep in each other's arms. You teach me new ways to have orgasms, focusing on my pleasure like a personal mission. I learn to relax into and enjoy what you are giving me, letting go of the idea that my sexuality was ever about anyone but me. We roll between the sheets with a comfort outside of our familiarity. By the time we are hungry and have to get up, I am yours.

"I think I am in love with you." You say as you squeeze into the tiny dinette in my Airstream. You take the glass of wine in your hand and look at the fancy cheese plate spread I set out in my less than fancy life. I laugh at you because it is too soon for you to say that, but I hear my own heart jump in response.

KIDS

March 2017

The morning after our first night together, you flop down on my bed and inform me that you'll never get married or have kids. I stop preparing breakfast and look up at you. With a calm and firm voice, I say, "Oh. Well, we probably should not date then, because I want those things."

You stammer and try to take your careless words back, saying that you could probably be talked into marriage, but the 'kid thing' would be hard for you. You explain that you have never dated a woman who wanted kids before and it is against your environmental values to reproduce. You would have to think long and hard about it, but you wanted to keep dating me.

I shrug my shoulders and decide that I won't attempt to convince you of anything. This is your debate with yourself and you will need to spend some time deciding what you want. I say instead, that I am thirty now and don't have years to waste on someone who will not make up their mind. That would push me past my biological clock. So, I will give you two years to figure out what you want and if you are open to a having family.

You blink back at me like you have never seen the kind of creature that is standing in front of you before and then break into your most charming smile, pull me onto the bed next to you, smothering me in kisses. You will take whatever years I will give you.

Over the next few months this conversation resurfaces. You try to debate with me the dying planet and why humans are a plague. I do not deny these things, because we have the same opinions and values around the environment. I can see your perspective and do not disagree. I just want a baby; not now, but eventually.

You call your father one afternoon and relay the conversation to me over dinner. "I asked him how he decided to have kids with mom."

You have an older half-sister that your father adopted and raised as his own. He didn't want any more children, and was content with his daughter, but your mother pushed for more.

"We decided to make lists. She would write all of the reasons to have one and I would write all of the reasons not to, then we planned to sit down and exchange them. I went through each of my reasons, two pages long. When she read me her list, it simply said, 'You'll see.' The debate ended there and parenting has been the best thing in my life" he said.

I knew that he had won the debate for me with that story. You beamed with pride at your father's words. They were powerful in many ways that day. You were not ready to admit it yet, but I knew. I was also impressed by how thoughtful you had been. I was impressed that you would call and ask your father for advice, and that you were reflecting conscientiously on this big debate. I loved hearing about how you worked through this for yourself and was impressed by how you shared it with me. I was proud of you too.

▲

Eventually you settled the debate by telling me that you wanted me enough to give me anything and you would give me children if it meant you could keep me. In Costa Rica, you would be beg me to take my IUD out so we could start trying. I wondered then if it was because you felt me slipping away and thought that if I had your child, I would be more motivated to stay. I will never know, because we never had that child.

"R" RATED OUTDOOR ADS

Spring turns to Summer 2017

We have only been dating a few weeks, but you are excited to show me all your favorite places in the area. You have been living in this town for eight years and I have only been here for one. We spend our time together day-dreaming about all the adventures we will go on despite your busy work schedule. This weekend you manage a couple days off in a row and choose a lake without a trail. I am eager to prove to you that I can keep up and you are eager to share this place with me.

You treat these secret lakes like they are sacred ground, guarding them jealously, in the same ways you guard me jealously. There is something romantic about your possessiveness, of the land and of me. There is something almost pagan in your worship of us both. It is as if I am just an extension of this sacred place to you. It's my land. I was born here. I was raised in these wild places, and by having me, you somehow consecrate the earth that drew you here.

I listened to your stories about the first time you drove through Oregon. I watched the look in your eyes while you talked about the first time you saw the openness of this landscape. The majesty of the mountains captured your wildish nature and brought something out of your soul that you did not know was dormant within you. That part of my soul has never been dormant, because this place is my home. I have no idea

what it's like to live in urban sprawl amongst hills that claim to be peaks.
I feel completely native to these lands, as if the trees and rocks and vast
landscapes are my backyard, my birthright. You look at me the same way
you look at these places, with lust and awe. You only want to keep them
wild.

We pack up and head out in the early morning, starting with a good
pace up the trail. When we reach a grove of trees, you slow and begin
to look around for signs of a walking trail to the lake. After wondering
about a bit, you decide the season is too early for this tiny footpath and
we begin bush whacking. It is early season in the mountains and we are
no strangers to the patchy snow still lingering from winter. We are both
hiking in sandals, but this does not slow us when passing over the patches
still lingering in the darker parts of the forest. Once I even slip and fall.
Laughing together at my clumsiness, we are still drunk on love drugs.

Eventually we reach the lake and begin to scout a camp site. There is no
one else here and we find a nice dry beach on the far side with a waterfall
to our backs and the lake at our toes. The dogs are skipping in and out of
snow and water, muddy messes of beasts, thrilled at their freedom, just
like us.

We pitch our tent and wander up the hill to see the falls. There is so
much water this time of year while everything is melting. The area is
lush and fertile, like our new love. You catch me in your arms as I try to
run from the spray of the falls, but I win and you follow me down the hill
just enough to find a dry-ish log for lingering. We are alone in a beautiful
place with no one to catch us in our scandal, so you begin kissing me with
strength, undressing me in this sacred place.

Romance quickly turns to comedy as you discover the long underwear I
am wearing as my base layer. It wraps me completely from neck to ankle
in one solid cloth, like a chastity belt given to me by the impending cold.
After rolling me this way and that, while I laugh at your conundrum,
you are finally delighted when you discover the butt-zipper on the back,
surely not designed for your purposes. Laughing hard between our lusty
breaths, we joke about "R" rated outdoor gear ads, imagining all the places
we might get away with scandals out here in these woods, bending me

over logs and hot nights inside tents on top of snow.

Later we make our way back down to the shore and I take a picture of
you cuddling my dog, Nellie, and I hold this memory in my heart, as you
wander off to fly fish in your own private paradise.

▲

You are so eager to share with me your knowledge of these remote places.
You tell me stories about how you drove from your hometown in rural
Pennsylvania with your college girlfriend back to her hometown in
Eugene when her father needed help on his farm. You tell me about the
first time you read Ken Keasy's <u>Sometimes a Great Notion</u>, your favorite
book. I watch your eyes while you describe the first time you saw this
land, stretched out before you without evidence of humanity in sight. You
had never seen anything like it before and you knew you would never go
home again. It was not long before you moved here with her, to this town
and then never left. What was supposed to be a year for you has become
almost a decade.

With our mutual wanderlust driving us, we choose another hidden lake,
again without a trail, underneath a mountain that I have been wanting to
climb. We trek together, finding the lake through some real trail-blazing.
You were encouraged with my outdoor savviness last time and are ready
to see just how far we can push the limits together.

When we reach the lake, tucked in the nook of the mountain, I strip
naked and spend the day sunbathing on my sleeping mat with a book and
a cider. You fish on the other side, because again we have the shore all to
ourselves. It's not long until you give up your fishing in light of distraction
and come to lay naked beside me in the sun. When we are well roasted
and too warm to tolerate the mid-day sun any longer, we wade out into
the frigid water, swimming to a sun-soaked rock on the opposite side of
the lake where you pin me again.

Early in the next morning, I get up early for my long trek up to the
summit, leaving you to fish alone in the quiet, the way you told me you

like it. When we meet later at the trailhead neither of us have completed our individual quests. We reflect in our quiet time alone and I am reminded that I do not like climbing alone and you are reminded that you do not like to fish with someone else waiting.

Passively, outside of conscious thought, we silently make the agreement not to do these things anymore. You slowly give up fishing to sunbath with me and I slowly give up climbing to lay by lakes where you think you might fish.

I try to bring books and wear clothes to keep from distracting you. You offer to learn to climb with me, but these things do not alter our magnetic inability to untangle ourselves. It is the beginning of becoming one and the resentment that followed. It was so satisfying at first, led to a rot in the soul of our relationships that became cancerous. Neither of us strong enough to resist the pull to let go of everything else for the sake of clinging to one another.

I SHOULD HAVE LET YOU LEAVE

June 2017

"I don't know what happened Chris." I finish another cider. In a town of beer drinkers, I have to find something palatable when we end up at a brewery. "He just vanished. One day he is asking me to stop by his brewery on my way into work every day and the next he is completely gone. I tried to text and call. I even stopped by at our usual time and his boss gave me some weird sideways look like I was stalking him, as if he doesn't always ask me to come by. Fucking asshole. I'm over it. Even if he does call me now, I'm done. I mean, who the fuck acts that way anyhow?! We've been together every day since March and he doesn't have the decency to tell me it's over? Just complete radio silence. I spent all day in a panic, but now I am just pissed. Fuck that guy. I mean it! If he calls, I am not taking him back."

"Well, cheers to that!" Chris is all too happy to hate you.

"Oh, shut up Chris. I know you're dying to say it."

"As much as I love to give you shit, I would never say 'I told you so.' I really am sorry he treated you that way. You deserve so much better... but maybe, I did kind of tell you he was an asshole from the start."
"Well, that's a little pot- kettle don't you think?" I reach over abusively and he dodges me.

After another round, I am sufficiently inebriated and should not drive.
I take myself and Nellie home to our little airstream in the meadow. It's
20 minutes outside of town up a winding forest service road and I could
probably make the drive in my sleep. It's a good thing too, because I am
not making great choices tonight.

Nellie and I crawl between the sheets and bury ourselves in my down
comforter because these mountain nights are still chilly even in June. We
fall asleep easily aided by the alcohol.

▲

It is still very dark, so it must be early, but I hear your voice.

"Grace, please just let me come to bed. Please. I'm so sorry. Can we talk in
the morning? Can I please just come to bed now?"

I am groggy and hardly know what's happening, too groggy to remember
that I am angry. You take off your shoes and pants and crawl between my
sheets, wrapping yourself around me like a vice. Then we drift back to
sleep together.

▲

In the morning, I remember all my wrath from the day before. I am
awake and on my elbows with eyes boring into the side of your sleepy
face as you slowly come to back to consciousness.

"Ok just give me one second to wake up," you mutter.

I do not move, or answer you. This seems to help you wake up faster.
Maybe it's the adrenaline we both now have, mine a product of anger and
yours a product of anxiety. Somehow we are both very articulate for two
hung over fools.

You launch into an explanation of how you got anxious and started having doubts about us. You told your boss and co-workers, that you broke up with me. Then you went out drinking with your friends. At some point you found yourself at Charlie's house drinking beer on his porch. Charlie is going through a divorce. It has been messy and sad to watch because he is so likable. He is charming and funny. He is self-reflective and seems like he can see into your soul when you are talking with him. Charlie is also completely unable to hold a job and spends all his time with people ten years younger than him. I can understand why his wife is leaving, even if I do adore him. He's a romantic that will never grow up and that is why his marriage is ending.

On Charlie's porch, you spilt all your secret fears and anxieties about marriage, divorce, and me. You asked him what he did wrong and what he would do differently. You explained to him that you have not spoken to me in three days and plan to end our relationship. Charlie explained that he wishes he had tried harder, been a better husband, and worked on things.

At his urging, you got in your truck and drove up my forest service road at 1 AM, more inebriated than was safe, to find my little silver bullet in the woods. Remembering the revolver, you gave to me to keep next to my pillow, you approached gingerly, with caution. First calling out to me, then knocking on the door. Three times you knocked and I did not respond. So, you carefully opened the door, to sit on the edge of my bed, pleading with me.

Nellie did not move or make a sound, and neither did I. Eventually, I lifted the edge of the covers to let you slip in, allowing a morning congress to decide our fate.

▲

"Can I have my gun back?" You asked me. "It's obviously useless if you didn't even hear me drive up, knock, and let myself in."

"I told you that when you gave it to me. I don't have it in me to use it anyway. Go ahead and take it home. It would be good to not have to exchange it with you the next time you decide to leave me." I stab back, still barely quelled.

I grab the long silver barrel from within arm's reach. This is your prettiest gun, you said when you asked me to keep it here. You wanted me to have a beautiful lady's gun. It is also the largest handgun you own. Revolvers are ostentatious. The technology for hand guns has changed so much that these are just showy now. They make a statement, but there is no reason they need to be this size anymore.

It's not loaded. I would not let you put bullets in it. I grew up around functional guns, but we never kept them in the house. I never liked having it so close to me. Guns were for working, killing rabbits and other vermin that threaten the crops and farm, but not people. My family did not grow up with that kind of fear. We were taught hospitality, to share. We only protect our things with door locks and our faith in humanity, and mostly this works.

"You don't have to use it, you know. If someone is harassing you, often they just have to see it. Or at worse, fire it to the side, and that's usually enough. You don't have to aim at them;" You said when I told you I could never shoot anyone, for any reason. "I would just feel safer if you had it out here with you. You are so far away and there is no lock on your door."

I do not feel unsafe out here in the woods. I know that the biggest threat to me is other people and this little meadow is hidden and remote. No one comes out here and outdoors people are generally happy to leave you alone because they want to be left alone too. I promised myself I wouldn't believe those narratives about women being unsafe in the world a long time ago, but I agreed to take the revolver anyway, to make you feel safer about me.

Now that you see how useless it would be to me, I am happy to return it. So, lifting it by its long silver barrel, I hand it back to you feeling smug, for more than one reason. You take the handle in your hand, and it fits in your palm in a way it never would in my small hands. I haven't yet decided if I will forgive you.

We spend the next four hours in bed, mostly with me ranting about how your behavior was unacceptable and I would never allow you to treat me that way again. I explain to you that you can have all the space you need whenever you need it, you simply need to communicate that you are taking it, instead of disappearing and avoiding. You make promises and apologies, but I am still so angry, so hurt. You humiliated me in front of your co-workers and friends, acting as if I was come crazed, jealous stalker. You spun a story about me to hide your own ineptitude with communication and boundaries. You made me look foolish to cover your own mistakes.

Eventually, your begging wears me down and my anger gives way to sadness. We miss our backpacking trip and my sadness grows to include the loss of the weekend and the happiness we could have shared this morning. I am sad that we are having this conversation and that I have wasted days on these feelings. I am sad that this was so all so avoidable. I am exhausted with the frustration that you did not trust me to care about your needs enough to tell me what you wanted.

It is my sadness that you find most intolerable. No amount of apologies will give me those few days back or make these feelings vanish immediately. I know this and accept it, but you find it hard to cope with this truth.

▲

Three years later, when I look around the playa at my scattered dreams, I remember this and know that I should not have taken you back that morning. I should not have let you crawl back into my bed and beg for forgiveness. I should have told you that once a line is crossed it cannot be uncrossed. I should have said that some behaviors are reflections of larger problems deeply laying at our core. I had seen yours, and the sadness at what I found there was overwhelming.

You would leave me time and time again, because you could not ask for what you needed. You would punish me for your unmet needs and I would try everything in my power to break this cycle. Eventually my bruised and battered heart would no longer open to you when you came back. The promises you made on that morning would prove to be empty. On this playa, I realize I should have believed your behavior rather than your words, but my own demons kept me from my truest knowing.

OUR FIRST CHRISTMAS

Fall and Winter 2017

It has been nine months now and I can count on one hand the number of nights we have spent apart since that first Sunday in my Airstream last spring. We are talking about me giving up airstream life to come live in your house downtown. It was a smoky nasty September and I am starting to think about moving indoors again anyway.

Buck does not like me, but you and Bo don't really like living with him anyway. You and Bo are always standing in the kitchen and gossiping about how Buck cannot clean up after himself and how annoyed you are with his depressing disposition. I always ask silly questions like, "Why don't you just talk to him about it?" but there are always excuses not to do so. It's like watching an old married couple that just needs something to bitch about together in order to keep their relationship alive.

The analogy reaches further than that I remark to Jess one afternoon. "The way they orient themselves around one another. The way they enable one another's lifestyles. Hank needs someone to worship him, and Bo needs someone to enable his peter-pan refusal to grow up." The familiar cadence in the way you live together makes me wonder if there could ever be any room for me in this house with the two of you. It feels like I am the other woman to your roommate, an after-thought.

Jess does not say much. She stopped saying anything about you months ago. She also stopped visiting after the last time she was here.

When she visited last, it solidified in her mind what kind of man you were. We were camping together at the airstream and after we had all had enough to drink, you stormed off into the woods. I can't recall all the details. I just remember that Jess and I were laughing and for a moment I was focused on her instead of you. You became angry about something I said and then you were gone. I went after you because I was anxious about you leaving me again. When I brought you back, Jess said nothing, but she never came back to visit us again.

I am still pretending that I haven't noticed these changes in the distance between us and prattle on about other things, asking her about her life, a much safer subject.

▲

Eventually you do ask Buck to leave, citing me as an excuse and solidifying his dislike for me permanently. As we make plans for me to move in, I begin to notice the general neglect and uncleanliness of the house and begin attacking various projects long overdue. I'll be damned if I move into a place with dirty floor boards. I start to deep clean the kitchen and rearrange the spices. I sift through the overly full cupboards and stack the unnecessary junk in piles for you and Bo to assess before a goodwill run. You bought this house furnished and it has seen a turnover of girlfriends and roommates in the years since. The collection of useless and unknown junk has amassed into a clutter that threatens my minimalist sensibilities with a panic attack. Also, I am nesting and excited to build our little life together. Bo is not impressed.

Bo begins complaining about me to you, without telling me, a pattern I should have anticipated when I witnessed how you both dealt with Buck. I ask him if everything is alright, and he answers with things like, "Of course!" and smiles. Then later I hear about it from you. You are always taking his side. I feeling that you already have a wife and I am just the mistress moving in grows, and I feel more and more alienated for you.

There is a veiled, awkward agreement that Bo will not pick a fight with me in order to preserve his relationship with you and you won't upend the status quo in order to preserve yours with him. I began to feel the familiar feeling of exclusion that will haunt the rest of our relationship. We begin to argue more and more until the dreams of moving in end with me finding another room to rent across town.

The room I found on the other side of town is an awkward fit. My roommates know you and put limitations on the number of nights you can spend with me there and your dog is not allowed. This forces us to spend as many nights at your house as ever before and the futility of the arrangement becomes increasingly clear. I let the boundaries fall and it's not long until we are discussing my moving in again.

You begin to resent me for "not having my own friends" and for trying to be close to yours. You resent that my relationship with your peers challenges them in the same ways that attracted you to me. I was different than any one you had met before. You said it was the reason you loved me. But in this regard, you want me to give up my idiosyncracies, so that they not create conflict. I don't really want the conflict either, and I also can't understand what I am doing that is so offensive. I don't call them out or pressure them to change. It's as if my very presence is offensive by illuminating ways that they are content to be in the dark. I don't mean to, and I don't want to. I just am.

You used to tell me that you wanted a more authentic and kinder life. You wanted to grow into a better person and being around me challenged you to become more than the irritable, atrophied version of yourself that you had curled into in the last few years. I never tried to change you or your friends. I did try to live in accordance with my own compass, a very dangerous thing. Your friends did not want this kind of change the way you claimed you did, and they resented me for shaking things up.

I officially moved in by the time Christmas approached. We went to my family farm for a tree so that you could meet my people for the first time.

Grandpa loved you. I was shocked and delighted that he finally approved of someone I loved. You were charming and sociable, and even showed interest in all things farm related. You talked about the tree farm you worked on back east and seemed to idealize our little farm. Grandpa liked you despite his persistent intention to not.

We picked out a tree and drove it back home to spend the evening decorating. We wrapped lights and unpacked the boxes of carefully preserved ornaments I have been collecting since childhood. I am excited to share all of this with you, my family and my traditions, but when Bo arrives home, he is obviously upset.

In response, you interrupted our celebrating by following him throughout the house mocking me and my silly interest in Christmas. A sudden change from our otherwise festive day. Torn between two camps, you try to placate his mood and make a memory with me simultaneously. It doesn't work. I go to bed hurt and embarrassed, feeling judged and alienated.

A week later Bo comes home with a tree also. It is a sad, Charlie Brown twig with one small cluster of green protruding from the end in a laughable mockery of growth. He proudly places it on the other side of the living room and hangs scraps of bikes and other mechanical objects from it. Your friends all laugh at his obvious opposition to the pretty little tree I had created. It is fun for them to mock the contention between us and you laugh along with them. I buy him a bike ornament as a peace offering but he does not say thank you. I even try to laugh with them, but they stop when I join in. I feel like I'm living a high school nightmare and you abandon me to it. Your quiet coaching on the side on how I could win them over and what I need to change to be more accepted only signifies your tacit compliance with this immature system. It is the loneliest Christmas season.

▲

Several years ago, I decided that I did not want to participate in consumerism style Christmas exchanges anymore. My family had some

difficulty adapting but has successfully managed in the last few years.
We agreed this year that we would keep it this way between the two
of us also and decided on activity-related gifts for future adventures.
You would buy me ski boots, since you work in the industry and get a
discount, and I would get you climbing gear, since I work in that industry
and can still use my pro-deals. We concluded that this would give us years
of fun doing something we both enjoy without the pressures of frivolous
holiday shopping.

We go to the mountain shop together, fit you for a harness and shoes and
I order your gear. As it arrives to the house, I wrap it up, and begin to
pile it up under the tree. I wrap each box separately because it's pretty
and more fun to have more boxes. You take me to the ski shop and have
my high arches fitted for fancy insoles and then order my boots wrapping
them up to fit under the tree as well.

A few days before Christmas, I go to the dispensary to buy you a small
pipe which I also wrap up and place in the branches on the tree. It's
a small, inexpensive gift and I think nothing of this breach in our gift
exchange agreement. I bought it because of a recent argument where you
finally tell me that you are a smoker. You had been lying to me about it
since the inception of our relationship because you believed that I would
not have dated you if I had known. I confirm this assumption and am
upset by your lies. So you agree to quit, saying it was really only for the
marijuana anyway.

I eventually begin to feel guilty about asking you to change your
behavior. I know better to than to ask a man to change for me, but I hate
smoking and you had lied. Instead of dealing with this issue, your lies and
my boundaries, I buy you a small pipe so you can keep smoking weed and
I can feel like I'm being supportive.

When you find the small package, tucked between the branches, you
are thrown into an anxiety fit. You stand in the living room with Bo
wondering about the small package. What does the presence of this
package mean? Does she expect other gifts? Was this whole arrangement
a rouse to set you up for failure? You begin writing stories about me in
your mind that drive you to break into the package like a child, snooping

in their gifts before the big day.

When I come home that evening, I notice my carefully wrapped little package is askew and the wrappings disheveled. I can see that you have opened it and hastily rewrapped it. You are chuckling in the kitchen with Bo when I ask you directly what happened. You lie. Again. You are angry that I caught you, so you act offended that I would accuse you. Bo looks away with a wry smile, tacitly complying with your deceit.

I recognize your lie and I am hurt. I wanted so badly to surprise you with something thoughtful. Tomorrow is Christmas and I don't want to fight. This whole month has been one sad moment after the next, with arguments piling on top of others, and each time I reach out to you, I feel less seen, less heard, and less important. My heart is sore and I feel lonely when I head upstairs to bed, leaving you with your other wife in the kitchen to continue laughing at my expense.

When you follow me, much later, we discuss what we might do in the morning and agree to open presents in the evening when I get home from work. You said that you planned to work so I should go ahead and pick up the Christmas shift. Later, you make plans to go skiing with Bo instead. I'm not upset about the skiing, but I hope that we can have some time together tomorrow night.

In the morning, when we wake up, you run downstairs like a child to the tree and with Bo, and begin tearing into the gifts that have continued to accumulate from your family, while I slip into the shower and prepare for work. You are both laughing and comparing what your mothers have sent, making plans for your ski day. I can see now that you never planned to work. This is the way you have been doing Christmas since you moved here from the east coast and you did not want to change your traditions for me. I would not have resented you your fun if you had only been able to tell me the truth when we made our plans. Instead, I go to work and then go out afterwards with my lonely co-workers, bitter and sad about our first Christmas together. They buy me drinks and tell me how I deserve better, but I have no intention of leaving you even now.

I know in this moment that you are not ready for the kind of relationship that I want with you, but I love you. The way I moved the spices and the Christmas tree become a wedge between Bo and I that will never mend because he will never talk.

For the next six months until we move to Costa Rica together, he never once cleans the bathroom and leaves his loogies and blond hair in the drain every morning before going to work. It's a passive-aggressive protest against my presence in the house. You complain about these things to me, but never confront him. I eventually ask him to do a chore because I get tired of being the maid, and he resents me even more. He won't cook in the kitchen and often comes home from work to sit in complete silence in the living room, ignoring me entirely, until you arrive. Then he smiles and strikes up a casual, pleasant conversation with you as if I am not in the room at all.

You tell me that this is all my fault. I should just do this or that or something else to get him to like me. There must be something wrong with me if all your friends hate me, you say. I shouldn't ask such personal questions or be so assertive with my opinions. I should just try to be more likable. I began to shrink into a smaller and more nervous version of myself, growing quieter and less like me every day. I believe you that I am just unpalatable and no one likes me. I am too offensive and rude and if I can just figure out how to be better, then everything will be alright. Then they will approve of me and we can be happy together and I won't feel so alone.

Or perhaps we just need a vacation...

LA CASITA

February 2018

Our plane touches down in LA and you take my hand on the off ramp leading me towards the airport bar. I have been through so many airports in my life, but I have never visited the bar, or even restaurants. Airports are so egregiously over-priced that since I was a child taking flights from one parent to the next, I would never have considered such an indulgence.

"We're on vacation" you say. So, I follow with the excitement of permission.

We are heading to Baja, Mexico together; our first real vacation. Your work has been driving you mad. Your drinking binges have been escalating into late nights, where you don't answer your phone. Sometimes you come home bleeding, with incoherent stories about how your hand has ended up so mangled. I stay up to clean the blood off the floor and walls after your emphatic tales of heroism that I never quite believe.

Sometimes, I make the mistake of expressing my disapproval or concern and then your gregarious charm turns to darkness. You threaten to throw me out and try to end our relationship. I cry and plead and get angry along with you. Bo listens from his bedroom without intervention. It's humiliating and I am sleep deprived, tired in my soul.

You always apologize in the mornings, telling me how stressed this new position at work has made you. You aren't managing well, but you love me and you're trying. I try to encourage you to take real weekends where you don't answer your phone. Maybe try to trust your colleagues and don't rush to the brewery every time there is a crisis. You can't maintain these kinds of boundaries daily, but you do agree that you need a vacation.

"You're the most important thing in my life." You tell me. "I know I need to figure out how to spend more time with you."

So, you carve out 10 days for us and we book this trip on a budget, eager to discover if we enjoy this kind of adventure together as much as we enjoy the others.

I believe you that these moments with work are truly a crisis. You have explained to me that you are adjusting to your new role as head brewer and that the demands your boss has placed on you are unfair and he doesn't understand them. You are underpaid and over-worked; simply doing your best to keep your head above water. I believe you and hold my breath for the time when a work/life balance is possible. After almost a year, this trip is the way you are showing me that you are really trying to put our relationship first.

▲

When we deplane in Baja, we head to the car rental to pick up our little adventure-mobile. We have planned a road trip from here to the mountains of Santiago, followed by kayaking in La Paz and beach camping, and then on to Todos Santos, a sleepy little artisan hub on the pacific coast.

The first few days of our adventure are beautiful. We camp at an eco-village, visiting mountain oases and hot springs. We hike up these rivers as far as our flip flops and sense of wanderlust will take us. The palm trees are the only observers to our naked, riverbed sunbathing, and cliff jumping. We make love in the shade of the palms just like we did last summer on the banks of our mountain lakes.

Afterwards, we head to La Paz for our scheduled kayaking event. We debated this trip because of the cost. Neither of us is making much money these days. I am still bartending to supplement my renewed practice and you've said, "brewers never make six figures." This is our splurge, the most expensive part of our journey, a three-day kayaking trip up the coast of the Caspian Sea. Your friends advised us that it's worth it.

When we arrive in La Paz, the winds pick up and shut down the port. Our trip is canceled. Instead of being distraught we make new plans to camp up the road at a local beach for the night. We park a little way away from the cluster of RVs grouped together for the sake of privacy. We have a cocktail at the beachside bar and head to bed around dark.

Sometime around midnight, a group of locals roll in and begin singing loudly in Spanish from the bonfire they lit surprisingly close to our vehicle. There is a baby crying and we lie in the back of our SUV holding one another for hours, wondering how long it will last.

Around 2AM, they start their car and begin spraying our rental car with sand and rocks while doing doughnuts so close they nearly hit our front bumper. Now, we are wide awake and frightened. Scrambling to get all of our things from the front seat back into the back of the car, which we've converted into our bed, we drive away without getting out of the car, forgetting your flip flops in the sand. We do not even notice their loss until the next morning.

We had heard stories of the La Paz locals hating tourists and this beach being a dangerous one for camping. Suddenly, we understand why all the other RVs are parked together in a cluster.

We race up the road to the parking lot at Bahia Ballena to finish out our mostly sleepless night. Deciding the next morning that we don't much like the area, and head to the opposite coast and Todos Santos.

▲

Todos Santos is beautiful. We fall in love with the quaint, artist town. We find a cute little yurt style room at a local hostel, owned by some world traveling Italians. I spend the afternoon wandering through galleries of various kinds, finally stumbling into La Sonrisa de la Muerte, a small artist owned co-op, whose principal operator is an Argentinian woman who moved to here to do wood cuts.

Her simple, elegant, traditional, Mexican style, is intriguing. She has various types of animals and katrinas in unique colors and shapes. The walls are lined with prints from various artisits, but hers stand out to me. I could spend hours in here. A particular piece catches my eye, A Zebra and Meerkat drinking beers, lounging in front of a camping trailer. The mostly black and white print is accented by a striking shade of gradated blue sky in the background. I want it, but it is too expensive.

I debate with myself for a while, asking how much it is and reflecting on my budget. I want to buy a piece of art for our house. We had discussed this before our trip, but this is more than I had wanted to spend, even if it isn't really much. We move onto some smaller pieces that are clearly made to be displayed together but I can't afford all of those either. After pointing out the two pieces that you like, you leave the shop to find a beer while I make my choices. I can see that the artist is disappointed about separating them, so I linger a while longer with my internal struggle. When she returns, in her broken English, which is much better than my non-existent Spanish, she explains that she has just the thing for me in the back.

She leads me to a small door at the back of the shop, disappearing quickly, she reappears with the 3rd of what will become 50 prints of a new piece she's just created with the same four animals. The rabbit, the coyote, the chipmunk, and the anteater are in a garden around a table drinking cocktails, surrounded by cacti and monstera plants in pots. It's titled Quatro Abrijas Beben Margaritas. I adore it! She packages it up in a tube to keep it safe on our journey home and I am thrilled to share it with you.

The next day we set out for more beach camping near Pescadero. When
we arrive, we find a long stretch of sand and three small huts woven
out of drift wood. They are not quite large enough to stand in, but
long enough for us to lay down. We find our bottle of tequila and the
Pineapple juice and sit with our backs to the hut hung with a hand-made
sign reading La Casita. The letters are yellow, outlined in black, and it
dangles from a rusty wire above the door way. We sip our cocktails and
watch whale spouts making their way up the coast line. Finally, we roll
out our sleeping bag wrapped inside a driftwood shell as the sun sets
against the pacific, a perfect afternoon.

CHOICES

March 2018

"Hi bebe, how's the fishing?" I respond to my ringing phone.

"Great! I just quit my job!" You announce into my stunned silence.

"Oh? Ok, um, I guess you've been talking about it for some time. Did you want to talk about it or anything?"

"No. It's done. I just called Patrick and told him."

"Oh. You already did it?"

"Yeah. Is that ok?"

"I mean, I'm surprised, but we don't share finances. Are you financially ok to do it? Like we don't need to figure something out with the house or anything?"

"No. I have about 60 grand I pulled out of the stock market when Trump was elected. I'll be fine for a while. I want to put our relationship first. I want to be a good partner to you and I've been so stressed that I haven't been treating you as well as I should. You're the most important thing in my life. I love you more than anything else in the world and I want us to work."

"Ok. I trust you. I know you've been unhappy for a long time, so if this is the first step towards something that's a better fit, I support you. When will you be home?"

"Thanks baby. I love you. I'm heading home now. See you in a bit."

"Ok. Love you. Bye."

I hang up the phone in semi-stunned silence. I suppose that this should not be too shocking. You have been telling me that you are so unhappy and that this position you took just before we started dating has been driving you to drink too much. You have blamed this job for your impulsive and often aggressive behavior that has been escalating since I've known you. You have told me that you were always a good partner to your girlfriends before, and you're not sure why you get so angry with me. You have told me it's just the anxiety of this job. You have to blow off steam and that is why you stay out so late and come home so drunk. I have so desperately wanted to believe you, that I have been waiting. I decide to continue to wait to see what is true.

▲

Monday you tell me that during meeting with Patrick, he declined your offer to continue to work with the brewery until they find a new head brewer. You tell me that you offered to stay for up to two months and help with the transition, but Patrick declined and you only have two weeks left there. I am stunned by Patrick's choice because you have told me that you are the last remaining brewer who is trained on their ancient system and who is familiar with their staple recipes, but your work is none of my business, so I say nothing.

Tuesday you come home with several binders from the brewery. You stack them in our room on the desk and explain to me that these recipes are your intellectual property. You do not want the brewery to have them after you leave. You plan to alter the ones you created and return the binders with false copies. I note that this seems unnecessarily vengeful, but again say nothing.

Wednesday, you come home with six pony kegs and stack them in your closet. You explain to me that this is the yeast culture that you and your mentor created. You have been using and reusing this yeast strain to make the staple sour that has put this brewery on the map. You tell me that you called a lawyer and he said that you have more right to this culture than the recipes even.

Thursday you tell me that you don't even really need to work next week. You've done all you can for the brewery and the boys are on their own now.

A few weeks later, I notice that you still have the brewery's laptop. I ask you about it, but you shrug and say you'll give it back when they ask.

A month later, Whitney, the owner who sold the business to Patrick shows up at our house and appears angry. I leave the kitchen and retreat into the back yard to give you space to talk. She leaves with the pony kegs from the closet and the last of the binders from our room.

You sulk into the back yard and tell me that Patrick called her and sent her to talk with you. You say that he's been smearing your name all over town, lying, and telling everyone that you quit without notice. You are angry that he's slandered you and I'm empathic, even with some reservations. I suspect that Patrick's side of the story might have some truth in it.

A few months later you still can't find work. Despite the rave reviews that the other brewers in town give you, it seems that there is always something at the end of the process that ends your prospects. You tell me that Patrick has had you black listed and you are starting to worry about work.

"I'm giving myself until the end of July to enjoy the summer before I really start to look." You say. "How would you feel about moving somewhere else? I'm tired of this town anyway."

I watch all this pass and say nothing because I do not know what to believe. Some things seem to be in poor taste, unkind even. You have told me how indispensable you were over the last year, that making this transition in a week seems to be either a slap in the face to the brewery, or that maybe you weren't as indispensable as you made yourself seem. I suspect that the truth is somewhere in-between and the story you are telling me is the one that suits you for the moment. Again, I quiet my intuition in favor of wanting to believe that you are basically good natured.

▲

June 2018

The last few months since you quit have passed as tranquil as you had promised with chickens clucking in the garden, back yard BBQ's, and fire pit sing-a-longs. We are happy again and all your promises of decreased stress equates decreased drinking seem to have been true. I can almost relax into our new life and I have begun to make steps of my own to make a permeant situation for my career.

"Baby, I want to talk to you about something." You approach me with obvious trepidation.

"Ok. What's up?" I ask sitting across from you in the sunshine on our patio.

"Would you ever consider living abroad with me?" You ask.

"Of course!" I respond without hesitation.

"Really? That's it? That's was so easy. I wasn't sure you'd be into it."

"Definitely! I've always wanted to live abroad and I think trying it out before we settle down and do the kid thing is a great idea. I know you tried it in South Africa before, but I've never had the chance. I would love to find a way to make it work, but why are you asking me now?"

"Well, I just had an old colleague reach out to me. Do you remember the brewery in Costa Rica I went to help set up, when we had just met? Their head brewer just quit and they're looking for a replacement. Would you be interested in going there?"

"Hmm... it's not exactly on my list, but I think I can do anything for a year at least. Even if I hate it, it's only a year."

"Really? Ok. Well, I'll call him and tell him we're interested and get more information." You look at me with astonished eyes, surprised at my willingness. I smile back at you and start thinking about the steps I would have to make to move my career to an online portal.

BEFORE WE LEAVE

August 2018

Tonight, is one of our last in Oregon. We have made the choice and set in motion a plan of action that would be hard to reverse now. We are leaving soon and feeling nostalgic for our house and our yard. I make a cheese plate to delight a connoisseur and we are enjoying it with wine on our patio watching the nesting sparrows in the birdhouses we built together.

You find the ukulele I bought to take to Costa Rica, intending to use my spare time being creative, making music and painting and begin plucking away gently as we relax into the absolute calm. We are the happiest we have been since the beginning and it might be in large part due to having an adventure on the horizon. The air is holding our unspoken contract. Now, is not the time to argue. We must be united before we embark on this wild ride. The air is electric with our love and our vigilance, connected in our hope.

We are on the precipice of something that will show us everything we need to know about who we have become in this relationship we created together. We have made promises, set ourselves up for success to the best of our ability, and there is nothing now but to go and see.

You look at me across the table as if you are trying to divine the secrets of our future, trying to read them like ruins in the flecks of gold in my green eyes. Maybe you are searching for reassurance, but I can't give it to you because our stability is still too fresh for me to fully trust.

Your eyes are dark like chocolate and then never give anything away. I stare back, wondering if I am making an unwise decision to leave the country without more evidence of your stability. I am hopeful it will continue, but I still have not forgotten the long sleepless nights of last year, the arguments, and the blood. I set this aside in my mind in order to hold onto my hope like a buoy in the ocean. There is no land in sight now. Will you be good to me out there, far from everything I know?

"I need something from you." I begin.

"Anything." You reply, setting down the ukulele.

"I know that I said I could do anything for a year and you know that I want this to work as much as you do. I really believe this, and I'm gonna try my hardest. But I need to know that if something happens, if we get there and one or both of us are miserable, if things are terrible between us again like they were last winter and we're fighting all the time, that you will choose us over your job. I need to know that you won't sacrifice me or our happiness together to force this to work. Can you promise me that we will come home if things get bad between us? I don't want Costa Rica to ruin what we have now."

You reach across the table, take my hand, and looking me in the eye, promise. You promise that no matter what, we'll be ok together. I exhale relief, and with another deep breath in, we return to our repose.

FIRST WEEK ON THE ROAD

September 2018

We step out onto the playa with a bottle of champagne in one hand and orange juice in the other. We came to say goodbye to our desert. We left town 5 hours ago and have many more miles to drive today, but we had to stop to let the dogs out and where better to do it than here? Fresh faced and in love, we are finally leaving on our grand adventure.

We spent the last three months discussing different ways to make this transition work for us, the benefits, the risks. I told my employer and begun transitioning clients to an online portal as an independent practitioner. You have been so much better without your job and listened when I asked you not to drink during the day. You began acting like Morning Hank all day long. Morning Hank was so kind and attentive. I didn't miss Evening Hank.

When we embarked today, we were nothing but smiles and laughter and love. We have our two adventure pups in the backseat and nothing but a month of travel on our horizon. We could go anywhere, do anything, and we were confident in us. We toast to our wild life and laugh arrogantly at what we left behind.

▲

We camp in Nevada and then Arizona before crossing our first border
into Mexico. We covered a third of our mileage in two days in the states,
giving way to an ignorance about our speed of travel and the time we
actually needed to cover the vast distance of Mexico. We are nervous
and I speak no Spanish, leaving the entirety of our border crossing
responsibilities to you. It was a heavy burden and I feel ashamed of my
linguistic limitations.

In Mexico, we proceed through Baja, familiar territory to us because of
our previous travels. This was the place that made us believe we could
move to Latin America indefinitely. We love Baja, everything about it: the
crashing waves of the pacific, the crystal blue of the Gulf of California,
the culture, the food, the weather. So, our first week was spent reveling in
what we knew we loved, and then we boarded the ferry to Mazatlán.

▲

I love architecture, particularly churches. So, I could not allow us to drive
through any town in Central America without stopping to see la plaza
central and Mazatlán was no exception.

Catedral Mazatlan Basicila de la Inmaculada Concepcion is a hodgepodge
of various architectural eras. It was started and stopped in construction,
partially destroyed and rebuilt at various times and for various reasons.
What stands now is no single man's vision, but the smattering of time on
stone reminding us of our best intentions and how prone they are to be
thwarted by circumstance.

As we leave the city to find camping, we notice the change of landscape
from desert to jungle. The heat and humidity make the air around us
thick with unfamiliarity and we silently reflect on how this will alter our
camping experiences. Eventually, we find a sliver of beach and pull off to
park under a coconut tree, setting up our little home away from home.

We have mastered this transition by now, each knowing our part. So, we
get to work with efficiency. First pulling our bins off the memory foam
mat inside the back of the truck that serves as our bed, then tucking the

ones that do not carry camping gear up underneath the truck to hide them from potential weather or prying eyes. I lay out our double sleeping bag, which is growing increasingly useless in this heat, while you set up the camp kitchen, and we begin to plan dinner together.

Tonight, is different though, with the long ferry ride and being in unfamiliar territory, we opted to eat in town instead of cooking, so there is no need for the kitchen tonight. As daylight turns to dusk, I simply undress and crawl into the truck bed to hide from the pests that come out at this hour. I have created a custom mosquito screen to close us in and protect my delicate and reactive skin from the dangers of jungle life. Now, that we are out of the desert, I am glad I invested so much time into this function.

As I lay naked in the back of the truck looking out at the ocean, you linger around camp enjoying the salty sea air. Then we both notice a man with a machete walking the beach. He's not too close to our truck, but not very far either. I have not felt unsafe in our travels so far, but the presence of the man with the machete strikes me as odd. He seems to be searching for something, but I attempt to keep my mind from wandering the paths that might create more fear.

I can feel the tiny hairs on the back of my neck rise slightly as he passes. I breathe them back into place reminding myself that the narratives that Americans are fed about other countries are biased towards the extremes and inaccurate at best. But when he passes back the other direction and looks towards us, my hairs will no longer be talked out of their story. On the third pass, you have stationed yourself in front of the truck bed, between he and I, with your dog by your side. I have pulled my sarong over my body, and stay still, propped up on one elbow, where I am hoping to be invisible.

As the man approaches, I can feel my heart in my throat, and I hold my breath. As he comes closer, he puts his hands in the air as if surrendering and tosses his machete into a nearby patch of sea grass, signaling to us that he means no harm. I let out a small sign of relief and since I speak no Spanish, invest myself into reading his body language trying to understand why he has crossed the sand to our small hideout.

When he is finished conversing with you and returns in the direction
that he came, I hear him say something that sounds a bit like a non-
threatening swear and see him shake his head from side to side gently.
You then turn towards me with a chuckle and tell me that everything
is alright. He let you know that he and another man patrol the beach in
this area looking for nesting sea turtles. They use machetes for digging
up the eggs, returning them to the sand in the turtle sanctuary down the
street. He also warned us that it is not legal to camp here, but that we
were unlikely to be bothered. He alerted us to the dangers of parking
underneath a coconut tree with a potential storm approaching, motioning
out towards the clouds hovering slightly off shore. He offered to let us
park near his restaurant down the road, but you declined. That is when he
called you a turkey and shook his head, walking back towards the ocean.

We smile at one another, breathing out the air we didn't knew we were
still holding. You reach out your hand to me in reassurance and we know
that we are safe again, sparing all but falling coconuts. We see the man
pass several more times throughout the evening and into the night, and
we see his compadre as well, but we are no longer frightened by their
presence. We spend the rest of the night undisturbed.

▲

It takes us the better part of the month to get through Mexico. When
we began, the smooth roads in the states fooled us into believing that we
would be able to travel swiftly over long distances and have time to linger
in some places at our whim. As it turns out, the roads are littered with
topes and small towns. They are rough and we drive at least 4 hours each
day barely making any progress towards Costa Rica for your start date in
three weeks.

Each night camping increases the number of itchy, red bumps that cover
my body, until I slowly dissolve into a frantic, tearful shell of myself. You
feeling unable to save me from the unknown assailant, grow increasingly
frustrated with my inability to cope with the discomfort, and growing
slowly more scowling and aggravated. You begin yelling at me in each
city we navigate for the way I drive or don't drive, give you directions or

can't read a map, make a plan or don't have a plan. These itchy red bumps
and my increasing, unsolvable discomfort begin to push us into a state of
barely controlled chaos.

▲

As we drive into Guatemala, we begin by breaking the first rule: never
drive at night. You had heard stories of some night time car traps used to
stop vehicles and extort their drivers, but this border crossing took longer
than we had planned. Now it's growing darker, and we are hungry and
tired. As we climb higher and higher on these windy mountain roads, we
begin to understand that our beach camping is at an end and we need to
find a hotel.

As we work our way up the winding highway towards the nearest
town. We pass an Auto Hotel, the sign reads. Then we pass another and
another, each with gaudy painted hearts and pictures of romantic partners
wrapped in passionate embrace. We start to giggle and guess at what
these institutions might be. "Every day is Valentine's Day!" they seem to
shout at us.

Growing desperate for a place to stay, we decide to give one a try. As we
pull up, we are greeted by what appears to be three generations of women
that we assume own the place: middle aged woman, a woman in her 20's
that we assume is her daughter, carrying a child no older than a year
and a half. We ask to spend the night and they look from one to another
clearly confused. The rooms are only rented hourly they inform us. At
this juncture, we start to understand our error. We try another just to be
sure, but as we pull in, we notice a man with two young girls somewhere
between ages 16 and 20 waiting to greet the next visitor and we burst into
shocked laughter at our ignorance. Apologizing, we pull back out and
continue our desperate search for a hotel.

When we finally reach a town, there is a small hotel called Margarita. We
book a room, and upon entering, I become somewhat afraid to touch any
of the surfaces. A small step up from the Auto Hotels, I think. Crawling
into the bed, I am careful not to place my bare skin on anything but the

clean sheets. Then, giving way to my curiosity, I connect to WIFI and
research Auto Hotels, Guatemala. What I find confirms some of what we
had discovered from deduction. They were originally created as a place
for lovers to go to escape the single room dwellings that they would share
with their entire extended families after marriage. A place designated for
family procreation, a cultural necessity in family life of this kind. Over
the years they had transformed into places where drive-by truckers might
rent a room and a woman.

We discuss this as we turn down the lights and I feel the familiar
experience of my mind growing to accommodate this new information.
It feels something like humor, followed by shock and disgust, then
compassion. Finally landing on sadness as my mind expands to wrap itself
around the complexity of this issue. I try to set aside my judgements as I
reflect on the poverty and desperation in the conditions of the houses and
people that we have driven past in the last few weeks.

Sometime around 1AM, I hear a small knock on the door next to ours. I
hear it open and close. I hear her work. Then I hear the open and close
of the door again, and her small knock on ours. You are asleep and hear
nothing.

The laughter from last night lingers in our mouths the next morning as I
tell you about this, but it has a strange aftertaste now. I redirect my mind
to gratefulness that we found laughter at our cultural ignorance instead
of anger and blame over whose fault it was that we broke our safety rule.
As we leave the Margarita Hotel behind, my heart is sore and tired from
expansion and I am ready to leave this place behind.

▲

Our next adventure in Guatemala is a stark contrast to our first night. We
drive into Antigua mid-day and find the Jardin de mi Tia just as described
in the listing. We rented 2 nights here to give ourselves a respite from
driving, to explore the city and enjoy the colonial ruins.

Antigua is a romantic dream. Each building seems half ancient and half rebuilt and I quickly lose myself in an architectural paradise filled with miniature bathrooms and pokey corner hallways winding into garden courtyards. The wine and music, the diversity of languages around us, and the way the indigenous culture seamlessly mixes with the modern all blend into an enchanting fantasy turned reality. People in various colors and traditional clothing wander the streets next to those in modern clothes mingling the past with the present in an curious display of art and culture.

In this high mountain air, my skin heals and we sleep soundly for the first time in weeks. I recover some of my curiosity and hopefulness, and naively muse about our destination. We have 4 more borders to cross in the next week. We have seen so many places that we have loved. Places where I thought, "I could stay here forever." I ponder how I will feel about the town we are heading towards.

ONCE WE GOT THERE

September 2018

It has been a month since we left the states and I am a different person. After leaving Antigua, and being back on the road again, I feel like a tattered piece of cloth hanging out on a line, haggard on the edges and dripping with humidity. We shouldn't be arriving for two more days but I am so tired and uncomfortable that I beg to pick up the pace and push through both Honduran borders today. Assuming our arrival would produce a respite from the last three weeks of misery that are etched on my skin, I am dying to meet our new home.

You wanted us to pull into town in the daylight so I could see the place we had driven over five thousand miles to make our new home, but my pleas win out and we arrive at 8PM. When we pull in, we find the one unmarked, muddy street, pockmarked with potholes like my skin, slowing our speed to gentle roll. We attempt to communicate with Rico, the man who instructed us to arrive at the back gate, but he is unavailable. So, you find it by memory instead.

I can't wait to see our room, our bed, to begin nesting after our long, displaced month. You were promised a room in a hostel style environment rent free, as well as your wages to be the new head brewer here. As we climb down from the truck, my dog spots a smallish critter scampering into the bushes and she darts after the armadillo with urgency. I have never seen an armadillo before and am wishing for a closer look but she chases it off too soon.

We arrive in the house to find four men standing in the front room. They are leaning on the bar counter that separates the dirtiest kitchen I have ever seen from a living room with a small table surround by a couch and two chairs. The support beams are strung with a hammock and there are old surf boards in various conditions leaning around the room. The walls are mostly screen windows, which I assume means lots of light during the day, but it's dark right now. There is a large colorful mural painted on the wall that separates this room from what will become our bedroom.

You greet everyone with charm even though you are already irritated with me for my exhaustion and discomfort. We find that not all of these men live in this house, but that indeed, only men live in this house. Each other room is occupied by a man of similar age to ours. They are all single and working in various capacities for the community or the brewery. Rico lives in a small hut adjacent to the hostel house, named Casa Swell, but I will eventually come to call it The Frat House, less than affectionately.

Today I am trying to appear easy going and happy. So, when I see the brown toilet seat and am unable to differentiate if this is the intended color or simply an accumulation of filth over the years, I do not say anything. I just choose to pee outside. On our tour of the grounds the next morning, I find that the brewery has a bathroom and shower downstairs near the brewery and decide that this is where I will shower and do anything that cannot be done in the jungle. Our camping trip is not as finished as I had hoped.

Rico shows us our room and the boys eagerly jest about the peephole from the living room side that makes our room visible as long as it is lighter on our side than the other. I am sure they are joking, but there is in fact a hole and now exposed and overwhelmed are added to the exhaustion and discomfort I was previously feeling. I laugh along as if this is not disturbing because I know the rules for women in this setting and the consequences with you if I protest.

Under the guise of unpacking, I go to our room so I can try not to cry in the only space I have that's mine. There are no curtains on the window, so I hang a sarong. My body aches with bites. I am bleeding from waking myself in the night with scratching. I am sleep deprived. I am isolated from everyone and everything that I know and I have just walked into a shark's den of insensitive man-children who are making sex jokes about me within moments of our meeting. What. Have. I. Done?

Our trip became a game of endurance following that first night on the mainland outside of Mazatlán. Before this experience, I told you that I was confident that I could do anything for a year. Now it has been a month and I am not sure I can last another day.

My skin seems bent on betraying me, reacting angrily to any foreign plant or bug that touches it. It sends constant shock waves through my system in the form of pain and itch. The morning after we landed on mainland Mexico, I woke up to so many tiny bites enflamed and swollen that I thought I might actually have Dengue. I was almost feverish with the inflammation caused by allergic reaction and I have since used every available cream and antihistamine to no avail.

The only thing that seemed to calm my angry flesh was cool water and nights spent indoors. I punctuated these nights with cold showers until the bites could heal. You allowed a few of these stops on our trip when I was almost in tears, but it was outside our budget to find an Airbnb too frequently. Those nights allowed my skin to clear enough for us to continue and my optimistic attitude to return by focusing on the temporary nature of the road trip. Eventually, we would arrive and live indoors, I reminded myself often.

The days after our stops I was able to enjoy some of the sights and new experiences until we slept on the beach again. Many weeks after we arrived in Costa Rica, I would learn that the things that were biting me were known by many names, sand fleas, no see-ums, and that there were no screens that could keep them out. They are nearly microscopic and I would never be able to enjoy the beach that we moved to, because any evening that I was standing on it for more than five minutes they began biting and I was immediately plunged back into frantic swatting, followed by weeks of scratching.

Your skin on the other had seemed completely non-plussed by whatever creatures were present. Once you yelped, "Ouch! Something bit me!" as we were driving and then revealed a small red bump on your arm. This bump would disappear within the hour and I'd come to hate you for it and your lack of empathy. Nothing seemed to bite you and if it did, your body did not seem to react. Unfortunately, this lack of reactivity was reserved for your skin only.

The itching wasn't the only thing bent on driving me mad. The humidity began to cause cystic acne across my chest and face especially around my mouth where I sweat the most. The large, painfully swollen, raised bumps deep underneath my skin would multiply daily and face scrub or skin treatment was able to keep them away. These factors would bring the edge of my sanity into view and despite digging my heels in, I was sliding towards it, leaving long track marks in the thick, red, jungle earth.

▲

It has been weeks since we had sex, mostly because of my skin and discomfort. Though now that we have arrived, it's because of our roommates and the paper-thin walls. It is hard enough to be the only woman in a compound of single surfer bros, but even more difficult when they continue to make jokes about the peep hole in the wall to your room. Despite being sure that they would never look, the idea of it leaves me unwilling to be vulnerable in any capacity, even with you.

A few weeks after we arrive, you are starting to get used to the idea that we will never have sex again as long as we live in this glorified shack. Then the rains start. They are so loud on the tin roof that I look at you sideways, suggestively. No one is likely to hear anything over the sound of the rain pounding on the tin roof. You don't miss the cue and we discretely slip away to our room, one at a time.

Eagerly stripping off our clothes, I am on top of you within moments, careful to be as quiet as possible, while trying to be fast because we're not sure how long the sound will hide us or how long it will take them to notice we have both gone missing. It's like being in high school and trying

to hid from mom and dad again, except this time we are both adults trying
to preserve our sense of privacy.

I am just relaxing into the moment, when one of the roommates bursts
through the door. My worst nightmare appearing in reality. I am angry
and shocked, but mostly angry. I don't know what is exchanged between
the two of you because I am so angry at the interruption but I find
that you are pushing me off to the side of the bed where I slump over,
confused.

"What's going on? Where are you going?" I demand, sexually frustrated
and plotting the death of this particular roommate.

"Grace, you have to get dressed. The house is underwater." You say
tossing me my clothes.

I look down and see that there is at least an inch of water collecting on
the floor of our room and it is continuing to fill.

"Are you fucking kidding me?" I mutter as I pull open a drawer and throw
on a swim suit.

When I emerge from the bedroom after you, the dogs are running around
starting to panic, looking for higher ground. You are shoulder deep in
the brackish water from the incoming tide overflowing the mouth of the
river, outside the flood gate trying to pull it in tighter. The other boys are
helping and you are barking orders at me about packing up our important
papers to take to the brewery which is above the flood plain.

I put everything from the floor onto our sheets and start laughing, in
despair, shock, rage, or defeat, I am not sure. It was laugh or cry, and I
might have done a bit of both. I was still trying to act tough around these
boys, as if I had something to prove as the only woman there.

We toss the dogs over the flood gate and they intuitively swim towards
the brewery and we wade thigh deep in the muddy, water to wait out the
tide with thoughts of crocodiles and snakes in our minds. "My life has
turned into a Jumanji remake" I laugh inside my own head and finally

give into the chaos of it all. I decide this is fun, laughing at the absurdity of my new life.

Once at the brewery, no one mentions what that roommate must have seen, at least in part, and what everyone else must have known we were doing. I am grateful for the reprieve, the small sign of respect for our privacy, even if it was just for the evening.

NO DANCING

October 2018

We are slowly adjusting to our new life here in Costa Rica. Rico is doing his best to show me all the important places. We go to the nearest city to run errands together and I buy paint at the local hardware store. I ask his permission to begin muraling each of the bedrooms. I call it painting for sanity and everyone laughs nervously. He takes me to the rural town nearby and explains the way to find the best waterfalls and beaches. He is really trying hard to help me be happy here, but I know it is because they need you at the brewery.

Eventually, Rico invites us to the country wide brew fest in the capitol. He wants you to get to know the other brewers in the small community here in Costa. There may be eight craft breweries in total and like all the other communicates of brewers, they are all friends, relaying on one another for solutions to problems and the exchange of tools and ideas.

I'm excited. Despite living in our small town before Costa Rica, I am originally from the city and I miss the chance to get dressed up and wear red lipstick. Latin America understands my need to be fancy from time to time so, I pack the only nice dress I brought and we head out for the weekend to San Jose.

We arrive in the city and settle into our place deciding to go out for the best hamburger in town. Rico is always trying, kindly, to make me feel more at home. He can see that I am having a hard time adjusting and tries to make it easier. Rico knows that if I do not stay, you will not stay, and they really need you here. His kindness is real, but it also makes me feel like an accessory. Since he is the only one that seems to notice or care, I am partial to him.

After lunch, we go to the brew convention where everyone is talking about beer. I am used to it, because this has been happening our whole relationship. The only difference this time is that it is all happening in Spanish.

I am genuinely curious about most everything, which makes it easy for me to show interest in things that you care about even when they would not be otherwise interesting to me. I ask you about your work and what happens when things go wrong. How to alter the chemical process and though I am not a chemist, I enjoy learning about the complexity of what you do. I listen to the other brewers talk at conventions with genuine interest, because from a psychological standpoint, you can learn so much about a person by listening to anything they choose to talk about. This time it's hard to feign interest in a beverage I don't drink, that is being discussed in a language I don't understand. So, I find the only wine vendor in the place and proceed to spend an exorbitant amount of money on wine.

When we are both nice and tipsy, playing and flirting with one another like we used to, we find it's time to go. Rico has found himself a lovely Latina and the four of us decide to go for dinner at a bar with Salsa dancing. Rico loves to dance and I am excited to learn.

When we arrive, there are several men lurking around the dance floor and since you have brought the only available ladies for dancing, we immediately begin to dance with all of them. They take turns teaching me the steps and spinning me around the floor. It's easier than I thought at this simple level and I am having so much fun. I can't recall the last time I laughed this much.

When I sit back down next to you to catch my breath, your countenance has changed. You have a dark look in your eyes and I can see the storm clouds gathering. Alarmed, I ask what happened, and a story unfolds. One of the not dancing men told you to watch your girl, pointing at my dance partner. This small comment sent you diving into your darkest fears about me. What if I cheated on you? What if I fell in love with another man? A man who could dance? A more attractive, kinder, sexier man than you. What if you lose me?

You never explicitly tell me that I can't dance anymore, but you grow mean and cold. Punishing me for the crime that happened in your mind. I know how this night ends from here. You are already the victim and the fun is over.

You and I made an agreement back in the states about this. Your commonly jealous disposition has caused more than a few moments of conflict in the last year and a half; hostile conversations that did not need to happen and bar altercations that could have been avoided. I love to dance and know that it is a fundamental part of Latin culture. I also know that you are not comfortable dancing. You would not dance with me at your sister's wedding, forcing me to do so alone, with your younger cousins. So, before we left, I told you I would be dancing, with other men, and you would need to figure out a way to feel secure knowing that I will always be going home with you.

"You know I love to dance, and that you don't." I said. "We are moving to Latin America where everyone dances," I pause, "with everyone. I am GOING to dance. I would always prefer to be dancing with you, but if you don't want to dance, or don't know how, I will dance with other men. We need to talk about how to keep this from becoming a problem between us. I don't want to live in Latin America for a year and not be allowed to dance."

In that moment you could recognize your own demons. You were sober enough and reflective enough to admit it. "I know that I do that and I promise that I will work on my jealousy. Maybe I'll even learn myself" You chuckle. "I know you would never leave me anyway and it's stupid that I get so worked up over it. I don't want to be the kind of man that won't let you dance. I want to be a supportive partner to you. I want to be good to you."

These are words I heard you say many times while we were together, "I want to be a good partner to you. I want to be supportive of you." They kept me here with you when you weren't those things, because they gave me hope that you were trying.

"Isn't that the best we can hope for in partnership? Someone who tries and says sorry and keeps trying?" I plead with my wiser friends. They always responded with silence, knowing then that I wasn't ready to hear the truth about you and us.

Now we are here, in the very situation I had predicted. You are angry, punishing me, for dancing. Everything is ruined and I need to get out of this bar. I don't want to cry in front of Rico, or these strangers. I have to get out of here. I have to get away, but there is nowhere I can run from the inside of my own mind.

I stand up to leave, finding my purse and the door and stumble out into the street. I don't know where I am or where I am going but I am walking. You rush out after me and start to direct me towards the place we are staying. I am crying angry tears now. Livid that you took this moment from me. I have been so lonely and depressed and you took from me this moment where I was feeling real joy. I feel so very alone and trapped.

▲

I make only one more attempt to dance while we live in Latin America. When John comes to visit and we drive to Bocas Del Toro, Panama for a long weekend. We have heard it's beautiful and I am thrilled to get away from the surf break for some calmer, bluer water, and some snorkeling. A live band plays salsa in a Cuban bar the first night after we cross the border and John, having lived in Costa Rica for a many years before us, pulls me out of my seat good naturedly. When he returns me, he reads your scowl and rolls his eyes, moving to another part of the bar. He can escape you, in a way that I can't. You are temporary company to him. I live with you.

This time, I decide that it is not worth the fight and without knowing,
I begin to sit very still. Eventually it will become evident that the key
to my sexuality is the freedom to move and you will regret having tried
to contain it as our sex life dries up along with my smile and freedom.
Though by then, it is too late for us.

INTERNET

November 2018

I am on the PDX carpet flying back to you after a week with my family
on the farm. When I told you I needed to go home to visit, you were
dismayed at how soon it was after we had arrived, but you let me go
with some anxiety and a plan to have us in our new house by the time I
returned.

My trip was lovely. I saw family and friends. I did some painting and my
skin feels like mine again. I'm ready to come back and give this challenge
another try. I have renewed energy and renewed hope. I think I can do
this.

Our new house is about 15 minutes outside of town, up a 4x4 mountain
trail. It's perched on the side of the mountain and has a gorgeous,
panoramic ocean view. Best of all, there is a lovely sea breeze that cools
it down in the evenings and it is far from all the biting insects that live
closer to the beach.

It is becoming clear to me that you never really planned to leave The Frat
House. You had truly hoped that we would adjust to that life and be able
to call it home, so you make this move grudgingly, but out of necessity for
me.

I have arranged with the landlord to manage the other three Airbnb houses next door, doing the organizing and cleaning in exchange for a percentage of the profits that we can put towards rent, making this place extremely affordable. The landlord has promised to get me internet access in all the condos within a week of move-in so I can continue to see my clients as well.

With things beginning to look up for us, I am happy and nesting as we begin moving in. We find all the things we want between the three condos and set up the kitchen and bedrooms to our comfort. We decide not to use AC to keep our electricity bill low and I begin meal planning now that I have a proper kitchen.

Each morning, we wake up to the sounds of the jungle. Yawning howler monkeys begin their calls before dawn and it awakens the sounds of the roosters who are everywhere. We learn to love these noises, the new and interesting creatures that wander through the edges of our jungle lot. We feel like we are finally living the wild life we had dreamed.

▲

Within a few weeks, the landlord gives up the guise of having any intention of providing internet suddenly making it my person problem. Since I have only just begun to speak Spanish, the idea of negotiating internet access with the phone company is completely overwhelming. Fortunately, Alex, who is Venezuelan and Mau, who is Uruguayan, move in to the third house at the end of the drive and they embark on the same mission within days. They are both fluent in English and Spanish. Splitting their time between here in the winter and Colorado in the summer. Alex works from home and is just as concerned about the internet issue as I am.

On our first trip to the nearest city, we find that satellite internet is impossible because of our location and whatever service we have must be cellular. The nearest city is 45 minutes up the mountain and I make the trek about once a week for various things that can't be found in our beach town.

The next week, we tackle the issue for the second time and find that certain cellular plans are only available from certain stores. Meaning, I may have to drive 2 hours to the next city to get the access I need. I am almost in despair until Mau steps in. Using his Latin charm, he convinces the kind woman, Erica, who is helping me, to bend the rules for us. She agrees to see if she can work something out and asks me to return in a week. I am hopeful.

Meanwhile, each work day, I travel with you to the brewery and see my clients in the roof top, pirating their Wifi. It's not the most professional and it means that I linger at the bar the rest of the day waiting for you to be done working because we are a single car family. This arrangement does not really suit either one of us.

So far, I have made one friend here, Kristal. She is the lawyer for the brewery and she speaks fluent English. She is kind and makes sure to include me each time she and her friends make plans. But, they all prefer Spanish and I can't help but feel like a burden to them when they slow down to explain what I've missed in English. She also works 9-5 Monday-Friday. Right now, I'm lucky if I work 6 hours a week.

I have been posting flyers and trying to network throughout my local area, but most everyone seems more interested in using mushrooms to manage their anxiety than psychotherapy. It could not be more obvious that I do not belong here.

The next week, when I drive back up the hill, I do it alone. Erica can speak enough English to help me with my phone plan and is eager to practice with me. When I arrive, she does not make me wait in the long que, but beckons me straight to her cubicle. She tells me that she was not able to find me the router that I need this week, but she can definitely have it by the next.

I try not to seem too disappointed because Erica is working so hard to be helpful and it is not her fault that I am facing this issue. But it has been over a month now and this internet issue is starting to be a metaphor of my entire experience of Costa Rica. Everything here seems to be someone helping you get something basic that seems like it should be systemically less challenging than it actually is. Something is always owed, some deal is always being arranged for you, prices are never discussed up front, and convenience is not an option. In the end, I feel disempowered and indebted, which has does not suit my disposition.

You are working full time and back to the pattern of being on call for them at every hour, leaving me to manage everything related to our home. I cook, clean, grocery shop, find internet, and make all efforts to relieve you of any other stressors that might threaten your mood. I find that I am losing myself in just trying to make daily life work in a way that is tolerable for me.

The last time I make the trek up the mountain to see Erica, she is able to provide me with service through means of a small pocket hotspot. I still don't really understand what happened or why, but she turns on this magic black box that fits in my palm and tells me how to reboot it each month, with very specific instructions. She also calls me her friend and we make plans to have lunch on days that I come back up the mountain. I am grateful to her because she has shown me compassion when I was feeling lost.

When I return home that night, we find that the magic black box works! After a month of tears and frustration, I am finally able to have basic internet in my home.

My Home, the only solace I have in this place that feels so foreign. I begin to spend long days on the mountain alone with my bottle of rum and ginger ale. Sometimes, I do not come down to town for days until I have an appointment, like a Spanish lesson. I start to play games on my phone endlessly. I hide here, because the world outside feels so exhausting. It is exhausting to feel so alone and to work so hard at basic things.

Eventually, a friend who also lived abroad, tells me that this experience is called culture shock. She is compassionate recalling her own first experiences living abroad. You on the other hand, are not. You begin to resent our little mountain house. You resent your commute to town. You refuse to make it more than once a day, leaving me to decide in the morning if I will go with you to work or be here all day. You begin to grow critical of my sedentary behavior, criticizing me for not picking up surfing or another sport. You begin to criticize me for the time I spend alone, the meals I choose to cook, and my lack of language skills.

I try to relieve your anxiety about my moods. I know that your critique is fueled by your own anxiety, just like my mother's was when I was a child. I am practiced at reading the anxiety and soothing it before it becomes rage. I try to manage your mood to create space for me to have my own experiences. I remind you that when I have bad days, they are not yours to solve, that I do not expect you to fix me or fix anything. I remind you that they are mine alone and I am working on them. I remind you that I love you and our relationship is not in danger, but your anxiety grows anyway and with it, your anger.

As my culture shock grows into exhaustion, I can no longer emotionally regulate for the both of us. Simultaneously, your rage grows with your feelings of being out of control. Your drinking and our arguments increase. Until one morning, when you wake up and roll over to hold me in your usual apologetic fashion, expecting the assault from the previous night be forgotten in the morning softness, I say something new. I rebuff your apologies for yet another drunken evening. Instead of consoling you, I push you away. "I don't want to hear those words out of your mouth again."

The familiar narrative tumbles from your lips, but today, I won't hear it. "I'm just so stressed at work. They expect me to be on call all the time. There's so much pressure to perform. They don't understand the challenges of working in this environment with a jungle system! I want to be good to you. I just need to get through this last week."

But I'm familiar with these excuses. They have been the same since we met. Whenever you are stressed, you have an excuse to party to the point of belligerence. I just don't have the resources to regulate you anymore while I am isolated here alone in the jungle, wrestling with my own culture shock and career loss.

"I'm sick of apologies without change." I snap back, "Instead of saying you are sorry, I want you to change your behavior. Stop doing it. Stop yelling, stop punishing, stop drinking. Do something different! Anything different!" I roll over with my back to you and wait for you to leave the bed and the house.

You dress and head to work. True to my request, you stop making apologies but that does not your behavior does not change. If anything, it worsens. I begin to realize that those apologies and my gentle forgiveness has been providing you with just enough absolution. Without this enabling, you being to act out more. You punish me more, drink more, yell more. That forgiveness was the valve release on your addiction and without it, you begin to drown in the guilt and consequences of your own choices, washing me away with you.

ENGAGED

March 2019

It is our two-year anniversary and we are sitting on the fort wall in Cartagena, Colombia. I know that you have asked your mother for the family diamond and I know that you have bought me a small piece of turquoise as a place holder until she brings it to us next month. We are happy today, a reprieve from the tormented months we have passed since we left the states.

Over the last few months, my body has slowly fallen into disarray. My cystic acne has worsened covering my neck, back, and arms. My hair has begun falling out in handfuls in the shower, leaving my once bouncing curls limp and stringy around my shoulders. My eyelashes are all but gone. I no longer need to pluck my once full eyebrows. I spend most days bored and lost in my own depression, counting the hours until I can start drinking in the afternoon. You suggest we spend a month sober and I end the conversation in tears, admitting that a cocktail by the pool is the only thing I look forward to each day. I hate this because my budding addiction now robs me of my right to complain about yours.

None of this matters right now. Last night you danced with me at Havana Club, and today we are remembering what we used to be like together. We have always traveled well together. When you are on vacation you are your best self, calm, kind, patient, and fun. We do not argue and there are no frat boys around for you to impress by breaking your promises to me. Whether we are in the mountains in Oregon or the beaches of Baja California; breweries in the mountains of Panama or illegal Mezcal bars in Guatemala, you are always friendlier and more relaxed than when we are home. We have walked all the corners of this continent together and these hot Latin nights are no exception to the rule. It is nice to remember why we came here together.

The last six months have been hard. I have been miserable. We both have been drinking more, and the presence of the boys does not help. They seem to wait for revery weekend just to begin their party all over again. They don't care about the promises you made me about your drug and alcohol use. I am afraid they see me as the stick in the mud, controlling girlfriend, but they don't know who you become in our house when you come home high. You save all your worst venom for me in private. I am not as good at hiding as you.

Two years ago, I told you I would give you these two years to decide on me. I am in my early thirties and do not have five years to waste in a relationship with someone who knows I am not his life partner, as was your previous pattern with partnerships. You would spend five years with these women, all the while, knowing from the beginning, that they were not right for you. At least, these were the stories that you told me and I was in the habit of believing you.

Despite facing this anniversary, with my words looming in the back ground alongside the struggles of this move, neither of us is ready to make this decision. I am not ready to leave, but I can't imagine spending the rest of my life in this same state. You are unwilling to let me go, but afraid of this future too. We both want to keep our vacation selves forever.

You asked my dad and grandpa to marry me the summer before we left. You bought me a little turquoise chip that I picked out by a local artisan in town. Neither of us sure what I will say when you ask. So, this moment passes like all of our other travels, but this time we go home without promises. We know better this time.

A week later, while sitting in the river with a bottle of champagne, you ask me to marry you. You tell me that you wanted to ask me on the city wall in Cartagena overlooking the sea, but you were too nervous that it wasn't special enough for me. I quell your anxiety, as I always do, by assuring you that I do not need special. I just need you. Then I surprise us both with a "yes," mostly because I am still not ready to leave.

I begin to bargain with myself about my unhappiness here in Costa Rica. Maybe it is simply my idleness. I have never been good at creating my own structure. I rely on my work to do that for me. Perhaps my depression was really just my lack of work. I love my job and it brings so much purpose to my life. I moved here with a few clients to see online, but as they got better and I closed their files, I was unable to build a new practice with new clients. My mind has grown restless and my sense of purpose has slipped away. Or maybe it's the boys. There are so few women here and I crave their company now more than ever.

I use this logic to search for anything to blame for my distress apart from the actual reasons. I throw myself into wedding planning like it is my life's passion, but it does nothing to alter my disdain for this place. It has been growing like a cancer in my heart. I might have more to distract me than the rum bottle now, and my disposition even improves, but I cannot shake the sinking suspicion that this unhappiness isn't all about Costa Rica.

PUERTO VIEJO

April 2019

Most people invite their friends and family to come visit when they move abroad, everyone promises, but most never come. Unless you move to Costa Rica! If that's the case, then everyone you know will be jockeying for position during the best weeks of the year to utilize your spare room. We have had a revolving door of visitors since we got our own little place up in the mountains. Now that we've moved back to town, not much has changed.

First your parents, then John. Those were fun trips. Your dad and his new wife on their not-quite-honeymoon because they had not yet told your sisters about the marriage. John came next, and we went to Bocas del Toro after a week here.

Then my friends began to come. First, Michael came for a week. Then Jess was up in the Nicoya with her family and we explored the volcanos for a few days before connecting with them. Now Emily is In Puerto Viejo and I'm supposed leave to see her tomorrow.

You tell me that you have missed me while I was up north with Jess. This engagement has increased your affection lately. So, you ask if you can join me to Puerto Viejo. I'm happy to have you and we set out the next morning, excited to share our engagement news.

Emily has already been here at a conference for three weeks and is
missing her long-time partner, Eric. As we are sitting on the beach, a
beautiful surfer, with long dreadlocks and a dark complexation walks
out of the ocean carrying his board. His golden skin is glistening with
saltwater and his shoulders might be as wide as ours combined. His abs
look as though they were carved from marble and you would have to be
blind not to see him. He may have been an actual Greek god who just
emerged from his underwater kingdom. I am trying not to notice because
I am suddenly aware of your shifting mood.

Emily comments on some things she would like to do with him out of her
boredom and separation, while I divert my eyes and do not respond. My
hackles are up as I watch you watching her. The perfect storm brewing.
Then you shift your gaze to me. I exhale, as you take in my lack of interest
and the storm blows over for now. We go back to laughing and I am extra
affectionate because I know that your fragile ego just took a hit. I want
to do all I can to keep that pain from motivating you to do something
dangerous.

Later that evening, we choose a seafood restaurant with a Caribbean vibe.
We've been told they have the best Sopa de Mariscos in town, one of our
favorite dishes. We are sipping margaritas while waiting for our dinner
when you make some mention of how it doesn't make sense that the
objectification of women is wrong while it is allowed towards men and
begin an indignant pout.

You are hungry and the soup is taking a small eternity. Patience is
not something you do well and I can see the storm clouds gathering
again. I suspiciously eye the margarita in your hand and try to do some
intellectual deflecting. The truth is that I agree with you. I'm not really
into the objectification of any person, but I am also acutely aware that
the objectification of women has a different social context built on years
of oppression. Then, Emily calmly begins to explain the social context of
the objectification of women and we are making the mistake of explaining
what we believe to be a rational point to a rational person.

I catch the look of thunder in your eyes too late to prevent your tantrum.
Standing up, you stomp out of the restaurant and disappear into the night

leaving us there with the bill. I scramble to pay and catch up with your impatient form, arms crossed in the street waiting.

Emily slowly saunters behind, giving us the space she believes we need to resolve our conflict fully expecting this to be over shortly, but I know better. Out on the street, you are yelling at me about what a hypocrite I am and how Emily is a terrible person. I am quickly overwhelmed as is the pattern these days. Emily's presence behind me reminds me of the boundaries I used to possess and I decide that I need some time to calm down before continuing this discussion.

I ask Emily who is just outside of earshot, to walk with me on the beach and let you know we'll meet you back at the hostel. You stomp off. She and I walk towards the water. Once you are out of sight, the sobs come on so quickly that they surprise us both with their intensity. By the time our toes touch the sand, Emily is half supporting me to the nearest driftwood log to sit down. The minutes it takes me to find my breath feel like hours. When my voice finally returns, I explain to her the horrors of these tantrums and how they have worsened since we arrived.

"I just don't know what to do." I sob over and over again in my hands.

"I didn't realize it had gotten this bad, Grace." She replies, clearly shocked at how very delicately I am holding together a sense of normalcy. "Do you need to leave?"

"How can I?" I break into a new convulsion. "I have no money of my own anymore. No place to go. All my things are on his property. I have no car. I have alienated most of my friends, and I can't go to my family. If I wanted to go home, I would have no place to live and no way to pay for one until I have been working for a few months at least! Don't you see? I'm trapped here with him."

The words fall out of my mouth like a cascade. I had not even realized they were my thoughts. They are things that had been lurking just outside of my consciousness for the last six months. Things I could not bear to acknowledge. I did not realize until this moment that I had been working so hard to keep them away. Emily wraps her arms around me because there is nothing left to say.

I take the next two hours to catch my breath in order to be ready to face you. As Emily and I are walking back to the hostel, the first thing I notice is that the truck is no longer parked where we had left it earlier that day. I immediately search my bag for my muted phone to find a barrage of text messages demanding my location and the time of my return. I can read the increasing anxiety and accusation until the final one announces that you are leaving.

We walk into our room to find that you have taken the dogs and your luggage and left. I frantically text you back asking where you went and when you'll be back. You tell me to catch the bus home, a twelve-hour ride that routes through the capital and then back to the other coast again. My heart is in my stomach and I begin calling you repeatedly to plead with you to come back. I am afraid and my Spanish is still not good enough to provide me with the confidence that I will be able to catch the right bus home. I feel stranded, abandoned, and betrayed. You left me here without resources.

When you finally answer your phone, you are cold and punishing. You say that if I want a ride home, I have to meet you in the morning. This shortens my visit with Emily by two days. I lay down in our bed and spend another night sleepless. In the last two and half years, my number of sleepless nights are accumulating as fast as my eyelashes are falling onto my cheeks.

In the morning, you meet me and load my bag into the car without speaking. You are still visibly angry and I am still afraid. Afraid of you, afraid of being left behind, afraid of what this moment means for us. You still don't understand that this is a deeper betrayal, more public than any of the previous. Emily saw it. She was there and I cannot unsee the look in her eyes. This look reflecting her concern, reflecting my own fears. Our relationship is irrevocably altered in this moment and I cannot trust you anymore. You have shown me just how far over the line you will go and just how justified you feel in your punishing wrath.

We spend the next four hours of our eight-hour drive discussing this event. Your side first, because your side is always first. You talk about feeling abandoned by me. You are angry that I wouldn't correct Emily or intervene in her objectification. You talk about how my values are selective and my character inconsistent. I listen and empathize, apologize and console. I try to understand the hurt and anger you were feeling as you felt justified in leaving me behind.

Now it's my turn, but I do not receive the same empathy in return. For hours I plead for you to see my side as valid. When we finally sit silently, I am beaten down and exhausted. I don't even have the energy to sulk, so I let you place our hand on my thigh in mock connection, but I do not smile. I don't even look up at you. I can't look up at you with the hopeful eyes of love again, now that I know what you are capable of doing.

▲

A week later, we discuss this event with our new couple's therapist over a telehealth meeting. For the first time, it appears that you are able to understand why leaving your fiancée in a foreign city alone because of something her friend said might feel like a betrayal. You apologize and I believe that you may really understand and really be sorry. Unfortunately, it is too late. It has taken you a week to hear me. I am beginning to know that the toll it takes on my body to beg is more than I can hold any longer. It is not that you can't understand, it's just that the cost of convincing you is too high.

Our trust is now so fractured that no amount of golden hope can hold the pieces together. Like a beautiful vase that has been shattered too repeatedly, the pieces are all dust. I step back from myself, as if I am seeing my choice to be with you for the first time. I see it in the way that all of my friends have been seeing it for the last two years; a vain hope that things could be better, all the while, lurking under the surface is my life-long fear that this is all I deserve.

After this moment I never trust you again. It is not a conscious decision. It just seeps into my unconscious choices keeping me out of your reach. All the times that you have left me in bars or at parties, laughing at my

expense, culminate in this moment. They all collude to convince me that
your line of kindness and human decency is different than mine. I can no
longer hope to be treated the way that I want by you. No apology can
undo that truth.

▲

A tentative, but melancholy peace resides in our house for the rest of the
month. You know that something has changed and I sink further away
from you, from everyone.

COCAINE

May 2019

I am not sure why I am waiting. Except that I am always waiting. Waiting for something to change: you, this place, me, anything to bring relief. It never does. I am waiting because being trapped hasn't changed with my anger. I know where you are and I know what you are doing. It is the same as always and I hate you for it.

I wait for hours until, finally I cover my nakedness with a bathrobe and drive to the local dive bar and retrieve you. I pull up, looking as mad as I feel. In front of the entire town, I roll down the window and demand you get in this car right now. You look up at me innocently, telling me how you needed to be there for your friend. You give your half-finished beer to him and get in the car. Everyone is staring and I know that I look as crazy as I feel. I am the unstable, controlling girlfriend. The Prophesy you have spoken into being.

Once home, we start at it like always. I remind you of your promise, No drugs. You lie to me. I threaten to buy a plane ticket. Around and around we go. I promised a year. You promised no drugs. You are angry because I haven't tried hard enough to be happy here. I am angry that you haven't been supportive. I suggest moving home while you stay to finish your contract. You tell me if I leave, you can't promise to be faithful.

Something in me snaps, and I wander out of the house in the rain. Unsteady on my feet, I begin to walk down the muddy road towards the river, not even attempting to avoid the muddy, rainwater filled potholes. Still in my bathrobe, I can hardly see from the rain or tears. I don't know where I am going but I cannot stay here.

The swelling river calls to me and I wonder if it's strong enough to sweep me out to sea. I stumble into it and feel the water lapping around my ankles. It reminds me for a moment that I have been happy before. There was a time, in another life maybe, but I can almost remember it now.

I turn back towards the house and come in to find you on the sofa, reading, non-plussed. I collapse into a chair soggy and begin to sob, "I have no other place to go. I just want to die." I have begun spending time thinking about car crashes and drowning. I am embarrassed because it feels mellow-dramatic, but it's all true. It happened so subtly that I almost didn't notice. Or maybe it wasn't subtle, I just don't notice me anymore.

Now, I have your attention and this is how it has works. You are unconcerned until I am hysterical. Your tone softens and you move in closer with concern. You concede that this place is killing me and that it is destroying our relationship. You concede this because something must be blamed. You have been cleaning clots of my hair from the drain each morning. You have touched my feverish skin and spent many nights sexless because of it's rawness, heat, and itching. Finally, defeated, you agree to let me go home.

HOME AGAIN

July 2019

After nearly 24 hours of travel, my feet touch the familiar PDX carpet and
I send you a photo. I am relieved, almost giddy. You are sad and angry.
After everything that has passed, I simply could not have our wedding in
Costa Rica. I have come to hate that place. I have to hate something, after
all.

Jess is picking me up and I'll stay with her through the weekend for my
dress fitting party. She agrees to play designated driver from shop to shop
while we drink champagne and pick out Cinderella style dresses for me to
try. I don't have any intention of buying one, but any party with my girls
is a good party. I am starved for their connection and need to know that I
was not forgotten.

Once in the car, my girls are already laughing and greeting each other like
old friends. So many of them have met before, but would not necessarily
see one another without me as a reason. They all share stories of the last
time they saw one another, how we all met, and the crazy adventures I
pulled them into. They all talk about the fears they have conquered and
the limits we have pushed together. They remind me of how I dragged
them into the wilderness or up mountains for the first time where they
find your own power and confidence. My soul is full, remembering that
I was once a brave woman, that I had once inspired them. Encouraged

them and helped them find their best selves. I thought I could do anything for a year, but I learned that I could not be without my ladies. They give me purpose and remind me of who I am. It is them who fill my scared little heart this time and inspire me to find myself again.

After ample champagne, dresses, and a little too much of my thong visible, we talk about the wedding. I tell my ladies that, per a client's suggestion, I am making a family drama bingo card so that you and I can laugh instead of cry at the craziness only a wedding can bring out in a family. We have a box for your mother and for mine. We have a box for my grandfather and for each of your sisters. We even have one for me and one for you. We are all laughing as the girls ask what's in my box. I tell that that some point I'll start to yell-cry about something insignificant and then you storm off.

The girls laugh and roll their eyes at my box recalling the times they have witnessed me this way, and then they each begin to tell stories about the first time they met you. Each one recalls you losing your temper and then disappearing. Their smiles fade slowly as they look from one to another recognizing the similarity of their stories. Each one, on meeting you for the first time, witnessed your wrath. The messiness of a partnership is something everyone eventually sees, but they have each only met you once or twice. The humming of chatter fades as the same thought dawns in each mind. Jess and I lock eyes. Hers carry concern and say everything she would never say out loud, everything I am still not ready to hear, "Are you sure? Is this the right choice? Are you going to be OK?"

I change the subject because this is not the time or place to wrestle with these questions and I am out of choices. I gave up my career and financial independence to move with you from Oregon to Costa Rica. I do not have the option to leave anymore. Jess knows, but the others don't. I have thought about leaving you countless times while we were gone, but I did not have the money to buy a plane ticket, or a place to live when I came home. I know that you were vindictive enough to do any number of things to hurt me and I lived with the fear of what you were capable. It would be months before my job started reimbursing me for the work that I provided, contract work and negotiations with insurance companies are always slow. I am scared and trapped; so I am lying to myself and everyone because I do not know what else to do.

I silently promise myself never to be in such a vulnerable position again. The next morning, I head back to our small-town life and begin working on Monday with a sense of urgency and commitment to my career that I have never known before.

PDX

September 1, 2019

This month of separation has been one of the best in our relationship. I have been wedding planning and living in the land of hopes and dreams without the reality of you to wake me up at night with cocaine or drunk rages. We talk on the phone each evening and you are sweet to me. I know you are being careful with us right now because we are apart. I also know that it won't continue like this when we are together again. I miss you, but I know that this Hank is not the one that will be coming home to me.

I am driving back to the Portland Airport to pick you and your dog up from your long flight back from Costa Rica. Yesterday they delayed your flights due to a hurricane, but they also had to reroute you creating extra stops on your way home. You are not happy about this alteration and I can hear your anxiety about traveling rising at every lay-over.

Since it was your last weekend in Costa Rica, you and the boys partied in San Jose. As usual, you are not feeling your best for this comedy of errors today. Rarely have I seen you hungover. It just rolls into morning beers the next day mostly, but there hasn't been time for you to drink between flights today.

By the time you are ready to board your third flight, you are feeling the full weight of your weekend choices. You board the last one and de-plane twice before you finally send me the message that you are en route. Your arrival time changing from 8PM to nearly midnight.

On our last call, you were livid and any consolation efforts I made were an affront. I can't help you from here, so you hang up the phone with vitriol and I am relieved to still be a 4 hour flight away.

I arrive at the cellphone waiting area outside the terminal rest before you land. I pull in and nap a little waiting for your message. At 12, I get your text that you landed safe and sound and expect it to take another 45 minutes before you can deplane and collect our belongings. You say you'll call me again when you get to the baggage claim. So, I drift back to sleep.

At 1AM I jolt awake and realize the time. I frantically check my phone for missed calls or texts, and find nothing. I start to become afraid of how angry you will be if you have been kept waiting.

I drive to the baggage claim and begin to look around for you. It is a ghost town. I can see our bags left beside the carousel and quickly dash inside to collect them. I place them inside the trunk and roll forward to continue my search for you at another doorway. There are very few people, so I can get away with leaving my car for a few minutes without interference from the attendants.

I go inside to check the boards. There is another flight landing from Costa Rica and people begin to flood the terminal again. I wait a little longer, beginning to become frustrated at your lack of communication. All those people file out and into vehicles and drive away, still there is no sign of you.

I go back inside again, and venture all the way up the stairs to see if there is some delay or problem. Eventually another passenger catches me and tells me that they will tow my car if I leave it any longer by the curb. I dash outside exasperated and as I climb behind the wheel again, my phone finally rings.

"Where are you?!" I demand, irritated.

"I'm at Providence hospital." You say with a chuckle.

"Oh, shut up! Where are you?" I reply flatly.

"I'm not joking, Baby."

".... Stop it. Where are you?"

"I had a seizure getting off the airplane and two ladies saw it and called the ambulance. I am in the Providence Hospital ER."

I am speechless and all my anger evaporates and as begin driving. When I arrive, I quickly find my way to your room to find you a mess of lines and cords. You are still shaking and I have never seen a seizure before.

My eyes widen as I take in the scene and my crisis mode calm takes in everything at once. You reach out for me and I take your hand for a moment before I get to work. I make sure the dogs are fed and watered, and taken out for the bathroom. I take your carryon baggage to the car and prepare to meet with the doctor for a full update on your testing.

When the doctor arrives, he explains that there can only be a few reasons that you had a seizure. Based on the CAT scan and blood tests, you do not have indicators of a neurological issues. "The only other reason for a seizure like this would be if there was heavy drinking proceeding a period of time without alcohol. This could trigger a withdrawal response." He states, matter of factly.

"Well, he does drink a fair amount." I blink back at him with my large round eyes exaggerated by shock. I look down at you and then back to the doctor. "And he did just spend the weekend in San Jose with the boys."

The doctor tilts his head to one side, almost imperceptibly and asks me, "What do you do for a living?" His look is piercing and curious. It is as if he's trying to understand the situation more fully by reading me.

"I'm a mental health counselor." I reply, and as if hit by a wave, I feel heat rush into my face and neck.

His eyebrows raise, so slightly, the smallest crack in his carefully constructed bedside manner. Then another look replaces the surprise. It's confusion. He did not expect this answer or to have to tell someone like me, what I have missed: the obvious answer that suddenly seems very delicate. I am ashamed at my own denial. He is a mixture of concern and pity now, and I hear his diagnosis reverberating through the room in deafening silence. I know that I should have known before now. It is my job to have known.

In this short but irrefutable exchange between the doctor and I, I am forced to see my own avoidance. I am trapped between my hope and reality. You are an alcoholic. The fact now lays here just as tangible as your body in this hospital bed. We have been joking about it for years, but it is not funny now. Here, in this hospital room, no one is laughing.

In response to the earsplitting silence, you insist that this was related to the anxiety of travel, having to de-plane multiple times with the dog, but the doctor confirms that there is no evidence that anxiety can cause seizures.

With this sentence the doctor excuses himself, leaving no room for alternate explanations. Taking with him all the air in my lungs and my last tiny hope.

You fall back asleep holding my hand, still seizing every few moments until you're unconscious again thanks to the Ativan. The nurse tells me that we can take our time leaving. They don't need your bed urgently, so we can stay as long as we need. When she walks out the door and pulls the curtain shut, I am left alone with the pieces of on shattered denial and the image of you wrapped in tubes.

As I attempt to piece them back together, running my little fingers over their share edges, it feels like I am watching my life with you unfold in slow motion. I replay every moment where the stories did not add up. I see for the first time that the issues you had with your former employer were not as coincidental as you had led me to believe. The reasons you gave for the blood and the arguments were not your heroism or your victimization. Your insistence on walking or biking everywhere, based on the advice of a DUI lawyer you once met in a bar was advice that had saved you from countless consequences. Our cute, little airport bar stops were not luxury, they were necessity. It had all been a carefully constructed lie to preserve your addiction. This seizure, has flown like a boulder through the mosaic house you built for us to live in together and I am standing amongst the shards, seeing it for the first time alone.

I cannot un-know this truth. I am no longer allowed the luxury of avoiding what I do not want to see. It is inescapable and all my tools of denial are broken like the glass house at my feet.

Then the next terrifying thought creeps in, we are supposed to get married in three weeks.

▲

At 4AM I can no longer stand these thoughts alone. I need to move, do something, anything. I wake you up, and tell you it is time to go. We climb into the car with Ativan influenced sleepy eyes and ask me for a beer. I stare at you for a brief moment in shock, then deny you quietly, and begin driving.

We drive to my grandparent's house because it's the closet place we can get to and quietly sneak into their spare bedroom. They are supposed to be out of town, so I don't even call them to let them know that we are coming. I do not sleep, with your intermittent spasms in the bed next to me, and the sounds of my shattering world ringing in my ears. I lie awake staring at the ceiling until sometime long after dawn, when the shock finally gives way to exhaustion.

Only two hours later, I jolt awake and we begin to pack ourselves into the car for the drive home.

"Not the homecoming we were hoping for huh?" You chuckle from the passenger seat. I force a small smile and begin driving again.

THE LITTLE WEDDING THAT COULDN'T

September 20, 2019

The day before our wedding, we are on the front lawn of the rental we are staying in with all your family and our out-of-town guests. I am packing up the truck with the food that I prepared and the projects you built this week. Your father is helping me while everyone else is running in and out of the front door in a controlled chaos.

It has been a hard week for both of us. Last weekend, you chased me down the street yelling at me while drunk. I ran to Calen's house where I cried and spilt the whole story. I told him about your seizure and your drinking. The secrets that I had been keeping from your friends and family for the last two and half years spilled like red wine on white carpet. They were a stain I could not remove, but I didn't know what else to do. Then, I called your dad and asked for his help too. The two men that you are closest to were concerned and offered to be helpful. Your dad asked if he should cancel his flight for this wedding that seems to be cursed, but I begged him to come, hoping he could reach you in some way that I couldn't. When you found out, you felt betrayed.

I held my breath through this week hoping it would be filled with reconciliation, laughter, and joy at the pleasure of being together with the people we love, but you have been surly and irritable. You tell me that you're feeling exposed and don't want to attend your own bachelor party which Ben carefully constructed around your interests. You pout and your father mentions to me that you are nearly intolerable this week while you are building the arbor together.

I feel like I'm swimming against the current of your mood. Yesterday is the first day that I am feeling like I can tolerate you again. The space between us at night when we crawl into our bed feels endless, even as you wrap your body around mine. I feel an empty cavity in my chest growing more expansive with each suffocating night spent in this way.

I can feel the tension in the air this morning as we begin packing. I am not sure where its coming from, but its palpable. On the front lawn, as I carry one more container to the truck, I see you on your cell phone talking, but I am not sure to whom. A man is passing by on the street with his dog on a leash and I notice him before you. I also see your dog slowly begin to stalk towards the man. You are distracted by your phone conversation when he yells out, gripping his dog's leash, knuckles whitening. "Get your dog! Get your dog!" He says twice with increasing volume. I can hear the fear in his voice.

With phone in hand, your father and friends to bear witness, and loud enough for the neighborhood to hear, you tell him to fuck off. You tilt the cellphone from your ear and rotate your body to look him full in the face, squaring up your shoulders in a threat. The words that fall out of your mouth are quickly drowned by my own yelling at you to stop.

"Hank! Stop it! Just get your dog! Stop it!" I scream at you while the man scurries away on his way to the market up the road. My precarious composure cracking.

You finish the conversation I now realize was with your mother, and heave a sigh of regret. You're always so volatile around your mother. Then, rounding on me you refuse to acknowledge your inappropriate behavior. Your father nods in agreement with my assessment and you stomp back in the house to gather more support for your victimization.

On your way back out, the man passes again on his way home and you have another altercation. I am exasperated and teetering on the edge of my commitment already, but this outburst pushes me off the fence. I cannot imagine marrying you in 24 hours.

I am too exhausted by your mood swings and all this lonely wedding preparation to sign myself up for a life like this. I tell you to leave and your father and I finish packing up the truck alone.

When we pull out of the driveway, we pass the neighbor in his own front yard, on the phone with the police. Your father asks me to stop the car so he can deescalate the situation.

"Why?" I ask. "Maybe the police need to show up so that Hank can learn that he cannot talk to people that way." I state, indifferent and even hopeful that this is my way out.

"Oh no, you don't mean that. We can't have Hank getting arrested with the wedding tomorrow." he says, completely missing my desire to avoid that very event.

He climbs out of the truck, approaching the man. He apologizes for you, explaining that there is to be a wedding tomorrow and we're all feeling stress. His excuses for you are a little too accessible and sound a little too similar to my own. He climbs back in the truck as the mans' cell phone come down and he has used all his charm to put out that fire.

Ten minutes later, I find you with your mother at Calen's house. You are already drinking beer and telling everyone why none of this is your fault. Your mother nodding in agreement, eyeing me from the side. It doesn't matter to you that I won't look at you and that your father reminds you that the man had every right to call the police. You are lost to us, finding the easiest escape to the bottom of another beer can.

We finish packing everything and hitching the Airstream to the truck. Then we meet everyone at the rendezvous point at the established time. I manage to avoid talking to you until we are there. I realized that I can't spend the next 4 hours in the truck with you fighting about this incident and I notice the third beer can, mostly empty, in your hand. I ask you to ride with my mother instead.

"Please help her. She has the tendency to get lost." I ask.

You lie to me, saying that you asked her, but she didn't want you in her RV and then climb into your mothers' instead. By the time my mother has gotten lost and been found again, we are thirty minutes behind you and the Airstream is fishtailing anytime I try to drive over 45mph. I know it must not be weighted properly, so I call you and ask if you remembered to fill the water tank in the nose before we left.

You are angry at having your drinking party interrupted. "What do you want me to do about it, Grace?" You demand.

"I don't know, Hank. I just need help!"

"Fine. We'll pull over and unload it when you catch up." You shout, hanging up the phone unceremoniously.

When I finally catch up, your guys unload the sound equipment into your mom's RV, but it is still fishtailing. So, you grudgingly agree to drive it. My mother pulls in behind us and I climb into her RV as your mother's peels away with all your rowdy friends, followed by you in the truck with the Airstream, then us.

"You know that you are marrying your step-father, right?" she asks as I climbed into her passenger seat.

I am barely holding it together, "Yes" I breathe out defeatedly.

I did know. Until then I had fooled myself into thinking you were different. You could apologize; my step-father never did. Then, somewhere during the year in Costa Rica, your apologies had dried up. Maybe it was because I told you I didn't want to hear them anymore, because you never changed your hurtful, abusive behavior anyway. Perhaps it was because you could no longer look at your mistakes without raging at and blaming me. I don't know, but it has been a long time since I could convince myself that you were better than him.

With the Airstream is still weighted poorly, it doesn't take my mother and

I long to catch you. We see you swerve and both catch our breath. I begin calling you frantically.

"Are you ok?! Do I need to drive?" I ask, afraid to ask the real question, "Are you drunk?"

I already know the answer to that and you would not admit it if I asked anyway. You usually have a strict policy against driving after drinking, but if you don't drive now, you'd have to admit being intoxicated at 11AM. This is the reason your house is downtown, that you bike everywhere. I am reminded again of all the ways that you have sculpted your life to accommodate your alcoholism.

"I'm fine! I'm just tired." You lie again. "Just pass me, I need to let the dog out to pee anyway."

We leave you behind and find the nearest gas station with a fill site for water. I call again and ask you to pull in here so that we can fill the tank and end the fishtailing, but you are angry now and I am your favorite punching bag. You mutter something about it being too hard to find and I watch as you pass me on the way to the next meet up site where all of our guests in various vehicles are waiting to continue with the caravan.

My mom and I are the last ones to pull in and when we do, I walk over to you, obviously angry. I collect the Airstream keys and take it back to the gas station. I do this without speaking to you to prevent myself from saying something I'll regret.

I fill the tank which takes a full 20 minutes, but when I hop back into the driver seat, I see that I missed three calls from you. I try to call you back but there is no answer. My stomach is in knots. I know that there will be retribution for my inattentiveness. Whatever slight you perceived on my behalf is fodder for punishment for at least the rest of the day. I can no longer differentiate my fear of you from my loathing.

When I pull into the parking lot where I expect to see the same group I just drove away from moments before, the only people left there are my mother and my grandparents.

"Where is everyone?" I ask her.

"I don't know, they just all pulled out and started driving that way." She answers, pointing.

I've been left behind again. I am supposed to be marrying you in 24 hours, I don't know the way to our venue, and you left without me, again. I am livid and empty all at once. I peel out of the parking lot determined to catch up.

I call my own friends in the caravan who assure me that they didn't realize I was not in the front of the line and work with them to catch up. You are decidedly not answering your cell.

I find my way to the playa, driving much too fast on a gravel road and park far away from the various group circles that have started clicking together. I find the small group of friends that I invited and sit with them staring at the small fire in the center. I do not have the energy to set up the airstream alone.

When I finally venture into the group in search of a snack and drink, various people keep asking me, "How are you?"

The only response that seems to fall out my mouth from my dissociated trance is, "I don't know, how many times has your partner called you a cunt?"

I tell Charlie to go ahead and light the giant pile of pallets on fire tonight, "What are we waiting for anyway? Let's set it all on fire now!"
Only one person admits that in the last ten years it's been said in her partnership twice. "Well, Hank has called me that three times in the last six months. How should I feel right now?" I respond with no trace of emotion.

You choose not to speak to me all night, avoiding coming near me with the subtle charm of fliting from camp to camp in the highest of spirits. Finally, you wander into my camp and begin talking with Michael.

"I still haven't written my vows. I don't know what to say." You begin, looking for input. It would almost be a romantic gesture, if I didn't hate you so much right now.

"How about you start with 'I promise not to call you a cunt.'" I say clearly and directly enough to silence the circle.

You mutter something about not realizing I was there and slither back into the darkness.

"Maybe we don't need to put the C-word in the vows, Grace." Michael chuckles, trying to relieve the tension.

▲

That night I do not sleep. I toss and turn and finally get out of my mom's bed at 4AM to the familiar numb feeling of anxiety. It is the quiet kind that no one can see, that feels like an emptiness looming. It is the kind that keeps me poised and ready, not yet decided if I should fight or flee. My nerves are taught like the line that I am walking, the expanse below me like a gaping mouth waiting to devour when I stumble. I am naked and alone.

I see and hear everything, drinking in the silence of the desert at this hour, sitting with death-like stillness, staring. After a few hours, my mother gets up as well. Her own anxiety rooted in mine. She tries to convince me to eat. I don't recall the last time I've eaten, but I have no appetite. Out here in the dark, I feel frozen in time, my body needs nothing, as if I am not even alive.

I know that I cannot do it. I cannot get married today. Maybe I won't have to if the sun simply does not rise. Maybe by staying awake I can will the darkness to stay too. Now that we are all assembled here, I don't know what else to do.

I tried to run away yesterday. I called my mother while careening down that gravel road much too fast, trying to catch the caravan that left me behind. I told her that when I arrived, I would get in her RV and we would leave the playa. I had mustered up all that was left of my courage to make that phone call, but my words fell flat and so did the last of my self-respect. Now I am numb and out of solutions. I hate myself for it.

When she told me that I could not leave, that 55 people were gathered in the middle of nowhere at my request and it was irresponsible to leave them there, I deflated like a small balloon. I was also surprised. With the conversation we had while driving together earlier, I had expected her to celebrate my rebellion as the courage she never had with my step-father.

I had been so sure she would be supportive. She and I were in her RV together when we saw you swerving, driving the airstream drunk an hour after we had left Bend. She listened to me cry about how cruel you had been in those few weeks leading up to the wedding, calling me a cunt, chasing me down the street, threatening neighbors. I was sure that she would drive away with me right then, but she didn't. She refused.

Months later she admitted to me that she had called grandpa and he talked her out of it. I know that I will regret not having left yesterday for the rest of my life. It is the deepest betrayal of what I know to be right, the deepest betray of myself.

I do not know how many hours I sat awake at that tiny table in the dark, trying to be still so mom might be able to sleep. I do not know when I finally crawled back into her bed to try to scratch a few moments of rest before the sunrise brings the awful day to light. But as I begin to wake on this awful morning, the feeling of being frozen has not left me.

I walk out of the door stiff and cross the cracked earth to my airstream where you had slept. There I found the bottle of tequila that you had taken to bed the night before nestled in the blankets, tucked in like a baby, between the sheets, next to where they revealed your outline.

There were various broken items strewn about the small space from your drunken scramble to get into bed last night. My insides begin to turn from frost to smoldering rage. Like the coals of the campfire the morning after, with a little feeding I begin to ignite again. I grab these objects and throw them out the door onto the desert ground thinking about the night before, the last I saw of you at our rehearsal dinner party.

"Maybe you should start with 'I promise not to call you a cunt!'" My own words reverberating in my mind, drifting in and out as I throw the broken objects out of the tiny space that had been my home when we met, my sacred space.

This morning is absolutely perfect, in glaring contrast to the tempest inside me. The sun is high and though the air is still cool, I can feel the temperature of the arid sky slowly beginning to rise. After purging my space, I look out across the dry ground toward the mountains, holding the heavy sadness of my disappointment like a stone in my stomach. The ground has already become watery with the sun's reflection.

Yesterday, I called the photographer while driving and told her not to come. Any art that is created today, on this desert, is going to be gorgeous, but I will never look at it.

Then I begin to cry. The photos, the art, the beauty of it all, the work that I have invested to create something special, all a waste. There would be no art today. This thought struck my mind like an ax in my brain. It buried itself so deeply that it breaks through the stubborn pretense of numbness and racks my body with sobs. I collapse into the dinette because I can't bear to touch the sheet where you had laid.

I sit in my little tin can, so familiar, once a safe place for me, now desecrated with this memory. A place that will always hold the curse of this day. The tears begin to come with more force and I let them carry me back into the darkness hoping it will envelope me and I will not have to face this day.

I cry as long as the darkness will keep me but all tears pass, even when we wish they would stay. Eventually, all choices must be made. When they abandon me back to the situation at hand, I begin to pace my tiny hall like a caged beast in a space much too small for its wild nature. Then, Ben knocks on the door. Like a truly good friend and the appointed organizer, he came to ask me what needs to be set up for the wedding.

Snapped out of my dissociation, I stare back in disbelief that someone believes there will still be a wedding today. How could anyone on this playa not know that there cannot possibly be a wedding? How can my internal reality be so far from what everyone else is experiencing? It is as if I do not exist. I have a part to play and everyone is waiting for the performance of my life: blissful, if stressed, bride to be.

I dry my eyes and walk across the playa to begin giving instructions.

▲

I cannot run or hide from this day. It is a train speeding without breaks heading for a curve in the track. I am determined to manage my sentence without emotion. I cannot let your friends see me break. They would enjoy it too much. I return to my airstream to begin dressing as if I am preparing for a wedding. Calen comes looking for me, next.

I am sitting in my purple silk bathrobe, the one I brought for this occasion, alone at the dinette with a makeup brush in hand.

"What do you think, Grace? How are you feeling?" he asks.

"I will say whatever I need to say for this to be over as quickly as possible." I state, stoic and cold. "I just need this day to be over."

"I don't think anyone needs to say anything today. I can already see his 5-mile stare. I'll figure something out, but no one is getting married today." He replies and finds the door. He leaves to contemplate how to fill the role of officiator without giving away our secret. There is no wedding.

I walk across the desert in my lace dress. I hate it. I hate you. I hate this day. I cannot even smile until I see the faces of my friends, concerned and understanding. Their kindness melts me into a fragile place, where I can soften enough to go on with the pretense. My smile is meant to reassure them, but it grounds me; reminding me that this is not only traumatic for me, but for those that know and love me as well. I want them to be ok when this is all over, even if I am not sure I will ever be. They have witnessed too much. I have asked too much of them. Yet, here they are, gently smiling at me with compassion and understanding.

▲

Grandpa's prayer runs too long with too insincere an assurance to undo the Christian overtones, saying, "we accept all kinds." I lock eyes with Calen in the middle of the prayer. You are swaying reverently with folded hands and pursed lips. I wonder if you even hear what he has said. Calen asks me with his eyes if he needs to intervene. We both linger a breath longer as the end comes on its own. Exhale.

Calen then talks about needing to reflect on our life choices, the directions that we take, the paths we walk down, and I see in his eyes what he will never be able to say directly to you. "Is this truly what you want? This life, this addiction, this destruction?" It is the only warning he ever gives you.

The wedding ends and I reach to kiss you to cover the lack of pronouncement. There is no "kiss the bride," no "man and wife." How can I cover this so grandpa does not know? How can I hide this in front of all of your people? They are always looking for it to be my fault. I announce the wine and beer and head back to the safety of my trailer to change out of this ridiculous dress.

I do not see you during dinner and when Ben stands up to begin toasting, you are conspicuously absent. So, I make one of my own with the list of thank you's that I have accumulated for our community who graciously gave their time for this farce. I feel the weight of my guilt for having leaned on them for the creation of something so anti-climactic.

When dinner is over, the sun sets, and the bonfire begins. In my flannel and leggings, I can finally breathe again. It's over and everyone will leave tomorrow. I don't know if I pulled off my part. I have never been a good actress, but at least the curtain has fallen. You are elated and it becomes apparent to me that Calen did have the same chat with you that he had with me. Perhaps that is best, because you probably would not have cooperated. I say this to myself to justify your ignorance and to avoid the responsibility of telling you now. You are drunk anyway, it's not a good time to talk.

The flames grow higher into the night as more pallets are tossed on top. The stars are shining in the perfect way they do out here. The music list we created together along with the wine is having the desired effect. People are laughing and warming themselves in a happy daze. I am finally able to eat a little.

▲

I made too much food, I notice. I suppose we'll be eating a lot of potato salad over the next week. I walk to the fire with my cup of wine and sit next to our neighbors, chatting about nothing in particular. They know, I can see it in their eyes, but they are southern and would never say it out loud.

You are somewhere else again and I am relieved, until I hear you making bets. What am I hearing? Can you jump the fire? I hate you but not enough to wish you dead. Your college friends are not far away, cajoling you. You jump and make it across, barely, falling on your hand in the coals. You retract it so fast it is not burnt. God damn your athleticism. My white-hot rage is returning now as a cover for my fear. How much anxiety can I possibly swallow before I snap?

Then one of the college boys speaks quietly to the others who have moved closer to me to watch the scene, "He really has not changed, has he?" He states. "So impressionable, you could get him to do anything. Watch!" Then raising his voice, he calls out to you, "You only made it because you took it from that direction! Betcha can't do it from this side. There's no way!" His coy intent of trying to get you to jump the longer width of the fire is working. You begin pacing this side assessing the probability of making that jump.

Snap! Something inside me breaks and I round on him like a lioness, "You shut the fuck up right now or I'll punch you right in the dick." I state so clearly and with so much conviction that I am not sure I will wait to hear the answer. He claps his half open mouth shut like a mousetrap, takes one moment to look me directly in the eyes, He turns back to his friends, walking away from me and the fire.

"I'd love to see her punch him in the dick." Another one laughs, beer in hand.

"I told you not to get involved, man." I hear a from another. Slowly, they all pick up their camp chairs and head to their own space away from the fire.

In the meantime, you have been hedging your bet. Our neighbors catch their breath and look away, unable to watch. Ben approaches you from the side, "Hey man, you're scaring people. It's time to stop," he rests a hand on your arm.

I cannot fathom how he manages to convince you to walk away. I exhale. The neighbors reach over to grab my arm gently and ask me if I would like to come look at the stars with them. The three of us walk off into the darkness for a moment of peace before the night ends and I am left alone to face you.

You find me a few moments later, "Will you at least sleep in the Airstream with me tonight?" you ask sheepishly. I concede, because there is nowhere else to go anymore.

THE HONEYMOON

September 22, 2019

This morning, I watch everyone drive off the playa, leaving us to our "honeymoon." I sigh in relief as my grandparents, always the last to leave a party, finally load into their truck and drive their little trailer away from us. I am finally alone, next to you.

This weekend has been a slow train wreck and I have no energy left for crying. You are still unaware that we are not married. I do not have the energy to tell you and I am afraid that when you find out, you will climb into your truck and drive away from me and this airstream forever, leaving me alone on the playa with a dead cell phone and several cases of wine. I could not fight back now even if I tried.

I still cannot tell a lie, so as I lounge under the shade tent in my silk robe, I am silent. Waiting for the moment when the truth surfaces. You are icing the last wedding keg, and then pumping yourself an IPA from the handle. You are affectionate, but not aggressively. You are, at least, aware that I am fragile right now.

At some point you make reference to the ceremony and I cannot collude in this lie any longer. I tell you that we did not get married.

"There were no vows. No 'man and wife' statements. What did you think had happened?" I mutter, with no affect.

You take a few moments of stunned silence before yelling, "I hate you and I never want to see you again!"

I continue to sit, motionless. I am too tired to feel anything. So, I just sit, staring at the barren land around me. I cannot move. I cannot pack up or make any attempts at consoling you. I will not even entertain the possibility of doing it later. I do not care that you are suffering. I have held the weight of this alone for far too long and it is finally too much for me to bear. I let the columns of it crash around you, like Samson pulling the temple down on himself. I am your Delilah, not strong enough to keep the pillars in place any longer.

You slam the door to the airstream locking yourself inside. I exhale. I am alone with you close by, a familiar experience. I don't know how long I sit. Time doesn't seem to move, though I can tell by the sun that it passes.

Eventually, I move to the playa floor and strip naked in the sun. White dust on the fronts of my thighs and belly and breasts, my skin reveals tiny bumps from the cool breeze that blows, warning of the change in the seasons. It is both hot and cold here in an instant. It is beautiful and desolate and I cannot think of any more appropriate place to bury our love. I lay on the floor of the desert not sleeping, not thinking, until the chill forces me to move again.

I start to build a small fire with what wood is left as the sun begins to set behind the mountains to the west. I reach into the pocket of my robe to discover the Katrina figurines that Rico bought for us in Mexico. They are mismatched. He had bought a set, but in a mezcal stupor, misplaced the groom, returning home with only a bride. She is beautiful and I loved her the instant that I saw her. You were still in Costa Rica when you first sent the photos to me.

"What's the groom like?" I asked, after effusively approving of her.

A week ago, Mariano arrived from Costa Rica for the wedding carrying the replacement. He is much larger than her and does not match. They

cannot be placed next to one another on the cake as I had hoped.
Irritated, I had shoved them in this pocket intending to place them in
different locations to distract from their obvious incompatibility. I must
have forgotten them in mess of yesterday.

I pull them out now, touching their beautiful faces. They are of excellent
quality, handmade. I had wanted them so badly, but they were useless in
the end. I wondered where the original groom might be. I wondered if he
missed his bride. It felt wrong to me that they should be separated. What
a cruel punishment never to see one another again. I suddenly felt awash
with sadness that they would forever be separated.

When the tears subside, I dismiss my deluded, romantic fantasy and
throw them both in the fire to watch them burn to ash. I never want to
see them again. As I watch her white skeletal frame turn black with flame,
her terracotta construction crumbling back into the mud from which she
was made, the grief descends on me like the night sky.

You stumble out of the airstream without a word, walk over to the keg,
and begin to empty in onto the dry playa mud, creating a puddle of hop
smelling muck behind me. I do not look up at you or smile. I pretend that
I don't notice, I will not be fooled by hope again.

After this task that takes a surprising amount of time, you walk over to
me, and promise me that you will be sober until we decide together that it
is ok for you to drink again. I accept your promise because I cannot leave
you right now. I am still financially devasted from our year in Costa Rica
and then this futile wedding. I have nowhere to go. Also, I still love you
and am too tired to make any choices today.

MY FRIENDS

October 2019

We are home again, moving back into our little house downtown, but it is not the happy homecoming we expected. None of this has been the way we expected, not since that first night in the hospital. Nothing has been the same since. Like a slow-moving train wreck, a new trauma each week since you came home. Leading up to the biggest one of all, the utter humiliation in front of all of our friends and family last weekend on the desert.

Rob sends a congratulations text message and asks me if I'm free to grab a drink sometime this week. I think it might be good for me to get out of the house for a little bit, so we meet at one of our usual cocktail spots downtown.

I walk in and he jumps up, arms open, "Congratulations married lady! How was it? I saw some photos. Everything looked beautiful." Rob greets me enthusiastically.

"Hey!" I respond, not quite sure what to say about what has just happened, realizing I should have prepared a statement for the public. "Thanks! How was your trip?" I deflect, initially.

Rob wasn't able to make the wedding because he was home visiting family and I'm finding it refreshing to talk with someone who wasn't there to witness my humiliation.

He takes the bait and tells me about his trip home and his sisters and their kids, but it doesn't take long before he circles back to get the detail of the wedding.

"I didn't get married." I say with a smile, as if somehow this will make it less shocking.

He gafaws, "That's funny! But really, tell me all about it."

"I'm not joking." I repeat, my smile slightly fading.

"What?!" he sets his beer down and turns in his bar seat to face me fully.

Both our smiles have somewhat faded as I begin telling him how you left me in behind in the caravan and how you were drunk all weekend. Since it is still so fresh, I rely on my shock to keep me from expressing any emotion about this publicly. Rob simply stares back as he takes in the situation with insight as he always does.

"Oh Grace, I'm so sorry. I didn't want to say anything, but when you told me that he left you in Puerto Viejo, I knew he wasn't right. And all those times that we would meet for drinks and he would try to get me to leave you while you were in the bathroom. He was scary. I never wanted to go with him, but I was afraid of saying no to him. He's a scary dude. I'm so sorry he did that."

With that simple reminder I suddenly remember the small ways that you have been leaving me since we began dating. I am reminded that this behavior is not new, it was small at first and I forgave it, shrugging it off as a joke, until it grew large enough that no one was laughing, even to you.

"You know that you are always welcome at my place, right?" He adds on without hesitation. I can see that his offer is serious and I'm a little taken a back. It's not that I hadn't thought about leaving, it's just that at this point it seems to anti-climactic to slip out silently, when I couldn't walk away with dignity earlier.

"That's so kind, Rob, but I'm sure we'll work it out. We're going to see a couple therapist, and he's stopped drinking now." I sound confident in my hope, but Rob is not convinced.

"Ok, well I'll send you the information on the spare key when I get home tonight, so that you have it just in case you ever need it. I've been wanting a roommate anyway!" He states before changing the subject. Sure enough, later that evening I get a photo and instructions to his house. I thank him again, still certain I'll never need it.

YOUR FRIENDS

October 2019

Calen's girlfriend, Annie called me this week to ask what happened. She was not able to go to the desert, but when everyone returned to town, they all gathered at her house, and told stories of my heinous behavior. She called me to let me know that I owe some of them apologies. She sounds offended.

We are sitting at the local wine bar and she is telling me everything they said about me. They told her how I was irritable and bitchy. They told her that I was difficult and unsociable. They all talked about how my friends kept to themselves and would not get involved with anyone else. None of them talked about you.

"That's not MY son." Your mother said.

Only a small group of your college friends mentioned you jumping over the bonfire during the reception, or how you were drunk the entire weekend. They recalled how they had nicknamed you 'Man-of-the-Year' in college because you always had to be the best at everything. They remembered how easily influenced you were by those around you, almost as if you did not know who you were without being told. They wondered why I was marrying you.

Annie did not know what to make of it all and as she relays the reports
back to me. I feel overwhelmed with the judgment and misunderstanding.
I truly feel terrible that I have hurt any of the ladies' feelings. But with
your boys, I am not surprised.

▲

A few days later, I meet Rebecca for a margarita to apologize and I tell
her everything. I don't mean to tell her, but it rushes out of my mouth
with tears so fast that I cannot stop the flow. I tell her about the names
you called me the weeks before. I tell her about the way you left me in
Puerto Viejo, and then again on the way to the desert, the day before the
wedding. I apologize for being short and bossy out of my own despair. I
tell her it had nothing to do with table cloths or center pieces; I was just
so overwhelmed.

She tells me how sorry she is that this has been going on for so long. She
tells me that she had heard similar stories from your last girlfriend, but
that she had not wanted to believe them, because you are her friend.

She also tells me that I am right about all of your friends. She tells me
about the nights that she and Buck and Bo have spent around Jason and
Angela's fire gossiping about me. She tells me how she used to agree with
them too, until one night while we were out. She tells me a story about
how I said something that upset her and she uncharacteristically snapped
at me. Immediately after, I turned to her and apologized and never said
anything like it again.

She tells me that this was when she realized it had not been my fault at
all. She had been upset because I was talking about something that made
her look at a piece of herself she did not want to see and that made her
angry. She says she knew this was why your friends hate me. They cannot
maintain their avoidance around me and they hate me for exposing them.

She also tells me that they hate me because of you. You would never say
anything bad about me, and in feigned protection, you always tell them
to shut up when they would start. This was something else, she said.

Something so intangible and crazy-making that we both struggle to define it even now. She explains that it is the way you kept me separate from them. Something about it allows them to keep from knowing me in a full and complex way. You ensure that they can never connect with me so I can only ever be misrepresented and misunderstood, setting me up as the straw man of all their worst impressions.

Memories of our arguments come back slowly. You would scream at me, "Those are MY friends! Can't you call your own?!" You didn't want me trying to create relationships with this group of people that you cared so much about. You let them believe that you were the same as them because you need to be the same to be connected with them. Meanwhile, you lied to me about being the same as me when they were away, creating a losing, unnecessary battle in yourself between them and me.

I remember how you would say that you were tired of their ignorance and make fun of their obsession with conspiracy theories. I start to recall your laughter at their lack of education and difficulty retaining jobs. You mocked their belief that they should be able to make more money at their ski industry professions. I suddenly I can see that the venom you used to distance yourself from them while we were together was simply the projection of your own shame. You were not able to make these different parts of yourself compatible, your high education, east-coast, oil family status, and your blue-collar, ski-bum life. So, you kept me separate too. I feel sad for you that you could not love all these things without shame.

Rebecca tells me that she did eventually encourage the group to talk to me. She claimed I was reasonable and I would apologize. She was right. I would have done anything to take reconcile and be connected with the people you loved. She also told me that when she said this, they refused. They would never approach me. They did not want to make it right. It was easier to hate me.

I have never experienced this kind of rejection before. I am devastated and triumphant at the same time. I knew for all the years we've been together that they hated me, and finally, here is confirmation. The the validation of my intuition is liberating and I am sad for all the hours I lost trying to earn their acceptance.

When I come home, I begin to relay all I have heard to you, but you are angry with me. You can't deny it anymore, but instead of comforting me, you scold me. The familiar barrage of isolating comments ensues. Why can't I talk to my own friends? Why do I have to try to connect with your friends at all? Why does it matter what they think? Why do I keep getting involved with them? Why can't I just get along? Why must I be so difficult, so aggressive, so offensive to everyone?

I begin to see that the real danger of my connection with them is that it threatens their enabling relationship with you. When there is authenticity between them and I, it threatens your carefully constructed lies and the exposure of your addiction.

▲

The gossip tree continues on later in the week. Jason finds a time when he knows you will not be home, and comes to the house to talk with me. He walks in the back door as if looking for you and I offer to make him a cocktail. He sips his drink slowly while telling me that I was always bad for you and you weren't making me happy anyway. "So why don't you just pull the plug and save you both the suffering?" It is as if he knows that I am the only one still partially sane enough to make this choice, or maybe he's just too afraid to ever give you his actual opinion. His words could have been kind if he had ever taken care to know me. Instead, they sting like the judgement of a thousand fires where I was not invited and a thousand conversations where I left misunderstood.

He must have read the anger in my face as I take in the full weight of his accusations. Here I am, the scapegoat again. You bad behavior in the end, must be my fault. He grows visibly uncomfortable and concludes with a rant about how I should have known better. Nothing of this was out of character for you. Why am I so upset about it all?

I feel the heat rise in my face and I am running out of patience for his slow cocktail sipping. I narrow my eyes with all threat of a cornered dog and snap back, "Oh! So, it's not the alcohol that is the problem? It is the fact that I'm upset about it?! So, I should just be ok with him calling me a cunt and leaving me behind on the way to the wedding? I should just expect him to be abusive and shut up about it?"

Lasers might actually be shooting from my eyes and he can feel it because he is suddenly very thirsty and finishes the rest of his mostly full cocktail quickly, while backing from the kitchen towards the back door. There is a series of mumbled, nonsense that continues tumbling from his mouth. More for his sake than mine. We both know exactly how out of line his statement was, but only one of us needs it to continue to love you. He gathers what is left of his arrogance and asks me not to mention to you that he stopped by, confirming for me that all of your friends are just as afraid of you as I am. I never see him or any of the rest of that group again.

THE GUN

November 1, 2019

In the days after all the drama of leaving, I am been in contact with
your family and with Calen. I do not know what to do to get you to be
reasonable, to allow me to get the rest of my things and disappear from
your life forever. Your father advises me to leave you alone for a while
and let you calm down, so that is my plan until you text me.

In your first messages, you say that you don't want me to have anyone else
move the airstream. "I don't want some random guy with a truck on my
property." You spit at me. I can see the images that haunt your dreams.
Nightmares of me with other men. Nightmares that you have conjured
into truth.

You offer to do it for me and we begin to make plans to move it across
town. It is still early in the day and your tone is clear and direct. So, I
believe you. I am still naïve enough not to mistrust your moods. As the
day wears on, you stop responding, and in keeping with your father's
advice I give you space and go to a yoga class.

As I am leaving class, I receive a message saying you are ready for me to
come get it now. My yoga studio is close and so I let you know that I am
on my way. I pull into a spot on the curb next to the back driveway where
there are two gates, a person sized walkway and the one for vehicles. I

notice that you have parked your truck so close to the vehicle gate that a person could not get between them. Since I am still under the impression that your truck will be pulling the airstream, I am not yet alarmed.

I get out of my car to approach and hear you slam the back door, walking in my direction. I can see on your face from the length of the backyard, that you are drunk and I already regret being here. I haven't attempted to open the gate, because I agreed not to enter your property without permission. I am trying to be accommodating, to give you no reason to react. Again, with the foolish assumption that anything I could do would change your actions or decisions. I still play with the illusion of control, of my ability to deescalate your moods.

As you swagger towards me, I look down and notice a new lock on the walking gate. Then you are close enough for me to see a victorious look in your eyes. It is now that I feel the little hairs on my arms stand up. I notice your pocket and freeze. I can't believe what I am seeing. There is no way. You would never, but there it is.

Your revolver is ostentatiously shoved in your left pocket. Intentionally hanging out to make a statement.

You wanted me to see it. I know this because I am familiar with your gun collection. I have seen you concealed carry before. You have a number of smaller hand guns that I have watched you place into the back of your pants and cover with the very same hoodie you are wearing now. So discrete that no one would know it was there. You have often told me how a gun changes the feel of an interaction and though you want to feel safe, you do not want to escalate the potential altercations by sight of it. This is how I know this is intentional. You could have chosen any gun and you chose the largest handgun you own. "The prettiest one" you once said to me, when you asked me to keep it for safety in the airstream. The memory of you being concerned about my safety mocks me in shiny steel from your pocket.

I freeze. I'm shocked. "No one should ever carry a gun while they are angry," you had told me once, yet here you are angry and drunk.

"Is that a gun?" I say rhetorically, stunned.

"I just wanted to see what you would do now." You throw back at me, mockingly.

"Did you call me over here just to taunt me with a gun in your pocket?!" I stammer, still in shock.

"I just wanted to see what your plan is now." You point out the locks and the placement of your truck. It's obvious that I will never get my airstream out without your help or permission.

I call Calen because in my shock, I can't figure out what to do next. "He has a gun, Calen. He called me over here and told me he would take the airstream to storage, but he has a gun." It is as if my mind has slowed to a near stop. I stand here like an idiot waiting for instruction, from you, from Calen, from anyone. My mind is blank as I stare through the gate that now seems so flimsy, not nearly strong enough to protect me.

"You need to leave, Grace. You need to leave right now." Calen replies with calm urgency. He is decisive and clear. As soon as he says it, I turn and walk to my car. Momentarily snapped from my daze, I can see that this is madness. I drive to his house to talk with Annie.

Annie is burning papers in the back yard when I arrive. I fumble through the story quickly still in shock, but she is irate. She is ready to march over there with Calen and demand that this stop, right now. I just feel lost.

When Calen gets home a few moments later, she is on him about talking with you immediately. I begin to be concerned that our mess is going to create problems for them, so I excuse myself to let them work out their own plan. This is that last time that I see her.

▲

This moment becomes the defining moment of our ending. Over the next several months when I think of retuning to you, my friends and family frequently remind me of this moment. They are afraid for my safety. Despite the fact that I was not afraid, I will come to see it later as the way that you made the decision to end us. Something I could not do myself. Like a dog returning to its vomit, I will try to come back several times. Sometimes you will beg and I will return, and sometimes I will beg for you. But for the people that love me, this was the end.

I eventually know that when you made the decision to carry that gun across the yard, despite believing in my heart that you would never hurt me, you made an irreversible decision for us. One that everyone who loves me would never forget and that would separate you from them forever and, therefore, from me. I spend countless hours and days contemplating how to mend this rift, repeatedly unable to conceptualize a solution, but the truth remains that this choice is irreversible.

▲

That evening as I drive home, Annie's anger echoing in my shocked brain, I send a message to your father. I tell him that I tried to do as he said, but that you asked me to come by and that you had a gun. I was more scared for you than for me. You are so sick that you cannot even find the line of acceptable behavior anymore. I want him to call you, to make it better, to help you. It's what I always wanted him to do, every time I have called him.

Later you tell me that he did call you after that message, but only to let you know that he would hire any lawyer necessary if it became necessary. I washed my hands of your family then, because it became clear that they would be of no use taming the monster they created.

DR. LEWIS

November 2019

I am sitting on a beige love seat across the small top floor office from Dr. Lewis. It is not as cramped as it might feel with the vaulted ceilings and frosted window next to my right. He is a short man from New York and his diploma on the wall indicates that he has been practicing therapy for longer than I have been alive.

I am in this session without you despite the fact that he is our couple's counselor. I am trying to gain his approval to release me from our relationship. I am telling him in great detail about what we have experienced and even though I know better, I ask for his opinion.

He chuckles knowingly and gently, and then tells me that he does not believe you to be a "bad boy," but that it appears that we may have very different value systems. I want to have a family and a house and a career, he informs me. You want your freedom and an unconventional life style. I am confused by his assessment but try to listen anyway. "You may just not be a good match," he says, but agrees to continue to see us while we figure it out. I am start to dislike him just a little, but he is the only available option. "I am somewhat concerned about the issue of the gun, though." He concludes.

I leave this session and discuss it with people who have known us both, deciding that he has clearly missed the part of the story where I was wild too. He must have missed that parts where I lived in an airstream in the woods for a year before we met, or where I packed up my career and drove from Oregon to Costa Rica with you. Even more so, the part where you begged me to "pull the plug" so we could start trying for children right away. Our values and dreams were actually one of the few things that always seemed on track for us. So much so, they kept me coming back with the fear that I might never find anyone else like you again. Someone both wild and conventional, interested in finding a way to straddle that line and create something new.

I am irritated, but I also assume he'll figure it out over the course of the next few sessions and we are desperate. In this town, it takes a small miracle to find a couple's provider with addictions experience. I try to ask him for more than weekly session because of crisis, but his schedule and yours will not allow it.

▲

The next week we return together and I am sitting in the same spot on the couch, anxious because I can read your postured body language, ready to fight. Dr. Lewis is unaware of this and prattles on good-naturedly while we settle in.

He starts the session off by bringing up the gun. He does not believe it's a good idea for us to have them on the property while we are in such a state. He wants us to all sign an agreement that they will be removed otherwise he cannot continue to provide services, a basic and common therapeutic intervention in domestic violence cases. I recognize it and understand, and also see that you have no intention of understanding. You are combative, you quote the law, and finally you storm out when he suggests that they can be removed by outside resources if necessary.

As the door slams shut behind you and I am left in the office, exhausted, anxious, and furious, with a stunned Dr. Lewis.

He asks me simply, "Is he often like that?"

"All the time." I reply, annoyed that he needed this display to believe what I reported last week.

"Then why are you still with him?" He asks still in shock.

Perhaps I would have had an answer if I had not been so exhausted. I shrug and excuse myself, following you out the door. I drive back to your house alone, you must have walked, planning to remove the small count of items that I returned to their drawers when we decided to try again.

When I arrive, you are poised for battle, paranoia of protecting the property is obvious in the hateful lines etched in your brow. I know there is no use in arguing as you hurl accusations at me about how I colluded with this provider to attack you. I had planned this all along and was waiting to ambush you. You yell at me to collect my things and get out. I simply say, "I know" and remove the last of my undies from your drawer, find Nellie, and drive home.

I am so tired of this charade that I don't even wait a full hour before opening a Tinder profile. You are utterly replaceable and I am hollow with disappointment and disgust.

Two weeks later when we are sitting in this office together again, we have already decided on a contract that I have already decided I will not keep, and that I already know you will fail. It was an exercise in establishing proof for the decision I do not want to make, the one you made for me when you put that revolver in your pocket.

The contract is:

- No drinking
- No yelling
- No threats to leave or kicking each other out
- The guns must be locked, the combo changed, and given to someone else

- No dating other people
- Must attend therapy weekly

You started the session alone today because I told you I would not mediate your discussion with Dr. Lewis. I wait in the reception area in case there is extra time when you are finished. It takes 40 minutes for you to resolve your conflict with Dr. Lewis, a waste of an hour of my life. I come in to join you in the last 10, but I am already done. My body says what my mind is not yet willing to admit and I don't hear anything anyone is saying. The Doctor seems completely unaware of all of this.

In the following month, leading to our last break up, you never get your gun safe code changed and given to someone else. You don't even make an attempt, and I continue to drink on the nights that I don't see you.

THE LAST LEAVING

December 2019

It's Thursday afternoon and I have been thinking all week. I have been thinking since September. I finally know the answer and it is killing me. It kills me to keep my secret and it kills me to say it out loud because I know it will hurt you. I hate the answer. It's not the one I had wanted.

I am supposed to see you tomorrow; those are our usual plans now that I live at Rob's. I stay the night with you one evening a week and then again on your weekends. I thought that after moving out, I would stop crying every Tuesday morning, but that has continued. It has been destroying me to be so endlessly sad. I decide that I cannot continue like this and I cannot come up with a solution to ending my sorrow that includes staying with you. So, I call to ask you if I can come over this evening to talk, even though it is not our night.

You are immediately openly hostile and resentful in response to my text, which indicates to me that you already know what I need to say. When I insist that it is necessary to see you tonight instead of waiting until tomorrow, you act indifferent. Your infamous last resort. You use it only when you know that what I am about to say matters so much to both of us that the pain will overwhelm you.

I pull up to the front of the house and instead of inviting me inside you come out and lean over to put your head just inside the passenger window of my car. Another way that you signal to me with your body that you do not care about what I am saying and you see this as a waste of your time. I ask you to sit inside choosing to ignore your subtle stabs.

I have thought it all out, what I will say, and how I will try to calm you. I have thought about your responses and your pain. What I did not account for was your indifference. I have somehow maintained the optimistic view that no one could ever be as cruel as to utilize indifference as a weapon. Even after all our history together, I continue to be blindsided by this familiar tool. You won't even let me get out the words that will end it before waiving me away.

I am beginning to get louder and louder in my attempts to be heard and you are beginning to weave the old narrative, "You're being hysterical and it's unnecessary." I leave in tears and you tell me to come back another time, when I've calmed down, to collect my last few items.

PART TWO

THE LONGEST WINTER

December 2019

Dear Hank,   Dec 12

None of that came out the way I wanted. I wish you had just let me talk.
You can open your Xmas present whenever you want. It's a crockpot. I'm
going to write what I wanted to say because it matters to me to say it.

I love you so much and I have been bargaining with myself all week
about this. Everyone keeps telling me I'm trying to control the situation
and that neither of us can get better if I don't leave you. I think I realized
on Tuesday they were right.

I've been trying to figure out how to give myself the space I need to focus
on myself, on forgiving you and letting go of resentments and becoming
the person I used to be and want to be again. I was thinking about
asking for no contact between now and the time our contract is up, but I
realized that even then, the thing that keeps me from being able to work
on myself is fixating on whether or not we have a future together. If I ask
for more space from you, I'll still sit around ruminating about our future,
distracting myself from the work I have to do.

I realize now that if I don't end this, I will never focus on becoming
myself again, the person that I liked, and that we'll never really know if

you want to get better for yourself or just to keep me off Tinder. I want
to believe that 6 months from now after we've both grown some, that we
might get coffee and agree to try again, but if I actually want to get better,
I have to entirely let go of that possibility or I won't be able to focus. I
love you so much and I just want us to be happy even if it's not together
and right now I don't think that's a possibility.

I love you so much,
Grace

▲

And just like that, the last three years, the roller coaster, is over. You ask
me to send you a list of the things I need to get from the property and I
send this:

Here is the list of items you requested I send to you that I would like to
get from the house. I promise I won't go in without permission.

Exploding kittens
4 small colorful bowls
3 Mexican rugs
Double sleeping bag
Ski Helmet and goggles
Wine rack
Bathing suit and fuzzy PJ's
Body wash and face wash
My cacti (it would be nice if I could come in and get them, because they'll
die in this cold if you leave them on the porch, or I can come by when
you're there and you can hand them off if you don't want me to come in.)

Thank you,
Grace

▲

I collect the things one evening after work without incident and take them back to Rob's house. I unpack them into the drawers that I occupy now, in the tiny upstairs room that is now my home.

Home.

Then the tears begin anew. Where is my home? I left again. Will I ever have a place to put my piano?

I sit on the edge of this bed with a borrowed quilt and begin to replay the last few months. I reflect on the conversations that lead me to this choice. I think about how I called your father for help, and then stopped. I think about the last time I spoke to your sister. Her words were so stunning and stung so deeply.

"I just thought that with all that is going on with your husband that you would understand." I had stammered.

Then she repeated, "I do, but why are YOU doing it?"

I had loved your sister. You once told me that she had never gotten along with one of your girlfriends before. You were proud of me when we were with her.

"She talks a lot, and usually that bothers me, but she is always saying something interesting. So, I don't mind with her." She had told you.

I called her still hoping that someone could help you, even when you didn't want to be helped. She knew better.

A month earlier, her husband had relapsed and disappeared for 5 days, leaving her and her two kids to wonder about his safety. His parents were of no use to her and when she finally found him on a park bench inebriated, she was ready to scrap all 20 years of their life together. She missed our wedding and would never forgive him for it. I reassured her that she might get the chance to attend your wedding yet.

When I gathered myself after the ensuing bout of sobs, I walk to the corner of the room to close a half open drawer and catch my reflection in the mirror next to the dresser. My big green eyes swollen and red, making the green more striking by contrast. This is where I stood when I called your therapist.

I had searched for someone who would see you for addictions issues but everyone in town was full or a friend of mine. It had taken months to convince you to see someone on your own, evidence of me continuing to grasp at straws.

I was finally answered by a human, a good therapist, an honest woman. She told me the truth at the moment when I could finally hear it.

"He doesn't want to change in order to be better, Grace. He wants to change to keep you and that is not the same thing." She said, synthesizing the situation so concisely. She explained to me that you were not ready to change and take responsibility for your behavior, you were simply placating me. None of the things that you had done since the wedding were evidence of real and lasting commitment to change. If anything, they were evidence to the contrary, that you just wanted to pacify me so that you could go on with your life in the usual fashion. You did not want to get better, you wanted to be left alone. What's more, is that I couldn't get better either. Because I kept chasing your sobriety and demanding your commitment to self-improvement, I was neglecting my own mental health. I could not get better as long as I was unwilling to let you go.

I thanked her for her sound advice and wisdom. She had given me more direction in that five-minute phone call than any of our previous couple's counselors had offered in the hours we had spent with them and this was the spot where I stood when I knew that it had to end.

I retched with sobs again and stumbled back to the bed, glad that Rob is out of town again.

▲

I told Rob the secret I had been keeping when he came home at the end of the week, but I could tell that his surprise was feigned. He had already known that I had begun seeing you again.

It was humiliating that I went back to you after the incident with the gun. I couldn't bear to tell anyone. I knew what I looked like, and I didn't want my housing to be threatened. I wasn't sure if he would ask me to leave if he heard that we were trying to work it out. So, I just never mentioned it, and he never asked. Everyone was so afraid of you, and for good reason. I didn't know if Rob would decide that having me in the house was a liability, so as a compromise with my guilty conscience I never told you where I lived.

I told Rob that I had kept our address a secret, even though he never asked for confirmation of this commitment to his safety. I felt like I owed it to him for all the kindness he was extending to me. It was my penance for the haphazard way I had been throwing it away. I know that he worried about me and that he noticed how much wine I was drinking, but he never said anything. I know that you were scary to him. He had told me on more than one occasion. I know that my traumatized verbal vomit was funny to him, because it was laugh or cry, but he was worried.

I am going to need to find something to do with all the thoughts and feelings that I am trying to drown with left-over wedding wine. It's simply not fair to ask Rob to hear them all and I have so many things left to say.

Then, I decided to write you a letter. I decided that every time I want to call or text, I'll say what I need to say here instead, without the danger reengaging our vicious cycle or asking someone else to hold my trauma. It seems like the kindest way to protect myself, everyone else and even you. Maybe I'll eventually write one that I can send.

▲

Dear Hank,   Dec 14

I am sitting on my couch, binge watching old seasons of The Voice while
drinking a bottle of wine. I miss you so much.

I am remembering how you used to watch the YouTube highlights of
Britain's got talent when we were bored in Costa Rica? You were so cute,
getting so excited for the winners. It's such fluff television that makes you
feel so good, so hopeful. We needed that back then, when things started to
get very dark for us. The days were so short and we were so isolated. We
never should have moved there.

Sometimes I wonder where we would be now if we had never left. If I
had not given up my job and if we hadn't spent all our savings driving
from Oregon through six Central American borders to that tiny surf town
in the jungle. Would we still be happy? Would we be sitting in our back
yard watching the nesting birds, making fancy cheese plates, and sipping
wine? Would your alcoholism still have escalated to disaster? Would I
have left before we got engaged and spared us the humiliation of that
wedding? Would we still be in love?

I guess we'll never know,
Grace

▲

I'm glad these days that Rob isn't around to see me fall apart. I have the
house to myself while he travels. He checks in frequently, because he is
worried about leaving me here alone. He told me so last time he came
home.

"How was your trip?" I asked as brightly as I am able.

"It was really good!" He tells me about visiting his family and the
adventures that they had together. "It's nice to know that you're here with
the house too. I feel bad leaving you here alone right now though. How
has it been for you?"

"I actually think it's a good thing for me right now. Please don't worry about me. It's nice to have my own space to fall apart in, that way I can drink as much leftover wedding wine as I want without feeling like I have to justify it!" We both laugh awkwardly and he drops it.

Rob is letting me stay here while I get on my feet. My insurance reimbursements can sometimes take up to three months to receive for the services that I provide. So, when I came home in August and began working, I didn't start seeing any money until the same month I moved in. I was in such a hurry to leave when I finally pulled the plug that it was several weeks later when we even began to talk about rent.

Rob can afford his house on his own, he just likes having a roommate because he gets lonely. He's a great roommate, super clean, and doesn't ask any questions that I don't want to answer. It's the perfect soft landing for me right now.

He offers to let me stay as long as I need, rent free, until I can get my shit together. I have a hard time accepting this kind offer, but I don't have any choice right now. We settle on two months before I start to pay him rent. We don't even negotiate, I just agree to pay whatever he believes is a fair price, and he is always fair.

▲

We have finally broken up for the last time, and I know it, but you don't seem to see the difference. It was a Thursday when I told you, and you had just seen your new therapist for the first time that week. You liked her. You said you had felt heard by her for the first time in any of our previous sessions. I was glad for you. I think that may have been why I felt confident to end it. I think I felt like you finally had the support you needed and I could let you go.

You cancelled your next session with her as soon as I left. Proving her point and giving me the confirmation that you are not at all committed to your treatment. You still communicate with me daily to give me updates on your self-destruction because you know just how to hook me back into our loop.

▲

Dear Hank,   Dec 17

You are so mean. Every time I'm around you I feel crazy. I try to start
with poise and calm but within moments of you entering a conversation
or even just the room, I'm hysterical again! I'm so tired of feeling
hysterical.

Fuck you for suggesting we could ever be together again! As if this is one
of your previous breakups where you continued to bang for the next
year and she still pines for you! We are NEVER getting back together!
NEVER! That was decided the moment you cancelled your therapy
sessions.

Finally, after years of begging you to work on your alcoholism I found
you the perfect therapist. You even liked her, as of last week! But it
was all a sham. She knew it. She told me when I called her for couples
counseling. She told me she wouldn't see us, but she'd work with you if
you were willing. She told me then that you didn't want to get better, you
just wanted to keep me. She told me you wouldn't get better if I stayed,
and I said you wouldn't get better if I left. We were both right. You're
never going to get better. You'll never look at yourself in the mirror. And
I can't keep holding my breath.

I am running away from you as fast as I can. You have been a cancer on
my self-esteem, on my confidence, and on my career.

Get away from me,
Grace

▲

I'm starting to think about blocking your number because you don't respect my boundaries and I am barely able to set them anymore. But you think I owe you money, and I am having a hard time deciding if I buy your reality.

You sold your truck before we left Costa Rica and wired me the money so that I could purchase a small car for myself and truck for you. I found you a nice early 2000's Toyota Tundra for a steal of a price and I bought myself a cheap little city car. I only paid 3000$ for it. It's not very pretty, but it's economical and reliable.

"Could you please drive something cooler" you teased me at the time, "like a Subaru or something?"

"No way! This thing gets 40 miles to the gallon and takes me everywhere I need to go!" I quipped back. It's true that I've never wanted to own a nice car. I'm hard on my vehicles and don't want to feel afraid to use it. So, I've always driven cheap little cars that are reliable and perfectly adequate for my daily use.

When we got home after the wedding, I deep cleaned the house and refurnished the living room to make it feel less like the frat house and more like a marital home. I was trying to wash away the soil of that day from the walls and floor boards. As if I could scrub out the stains of the damage to our relationship.

I sold the hide-a-couch with peeling pleather and bought a big blue sectional and some new pillow covers for the throws. I moved our bed and dresser into the second bedroom to give us a new space for creating a new kind of partnership, all while you were trying to be sober.

I didn't ask you for help with any of the cost, because I knew it wasn't important to you as it was to me. I was clawing at the walls of that building trying to carve out the life I wanted to share with you from the remnants of the disaster behind us. I was redecorating my way into a space that felt livable from the closterphobia of my choices.

It didn't work and while I was leaving, I took nothing but a few pieces of art off the walls. You threw frames at me, shattering glass here and there.

I took them to the dumpster outside, but I left all of the furniture. Even things the I had brought with me before we were together. I had no use for it anyway. There is no room here in Rob's house for my furniture.

When I sold my car before leaving for Costa Rica, I used that money to pay for our gas on the road trip across 7 countries. I used it to supplement my income for months before it finally ran out and we were dependent on yours.

But after all this wash of mixed finances and bad investments, you still want me to pay you back. I couldn't lie to you when I was running away. You attacked the airstream with an Ax when you caught the inkling that I wouldn't pay. So, I begged, and made promises, and now I feel beholden. I feel like I have to honor my word, even if I was coerced. It's a silly little thing that keeps us connected, a little way that you still have power over me.

▲

Dear Hank,   Dec 20

I hate my car. I hate that it's this little link between you and I. You know this isn't the first relationship where I've had to buy my car from an ex. Remember when I told you about paying off 26,000$ of my ex-husband's debt over three years of marriage? Well, both car titles were in his name when I tried to leave. He made me pay him for that stupid car too. Asshole. Just like you. Only this time, you don't even have any legal claim to it. I'm just paying you to get you to stop harassing me.

I shouldn't do it. All of my friends say I should tell you fuck straight off. What about the year of lost income in Costa Rica where we boosted your career, leaving mine behind? It should all be a wash of mixed finances, but you have always felt like the world owes you something. Entitled, little rich boy.

God, you are like a looming cloud over my life that I didn't turn around to see. I could hear the thunder, but I just wouldn't turn away from the sun to see the weather changing behind me.

Honestly, I just don't want to fight anymore. So, I'll keep writing these stupid checks.

I hate you,
Grace

▲

It would be months before I finally stopped paying for that car.

▲

With Rob gone so regularly and the wedding wine supply dwindling I start to think about my future. It is clear that I have wasted years here, years that my body doesn't have for starting a family. I am beginning to feel the full weight of the anxiety that kept me from leaving for so long.

The sunk cost argument that women have with themselves when they sneak up on 35 is a trap that keeps so many of us in unhappy relationships. Over my years in practice, I've begun to notice that sometimes it's not even age related. I've met women at 25 who use this argument to keep themselves in partnerships, using excuses like, "I don't want to be an old mom" or "what if I never meet someone better?" The pressure for us to find a reproduction partner doesn't seem to discriminate based on age or social-economic standing. It seems that every woman who wants a child will eventually face this fear.

I know that it kept me by your side much longer than if I had been 10 years younger. Staying with you actually provided me some relief from the biggest fear of all. Now that I have made my choices about you, there is nowhere to run from this background noise, like a gong ever ringing in my mind. Will I die alone?

It's a terrifying existential crisis that I can't escape and so I do the next best thing. I determine that I will have that life. I will take control of it in the only way that I know how, with Tinder.

▲

Dear Hank,   Dec 24

I started a tinder profile again. I know that one of your friends will eventually screen shot my profile and send it to you because they feel that you should know everything I'm doing in this small town. That's what they did last time you broke up with me. I feel guilty about this because I know it will hurt you. I also feel angry that you have so many people keeping tabs on me like you own me. You lost the right to judge my choices when you showed up to our wedding too drunk to say your vows.

The truth is, no one here is like you. I miss your giant schnoz and wanderlust. I miss naked sunbathing by those alpine lakes with mountain views while you fly fish.

We have different ways of getting over this. It hurts when I see you, hungover, bags under your eyes. You look like shit and I can't keep you from yourself anymore. I just need to remember that there are men in the world that will be kind to me sometimes. Maybe I can go backpacking with someone else someday. Maybe someone will laugh at my jokes and think I have the best ass in the world. I need to meet new people. I'm sorry, but I'm not sorry.

I love you,
Grace

▲

It didn't take me long to find someone to go out with. I guess Christmas makes so many of us lonely and my face is still pretty enough even if I don't feel very attractive these days. I mostly just feel like a walking train wreck where anyone can glance over to survey the carnage at their leisure. But somehow I get a date, and plan to go out.

▲

Dear Hank,   Dec 26

I went on a date tonight with a really sweet guy. He listened to me ramble on for hours and bought me another cocktail. You never bought me cocktails. Our first date we split the tab and that set the precedent for the rest of our time together. I told him he didn't have to, but he said, "I'd like to." How do you like that?! He wanted to treat me. He wanted to hear me talk. I didn't really know what to do.

Funny story, I had actually met Jeff before. I met him in a bar sometime before you and I broke up. I mean, we were separated, but it was after we'd signed the contract. The 90 day contract that said no yelling, no relationship threats, no dating, and no drinking for both of us. I was so mad about that contract. It was unfair that I couldn't have wine with my girlfriends because you were a drunk. I was so mad at you that I didn't keep that contract at all. I was lying to you. I still went out for drinks on days that we weren't seeing each other, and I didn't feel guilty about it! Mostly.

The night I met Jeff, I was meeting a girlfriend at the bar and she was telling me what I already knew about leaving you. Then there he was, talking with his brother to my right. I told my friend I wanted to give him my number. She carried me right out of that bar and took me home, made me dinner, poured wine down my throat and put me to bed in her spare bedroom that night. I haven't been that drunk for a while. I was so sad. I thought my heart might break in half, but I hated you so much. I still do. It wasn't fair and I know I was wrong too.

Jeff was nice, but I don't know if I'll hear from him again. I couldn't kiss him goodnight because I was afraid. Honestly, it was just nice to be around someone so kind.

Love,
Grace

▲

I don't hear from that gentleman again and that's ok with me. I am definitely not ready to be dating. I know it and I'm embarrassed that this man could see it pretty quickly too. I keep my tinder profile for distraction anyway.

▲

Dear Hank,   Dec 27

It just occurred to me that it's been 2 weeks since I left you. I mean really left you. We have been back and forth before, but this time was for sure. I never really know how I know, when I know, except that it comes on quickly and without hesitation. I'm sure it felt a little without notice to you. It probably would have been more poetic if I had left after the "little wedding that couldn't" but I didn't. I was without resources and frozen with shock. I just couldn't.

Annie told me to; other friends asked me why I didn't. I don't really know why I made those choices. I was scared. Scared to start over, scared to be the fool, scared I'd never have a successful relationship, and scared I'd never have children. So, I didn't leave, whatever the reasons, until one day, I did.

I really do believe that timing is something strange and spiritual. When you know, you know. That's what I tell my clients when they come in talking about wanting to leave their husbands wondering why they can't make decisions. I tell them that they'll know when they know and we just work to quiet all the other voices around them so they can intentionally listen to their own.

I still haven't told many people. You'd think with all the drama, I'd be sending notes and accepting accolades by now, but I've only told the people I've seen. I haven't told my family. Maybe I'm ashamed to tell them and afraid of the justifications I'll have to make to get them to understand. Maybe I feel like they're all too tired of hearing about it. Or maybe I just don't trust myself yet. My co-worker said she didn't believe me. It hurt, but I don't blame her. I've been back so many times before. So many reasons to leave and yet I never left. Why would I go now, right after you started therapy? It doesn't make any sense, but I think our humanity rarely does.

I'm sure all your people know by now and that's ok. I don't want to see them anyway. I know they think it's all my fault. Maybe it is. I don't care anymore. Except, I do.

Whatever,
Grace

▲

You might be beginning to see that this is the end, because you send me a message and ask me to meet you in the park. I probably shouldn't agree, but I can't say no to you when you're being sweet.

▲

Dear Hank,   Dec 28

Today you wanted to meet me in the park. You said you wanted closure, and you promised not to say anything mean. It's been weeks since leaving you for the last, last time and I am reluctant because I know that I still want you. I don't trust myself.

I have to kill the hope that drives me to believe that you will be better, and that this will ever be what I need. That hope is dangerous to me. It's what keeps me up at night thinking of solutions and books and different ways I can say something or approach you. It keeps me wrapped in the lie that I have any control over your addiction, your harsh words, or your choices. I have to admit that I am powerless over you. I cannot make you understand, or motivate you to change. I have to let go of hope in order to find myself again. I have to acknowledge that your addiction is not about me.

I already know what you'll say. I know you'll beg me to stay, tell me that you love me, and that you'll do anything, but you already fired your therapist. I can't do this anymore.

I love you, but no,
Grace

▲

I stand in the park, watching you and your dog walk across the lawn towards me with your familiar casual gait. You are still the most beautiful man I have ever seen. You are wearing the flannel with orange that I bought for you before the wedding. Orange is your favorite color.

You hand me my maps and I hand over your father's climbing gear.

"I love you more than I have ever loved any woman before." You say to me. "I have tried harder with you than I have ever tried before." I know this is true. You have been telling me this for the last 3 years.

I want so desperately for this to be enough. I want love to have been enough to teach you how to be kind. I want love to have been enough for you to be sober. I want love to have taught you how to value and support me, but it didn't. Love is simply not enough.

I am in tears and I can't speak. It's all I can do to let you hug me goodbye without grabbing hold oof you and trying to hang on forever. I have to walk away now, even though I didn't say anything that I wanted.

▲

At home again, I want to call you and tell you that we can work this out. I want to come home to you and our little life. I want to start a family with you and be happily married like we had planned for this season, but that life is gone. It's out of our reach now.

Why did you bother to call me? Why did you need to say such nice things? I've always been a sucker for you and now I'm second guessing this choice, again. After everything you've done and everything that my friends and family have seen, I am still so quick to hope again that you might be good to me.

▲

Hank,   Dec 28

Fuck you. Fuck you! F U C K   Y O U.
I wish you would let me go. I need to go. Please let me go.

I know that you loved me, at least you felt like you loved me, but you were the worst lover I have ever had, and that's saying something! I should have left you that night you showed up at my airstream in the middle of the night. We had only been dating, what, 3 months? You humiliated me in front of your co-workers and kicked me out of your house and then avoided me for three days. Just when I threw my hands in the air and said, "FINE!" You crawled back in and asked for another chance. The next morning, I screamed at you for 4 hours instead of going backpacking as we'd planned. We spent the day in bed trying to recover from the tumult. I should have known then what this was going to turn into.

I hate myself for letting you crawl back into my bed that night. I hate myself for all of the little betrayals I've made of myself along the way. I may hate me, but I hate you too.

But how do you predict being left at the alter? How to do you see that kind of betrayal coming? Maybe that's why I am so sick, because everyone else seemed to see it; everyone but me.

I love you and I hate you, please let me go,
Grace

My anger always comes to save me when I need it the most. When I was in my early twenties, I went to therapy for the first time. The therapist I found myself with reconstructed me from the pieces that I spilt on her floor over the 3.5 years we spent together. I learned that I wanted this to be my profession too. I wanted to give to other women the gift she had given to me.

In our time together she taught me that my anger wasn't the enemy, it was alerting me to the danger in front of me. My anger was my savior and it was there to give me the energy I needed to protect myself. Since then, I have made friends with that part of my soul. She always comes when I need her the most; when it's time act in self-preservation. This is no different, and I know that I need to retain this anger or fall into self-doubt. But it does not take long for my wrath to quiet down.

Dear Hank,   Dec 29

I feel hungover with doubt today. Did I make the right choice? Was I too hard on you? Did I ask too much? Maybe if I had done this differently, or changed my approach? Maybe I can still change it. Maybe I should have.

I called Michael after seeing you yesterday. I needed someone to remind me that I had made the right choice. Reaching my toes towards the floor to find the ground which seems to have fallen from beneath me. I recall Michael's words. He reminds me about his visit to Costa. He reminds me about when you left me in that bar downtown. He reminds me about the wedding.

"Do you remember the question you asked me two weeks before the wedding? That has always summed up the debate for me." He says. "You asked me if I had ever called one of my girlfriends a cunt before. You already know the answer to that question. I never have and I never would, because you just don't say that to people, especially people that you love."

The worst thing was that it wasn't the first time you had used that word. It wasn't the first time you promised never to use it again. So, when you promised that it would be the last, I just couldn't believe you anymore.

I know you loved me. Still do, I believe, but your love is this twisted, dark, and hateful thing. You love to possess, not to honor or cherish. I am not leaving you because you did not love me enough, I'm leaving you because you did not love me well.

I still love you too,
Grace

I suppose that's why we have friends, to remind us of what is true when we've forgotten. They still remember all the reasons I left and are happy to let me borrow their anger when mine leaves me for the softer feelings of doubt, despair, and grief.

Dear Hank,   Dec 31

I am so sad that we can't ski together and won't be traveling the world together anymore. There won't be any more naked sunbathing, fly fishing, back packing trips. I just can't live with someone who calls me a cunt and disappears for hours or days when he's anxious or angry and drinks his emotions away.

The frosting in our relationship was always perfect, but it was slapped on a half-baked cake. We had so much fun, but you couldn't be a kind, supportive partner in the day-to-day moments.

I would give anything for that to be untrue. I wish you had been more motivated to become that man, but your words were just empty promises.

I would have waited for him. You wanted this to be about how WE are wrong or how WE have issues instead of being willing to look at yourself and what you brought to the conflict.

I'm not perfect, but I know the devil inside of me. I own her and work hard on keeping her from hurting others. I don't always succeed, but when I fail, I apologize and try again tomorrow. I need a partner who can do the same. I hope you change your mind about going to counseling and working on yourself. I know that your friends and family don't see any merit in this course of action, but we can't be different until we start trying new things and you've already tried all of their things.

You asked me to compromise, but I'm done compromising. You shouldn't have to compromise on basic respect and kindness.

Love,
Grace

January 2020

I spent New Year's as a slowly dissolving, drunken whirlpool, sweeping everything broken and lonely into my wake. I found an equally wild and desperate man to help me lose a pair of underwear and one shoe in the basement wine cellar of a roaring 20's themed house party. I woke up with a real hang over to match the ache in my heart.

With all this distraction, I was able to forget about you for a few days, but by the end of my Monday work day, I was in pieces again. You texted me to tell me that I was the first profile that popped up when you opened your Tinder account this afternoon.

▲

Why did you send that to me? I glanced down at my phone right before
my last client of the day arrived and now, I'm just hanging on. I rarely
have a hard time compartmentalizing when I'm at work, but I did not do
my best job this time.

I know that it's not right to be upset; I was there first. The difference
is that I didn't bring it to your attention because I knew how hurt you
would be to know it. The last time you threw me out of your house, your
friend took a screen shot of my profile and sent it to you. You called
me in despair, completely devastated. You begged me to come back, so
I did. Now here you are rubbing it in my face, again proving that your
love doesn't come with care about my feelings, but with vitriol and
entitlement.

It's not your Tinder account that hurts, it's that you made it a point to
tell me. I have danced around your delicate ego, being afraid to see you
at bars on dates, hoping your friends won't tell you. Not because I'm
embarrassed, but because I cared that it would hurt you. You don't care.
You don't care enough to leave me alone. You are still looking for ways to
hurt me because you feel rejected and alone.

I lost my mind for a moment. I got on my app and swiped as fast as I
could until your profile showed up. I looked at the two photos you have
of yourself noting that they don't do you any justice. So, I sent you six
of my favorites. I sent you the photos that I have that make you look as
beautiful as possible. The ones that are etched in my memory. The ones
that I know will get you the most attention. Why did I do that? Was I
trying to prove that I was indifferent? And to whom?

Then you asked me if we could get coffee or take the dogs for a walk
sometime, or if I wanted to be left alone. I told you I love you, you are bad
for me, and I need to stay away from you. I need to be with someone who
is kind to me, whose friends like me and who understands my perspective.

Then you retched for the knife, using the old lines that cut the deepest.
You said you had accepted that we and our friends were just too different

for this to ever have worked. That lie drives me insane! That is the easiest, dirtiest, sweetest little lie that you have ever told. You tell it to avoid looking at yourself. You tell it to avoid the responsibility of your abuse, of calling me a cunt, of being an alcoholic, and of leaving me in countless bars and cities all over the world. You tell it so that you can feel better now instead of facing yourself. You're a coward, blaming fate instead of taking responsibility.

Please stay away from me,
Grace

▲

I sobbed with anger when I read that little lie. Then I did it. I told you to leave me alone, forever, and I blocked your number. I blocked it because it's been three weeks, and you still reach out to me every few days. If not to have me back, then just to stab at me.

Then I realized, you are never going to stop doing this. I don't know if you CAN stop doing it. I do know that every time your name pops up in my messages, I lose my mind, just a little. I also know that I'm tired of feeling crazy all the time. I'm tired of explaining myself. I'm tired of being gas-lit and I'm tired of crying. I'm tired of the way my body feels and the days that it takes me to recover from these interruptions. So, I have to make space between us that does not depend on your self-control.

▲

Dear Hank   Jan 5

I just woke up from a dream where we were happy together. You touched my face softly and we were smiling. We were talking about starting a family. In the back of my mind, just out of reach, I knew that this was wrong somehow, but for a moment I couldn't recall why. For that brief moment before I woke up, I had forgotten everything that had happened between us. It was the sweetest dream, but now I am awake.

Even in my sleep you haunt me. I can't seem to get away from you.

Love,
Grace

▲

I've been dating more and more to chase away the loneliness. It's the worst in the mornings when I wake up with an empty bed. Then terrible again at night, when I crawl back into it.

I went to see a movie with a man last weekend who I've decidedly friend-camped. He says he's fine with this arrangement, but in my experience that never lasts past their last hope of changing my mind. The movie we went to see was a mystery. I like that these old Agatha Christie movies that are making their way into theaters again. This one had a surprise plot twist, the suspected murderer is framed by the son of the rich man. One of the last scenes in the movie is the rich boy's father chasing the police down the driveway, waving a wad of cash as a threat or bribe, it's difficult to tell.

It felt like the murder knife went right through my gut instead of staying on the screen where it belonged. I saw your father throwing all his financial weight at your consequences, bending the universe to protect you from your choices. I saw the entitlement that ruined your soul. I saw the brokenness of a rich family that would consume those around then to retain their privilege. I felt it all.

Like the shattering of glass around me, I remembered all of the ways that I was a threat to this carefully constructed reality and was quickly tossed aside to preserve it. I went from savior to devil in a few short months when I started talking.

It was so odd to see it all play out on screen, as if this story had been told before and would be retold over and over again across history in different forms. It was chilling to witness, even though I know it well.

Despite all my dates, I haven't so much as let one of them hold my hand. Every time they get close to me, I cringe. I think of some excuse to use the bathroom, or move my body away from them. Some of them notice and back off. Some don't seem to care.

Usually, I'm quite the wild slut when I'm single. It's almost like a cleansing ritual after each major break up, but this time is different. Maybe it's because casual sex isn't as interesting in my 30's as it was in my 20's. Maybe it's because I just haven't met anyone I like yet. Maybe I'm just not getting drunk enough (in public.) I can't quite figure it out, but I might as well be that anxious little virgin self for all the prudishness I feel on these dates.

I mention this to my therapist and she tells me that I'm just not ready. Maybe she's right.

▲

Dear Hank,   Jan 7

Last night I had sex with someone new. It was the first time since I left you. I've been on several dates with him and he reminded me of you a little. He's dark haired and has a big nose. He's from the east coast and his favorite thing in life is snowboarding. He is a lot like you, but he is not you.

I knew by the end of our third date yesterday that this was not the man for me. He's too young in his mind and I did not like the way he smelled. I know that's terrible to admit, and he didn't smell bad, but there's something about the smell of a man that should make you feel a little wild. You always smelled sweet, like whiskey or fresh milled grain.

This morning, I expected to feel familiar anxiety. In the last few weeks since I started dating, every time a guy leans in at the end of a date to kiss me, my whole-body revolts. I get so anxious and awkward, even a little nauseous. I finally had to tell a couple of men this week that it would be better for me if they just didn't try to touch me. I felt guilty about my boundaries and told them that if they didn't want to see me anymore that would be ok, since there's no chance of sex in the near future. Oddly, they were all fine with it.

But that anxiety is not what I felt this morning. This morning I just feel empty. Everything in my room smells like him. I smell like him; my breath smells like him; my sheets smell like him. I showered, brushed my teeth, and washed the sheets.

It's not that the sex wasn't good. It was fine. It just wasn't you. It's not even that our sex-life was ever that amazing. People always assumed that it must have been really good for me to stay and put up with all the drama; that we must have been having the best sex on the planet, but we weren't. We are both pretty vanilla. A couple of plain lovers who liked each other's smell.

It's not his fault. He just doesn't know my body like you do. He doesn't know what I like and or how to read my body language. I suppose that's the benefit of sex with a long-term partner, you learn each other and so it gets better and better over time. Our sex-life was not perfect, but we knew and loved each other's bodies. Maybe what made our sex-life feel perfect is that it was ours and maybe I just miss you.

Afterwards he asked me to stay and I couldn't say no. It felt cold to send him home. He wrapped himself around me like a vice and I thought I would never sleep. Some women might find this romantic or sweet, but you know what a restless sleeper I am. He held me all night. I tossed and rolled and did not sleep. I remember how you and I used to fit together like two puzzle pieces. How I slept pressed up against your back, drinking in your smell and rubbing the tip of my nose on your skin. How If I woke up with a nightmare, I would reach for you. How you liked to be the little spoon. How sweet your face was while you were dreaming.

He left early this morning and reminded me that I don't have to freak out today because I've told him part of this story. I finally found sleep after he was gone.

It took years for you to learn not to wake me up in the morning and to give me my space to get up slowly. I don't want to have to teach someone new how to hold me, when to give me space, how I want to be touched.

I miss you,
Grace

▲

I never saw that man again either. I just couldn't do it. He pouted about it and I was reminded of why I felt he was too young to be my lover. The truth is that he missed his last lover too and we were just warming the empty space for a night.

▲

Dear Hank,   Jan 9

I don't recall exactly when I first realized you were a liar. I just remember that it was fairly early in our relationship. I don't recall what I caught you lying about, but I remember not saying anything when I noticed it. I remember setting it aside because it was such a tiny, white lie and I could tell it was from shame. I also remember pushing my chin just a little bit out and to the right, tilting my head at an angle to look at you, like my puppy does when she doesn't understand something.

I remember making the excuse in my head that many people tell silly white lies when they feel embarrassed. I remember thinking that this does not always correlate to bad character. I still think this is true for some people, but I have come to realize that yours were just ways for you to avoid responsibility. It was your addiction talking and my denial covering for you.

These thoughts were with me in yoga with your ex-lover this morning, the one I found you with at the bar the first time I left you. Yoga is something I used to love. I used to go twice a week and laugh and relax. I stopped going when we were together, but I started going again when we came home from Costa Rica. I signed up at the studio close to our house. The first day I went in, I saw her and startled. She teaches there and I had already bought my membership.

I came home to you and we laughed about it. We laughed at how obsessed with you she had been; how she used to go to your work and wait for you to get off, hoping that you'd have a beer with her. You used to call her your stalker. You would tell jokes at her expense to your co-workers, me, and your other friends. I was always confused about why she still hung around. I asked if you wanted me to say something. I can be so gullible. I genuinely thought that she had disregarded the boundaries you had been setting. The boundaries that I am now certain you never made at all.

I have fairly successfully avoided her in the studio. I go to classes that are not hers and don't talk much to anyone anyway. I do this now mostly because now she reminds me of you, and of how disregarded I felt when we were together.

Today she was teaching my regular class as a sub and I could not avoid her. I felt myself seething as I set up my mat, realizing I'd be spending an hour listening to her voice. I thought about how annoyed I am by her lack of boundaries. I thought about how she had disregarded the importance of our relationship, disregarded me! I could feel the heat of anger in my chest.

Then I thought, what if everything you told me about her was false in the same way that much of what you told your friends about me was false? What if you had never actually set those boundaries? What if you sought out her comfort when I was mad at you because you knew it was available? What if she was your back-up self-esteem plan; always ready to laugh and show interest when your partner was upset with you? What if you had wanted to preserve that and never said any of the things you told me you said? What if you had played us both and I was a fool for believing you?

I will probably never know. There are so many things I will probably

never know. You were Dr. Jekyll and Mr. Hyde. You once said that your
suspicions of me were so easy because you knew how easy it would be
for you to wander. I wonder if you did, perhaps not with your body, but
certainly with your heart.

I can see that this was not ever really about her, it was always about you.

Trust is such a delicate thing,
Grace

▲

I walked out of class that afternoon and pulled her aside. I apologized for
all the anxious and angry energy that I know has been palpably flowing
in her direction. I told her the whole story. I told her how you had talked
about her. I told her what I believed to be true and how I realized that I
was wrong. I told her how sorry I am that I had been cold and dismissive
to her.

She reached out to me and offered me a hug and her condolences about
us and the ways you had treated me. She told me she was happily in a
relationship and only thought of you as a friend with whom she had once
had a fling with.

I believe her and apologized to her for bringing it up. I asked her if it had
been the right thing to do, because I wanted to clear the air, but I didn't
want to her hurt her. I could tell that some of what I shared with her was
hurtful, because your actions often are. She assured me that she was glad
to know it.

I still avoid her at the studio, but when I am surprised to find her in one of
my other classes, I can focus now on my body and its movement instead
of on her and you.

▲

Dear Hank,   Jan 12

Gary and Char like to tell me how lucky I am that I got out while I'm so
young. We could have had 2 kids and then gone through a messy divorce
at 50 instead. Or maybe by then I would have lost so much of myself I
would not have left at all. I don't feel terribly lucky about any of it so far. I
feel like a fool.

I should have known better. I should have seen it coming. I DID see it
coming, but I stayed anyway. Sometimes I think maybe I should have
stayed for the 2 kids and the retirement savings. Maybe then I would have
my golden years of happiness and my kids to watch after me.

Then I think, "What if we had a boy? What if that boy turned out to be
just like you?"
That's when I knew I couldn't stay for the sperm and the college funds,
for the future my grandfather wanted me to have.

Tonight, I watched something on TV where everyone was dancing;
Dancing with partners like they do in old movies. I love to dance. The
last time I danced was in Boquete, Panama with John. You sulked and
punished me, angry that I had let another man swing me around the
dance floor. You had always refused to learn to dance. I guess I am lucky
that I didn't lose the next 20 years of dancing.

Love,
Grace

▲

My therapist mentioned in our last session that in the last few weeks,
while I haven't seen or heard from you, my pattern of speech is different,
slower and lower in pitch. She asked if I had noticed. I hadn't, but I have
been feeling different. More relaxed and comfortable in my mind in a way
I had almost forgotten. It's nice.

▲

There are still funny little moments when my anxiety returns. I went out this week with some old friends. One of them remarked that she always thought you were an ass because you had met them at least three times and never could recall their names.

After we had a few drinks, we were joined by another gal and decided to go dancing. As the three of us girls white-girl wiggled around the empty floor, I began to feel anxious. I would go back to Ted standing on the edge of the dance floor with his beer and make sure that he was alright. It was like a compulsion. I simply couldn't enjoy dancing with the girls.

I finally realized what was happening. I was worried that Ted be angry with Jackie later, the way you always were with me at the end of the night.

When I finally confided in Ted about this he laughed and said, "If I don't wanna be here, Grace, I'll just leave. I'm fine. I swear."

It reminded me of the night when you left the bar with Rob while I was in the bathroom. Then, I remembered the time you did the same thing in Arizona while we were visiting my family. You got my sister to play along and if it hadn't been for her husband and my sister-in-law, you would have left me there too. My mother came in and chastised both you and my sister for being so cruel.

I wonder how long it will take for me to feel comfortable having fun again, to have to force myself to stop looking over my shoulder and choose to believe that I will get used to having fun again eventually.

▲

Dear Hank   Jan 27

I'm still learning how to be alone. I don't know what to do with myself in this big empty house when Rob is away.

Next week, I am going to Hawaii to visit Gary and Char. They will be

there for the whole month and I invited myself to crash on their couch
for a long weekend. I need a jet setting fix and February always brings the
cold weather blues. So, I bought a ticket!

I think it'll be good for me to get out of town for a while; too many dates,
too many activities, too many ways to avoid the loneliness. I don't know if
I miss you, or if I just miss the easiness of being in a house with someone
who sees you naked on a regular basis. The casual way you have around
each other when you are partners.

I was laughing at book club last week about how I used to go next door
and porch-sit at the neighbor's house in my bathrobe. I hate pants and
the moment I come home from work they are off and I'm in my soft,
cozy robe. I don't do that as much as I used to, now that I live with a
roommate. I wore pants to book club.

I guess I don't have much to say, I'm just not yet used to not saying
anything to anyone at the end of the day.

Love,
Grace

▲

The cold weather always makes me feel mopey. I moved to this town to
get out of the cloud cover in the valley, but despite the sun, I still get sad
each winter. I have learned to assuage my seasonal depression with travel
to warm and sunny places.

I met Gary and Char before I met you. I was working at a bar downtown,
avoiding my career and several other responsibilities. They were some of
my regulars and found out that I was a therapist in hiding. We began to
talk about life and all sorts of things. Eventually when I quit that job and
started working as a therapist again, we began our own regular weekly
happy hour together.

One day, Gary asked me, "Do you think of us as parents, kind of?"

I wasn't sure if it would be offensive to say, so I denied it, "No way! You're so much cooler than parents."

Char laughed, flattered. Gary replied, "Well, we think of you as our adopted girl."

From then on it was official, they were my surrogate parents. They heard all the drama and all the fun. When I left you, they worried about me. I've relied on their guidance and validation ever since.

This year they were supposed to go with another couple to Hawaii for a month, but due to unfortunate circumstances, they were now going alone. As I sat with them discussing their change of plans, I interjected the idea of joining them. They were happy to share part of their vacation and their couch with me. It will be the first time I've flown anywhere since our separation. I'm excited to escape the cold and start doing some of the things that I love again.

▲

About a month ago, Nellie was due for her routine vet visit. She had been lethargic since we returned from Costa Rica, but I hadn't been able to decide if I should be concerned. The vet decided to run a blood panel just to check and found some concerning results.

It has taken the whole month of testing for us to discover that she has heartworm. Concerned about your dog, I ask the vet about transmission and whether your dog might have caught it as well. In a moment of concern and poor judgement, I unblock your number and send you a message about it.

The moment I sent the message, I regretted it. The polite dry conversation ended in a veiled threat. You asked me about some mail and thanked me for letting you know about the dogs. Then you told me you needed a payment schedule for the car and if I was able to provide it, you would continue to respect my request to be left alone. Then you mentioned a surgery scheduled for tomorrow.

Shortly afterwards, as the anxiety settled in again, I re-blocked your
number.

▲

Dear Hank,   Jan 28

You are so scary. Sometimes, I can't tell if you are really that scary or if
I just feel afraid of you. I know that there's a difference, but I'm not sure
which is true anymore. I don't feel like I can trust that you won't cross the
line of basic human dignity. I wonder if you would be so crazy as to show
up at my work. It's the only place you can still find me. You don't have my
home address. I avoid all of your regular bars. Would you come here to
get the money?

I keep reminding myself that you care more about your appearance than
anything else. You only want to be seen the way you construct. I keep
reminding myself that your friends and family told me not to worry about
the money. It's a small sum and debatable if I owe you anything. I gave
back the heirloom diamond you proposed with along with the setting
that I purchased for it. I left all the furniture I purchased for your house.
The cost of the car is debatable at this point. It was an just an unfortunate
wash of mixed finances by the time we were done. I gave up my career
and income for a year and you bought me a cheap city car when we
returned. Fair is fair.

The fighter in me doesn't want to pay you, out of principle. How dare
you demand money from me after I gave up everything for you. And how
about the expenses I'll be spending in recovering from the abuse: therapy,
rebuilding my finances, etc.

We used to have this debate about kids too. If I gave up my career to have
children and raise them, I would lose out on potential income from those
years. To me that meant that any pre-nuptial agreement that we signed
keeping me from your investments would be void. I needed to know
that you wouldn't leave me destitute and unable to care for myself and

our kids should something happen. But that is exactly what happened in Costa Rica. I was left without resources and could not rely on you. Now you are just as vindicative as I had feared, demanding money from me when we both gave up financial security to make that move together. I sold my car and used that money to fund the trip and now you want reimbursement.

I never wanted to take your house from you, but I was always afraid that this was how you would see it. You spent money supporting me; I lost money by going with you. Somehow in your mind I still owe you something.

Grace

▲

I wish that I hadn't sent you any messages. I relapsed and I feel the hangover. I am so afraid of you, but I still feel that I had to warn you about Hank. You were always making threats about killing him to avoid responsibility when he got old or sick. I was sad for him. He was a scared little herding dog who needed stability and consistency. He cowered under the kitchen table when you were drunk and angry. He was aggressive when you were anxious and you laughed at the behaviors that isolated him and stressed me out. You were proud of his surly attitude that matched your own and I have no confidence that you will take care of him. I wish I didn't worry so much about the consequences of your choices and the others that are affected by them.

▲

The relapse runs its course, hitting all the stages of grief as if for the first time: anger, then bargaining, and finally sadness.

▲

Dear Hank,   Jan 29

I miss you today. I can't tell if it's because I did eight sessions and am
feeling tired, or maybe because I haven't been on a date for a while.

We could have had everything you know, if you would only listen. You
were so good about some things. I told you once that I think leaving the
toilet seat up is super disrespectful and I never found it up at our house
again.

You always cleaned the bathroom. You were great at house chore sharing.
You did the dishes every morning and made me breakfast most days.

You simply couldn't hear me about the big stuff. You couldn't hear me
about the alcohol or using kind words. You couldn't hear me about
coming home when you said you would or just sending a text message
saying you would be late. You couldn't see that your friends hated me and
that the little lies were eroding us.

But tonight, I just miss you: your snuggles, your warmth, and your love;
flawed, twisted and possessive as it was. I miss being in love with and
being loved by you.

Grace

February 2020

Dear Hank,   Feb 1

When I type your name into my phone, the next suggested words are mi
esposo. Thanks Apple.

Today, I got on a plane for the first time since I left you. I wish you were here with me. I miss folding ourselves up together across two seats. I miss falling asleep on your lap or shoulder. I miss you using me as your pillow or blanket or both. Now, I'm sardined in between two strangers, instead of sharing with you.

I am not very patient. I want to be over this. I want to look back at photos of our adventures with poised contentment. I want to stop feeling sad and lonely when I reflect on the last three years, or feeling that I've wasted them building memories that can't bring me joy. I'm scared that I'll never meet anyone like you again. That my next partner won't love to jet-set with me. That he won't have an insatiable curiosity about other cultures and experiences.

I think the real problem is that it wasn't ALL bad with you. You were everything I had wanted, with some extra sprinkles on top. The extra was just more than I could take: screaming, fighting, kicking me out, coming home bleeding and lying, or carrying guns while drunk.

But the good was so good. You were tall and beautiful. You had a careless disregard for the rules in a way that fit with my own adventure lust. You loved to travel. You were willing to move to Costa Rica with me and start a new life. You were content to let me look at every church we drove past in Mexico and when you got tired of architecture, you would sit on the sidewalk with a beer and the dogs until I'd had my fill. You would backpack anywhere with water to fish and never dragged your feet about our next adventure. We could have been so happy together.

It broke my heart to leave you and no one understood why. After all you had done and all you had put me through, how could I still love you? Because in between the blood and lies and fear and pain, were quiet moments that were beautiful; planes to all the corners of Central America, Spanish pillow talk, dreams about the family we would make, and quiet snuggles in airports and tents.

You were my person and now you are gone. I try to keep up the anger in front of friends who had wanted me to leave. It makes it easier to be confident in my choice. I blocked your number not because I don't want to hear from you, but because I can't stand it. I can't stand that you're out there somewhere without me, mi esposo.

Love,
Grace

▲

This trip to Hawaii is surprisingly painful. I hadn't anticipated how many
things in these airports would remind me of you. I also hadn't anticipated
the perspectives that those long flights would provide.

▲

Dear Hank,   Feb 2

There is an older couple in the row in front of me playing rummy. They
are laughing and I am thinking of you. We played so much rummy on our
travels. You loved it until I started winning all the time. Then we stopped
playing.

You have ruined me for traveling forever. I have spent countless hours
in airports in my life. Flying back and forth from Oregon to Arizona
twice a year since I was two. I remember the PDX carpet before it had an
Instagram following, and it always meant I was coming home.

Years of traveling as a kid and then as an adult, and I never spent money
in the airport. I packed my own snacks and was completely self-contained
because airports are a total rip-off. As a captive audience, they can charge
you anything, and they do. But you always found the nearest airport bar
the moment we were through security and ordered me a 20$ mimosa
just because you know how much I love them. In hindsight, it was
probably because you needed a beer, but at the time it was sweet and felt
extravagant.

I miss traveling with you. It was the best part of our relationship.

Love,
Grace

▲

Reflecting on those airport bars and the seizure you had on your last flight home taints those romantic memories with the reality of your addiction. You hadn't sought those airport bars because it was extravagant and fun, it was another illusion to hide your addiction. There are so many things that were all part of the charade.

We lived downtown and you rode your bike everywhere. You said this was due to environmental consciousness, but was it? This town is known for DUI busts and you are rarely without any alcohol in your system, even mid-day. You never wanted to drive across town for an event. "It's too far to bike," you'd say and we would stay home. I was so naïve.

▲

Dear Hank,   Feb 4

It's a beautiful day in Kauai. I have been laying in the sun soaking it into my white, fish-belly skin. It's such a different color than when we lived in Costa Rica.

I was wondering out loud what waterfall it was that you can see from just about every angle on this side of the island, when this beautiful bronze man walked by. I only saw his feet before looking up. Then startling a little when I saw who I had stopped, I asked if he lived here and knew the name of the land features around us. When I tilted me face up from his feet in the sand and saw him above my hat, I felt shy. He was kind and answered me and glanced at the tattoo on my belly.

It's funny, when you are with someone you don't worry about how everyone else sees your body. To you I was always the most beautiful woman you'd ever seen. No need to worry about how pudgy or out of shape I've gotten, whether I'm eating too many carbs or not. You liked my little belly and held it while we slept at night. I never worried about whether I was attractive to you or not. Now I seem to worry about it all the time. Will anyone else ever see me that way again?

I hate being single,
Grace

▲

Realizations about your addiction aren't the only things that I'm reflecting on this week. I start to see the ways that my body has changed since we met, the ways I stopped caring for myself. I start to reflect on all the choices that lead me here beginning with my constant existential crisis.

▲

Dear Hank,   Feb 5

I love Hawaii. Every time I'm here I think about relocating. I start perusing the job boards to see if there are any postings in my field. There always are, something offering to pay for student loans, but I never apply. I'm always nervous that I'll get here and be restless. That island fever will drive me mad and I'll need to bolt.

The mountains are inspiring in a different way than the ocean. When I see the Cascades, I feel strong. I feel powerful. I feel alive. I feel the need to rise up and go, to meet any obstacle while measuring my choices with wisdom and fearless assurance.

The ocean brings me back down again. It calms me, soothes me. It makes me feel that life is as it is and there is no reason to fight or cry. It gives me the existential reminder that this is all there is and I must not squander it by rushing around, trying to control things that cannot be contained. It grounds me in my humanity and frailty, then sweetens this finite reality with the gift of a beautiful new day.

They are different forces with different effects on me, both so necessary.

There is a time to act and be powerful, and a time to let go and be still.

I wish I were sharing it all with you,
Grace

▲

These existential realizations bring my loneliness into full view. I can't
run from it here. There are no distractions from the emptiness that opens
inside me. It threatens to drag me in and it makes me angry.

▲

Dear Hank,   Feb 6

I'm so lonely. That's why I ended up with you, you know?

I want to be a great feminist. The kind that doesn't need anyone and
doesn't want kids and loves herself the most, but I'm too soft. I often feel
like a slave to the independent feminism of my generation. It makes me
feel weak when I admit that what I want is to love and be loved. I want a
family and a community. I want the white picket fence; I just don't want
to be trapped by it.

I wrestled with this the winter we met and failed to resolve it. Instead, I
fell into bed with you. I believe you were wrestling with this too. You had
left your last girlfriend and you were sad. We were just a pair of lost souls
that wanted to hide from our demons.

Now that you are gone the loneliness is back. It's as acute as it ever was. It
drives me to spend hours on dating apps in a dissociative daze. Even here
in Hawaii, I fantasize that some beautiful surfer boy will convinces me
to give up my life and run away to this island. It's something I've always
wanted to do, but never been brave enough to do alone.

But maybe if there was a man...

See! I'm a terrible feminist. I want all my freedom just so I can give it
away again, because mostly I just don't want to be alone.

I miss you, but perhaps I just miss someone.

Love,
Grace

▲

The tropical climate of this island along and all of this free time brings
the grief into focus. I can't escape the comparison game that comes from
familiarity and idleness. I find myself swirling through old memories with
every well-known scent and sound. I hear the sea birds and plunge into
visions of beaches in another tropical paradise. It's so visceral the I can
recall the even smallest details.

▲

Dear Hank,   Feb 7

Do you remember how terrible my skin was in Costa Rica? I have scars
from the cystic acne that covered my face, chest, and shoulders. I have
never had acne like that, even in adolescence.

I blamed the jungle. It was 100% humidity and 85 degrees and my body
was in revolt. That's what I would say.

Now I'm in Hawaii and it's not quite as humid, not quite as hot, but it
is still the jungle and my skin is beautiful. It's golden brown and soft. It
makes me wonder if it was really the environment that made my skin so
terrible, or if it was my own misery.

I know you harbor resentment towards me for that year. Obviously, I
have some towards you also. Do you remember when we were happy
before we left? Do you remember our promises? I asked you to assure
me that if I couldn't make it through the whole year, if it was worse than

we could've foreseen, if it was un-copable for one or both of us, that you would choose me. That you would be willing to come home. Whether the contract was complete or not. Whether it made financial sense or not. That we would be a team committed to our relationship and wellbeing above all else. You promised me. You said I was the most important thing in your life and would always be your priority.

Eight months later we were screaming at each other in the yellow river house. I was begging you to let me move home while you finished your contract, telling you that I'd lost my mind and might drive myself off a cliff. You replying that you wouldn't commit to being faithful to me long distance and insisting on finishing your contract. My worst nightmare coming true. I wondered out into the rain and thought about drowning myself in the river. How did we get there? How did we get here?

So many things happened between those two moments. So many nights of crying through the culture shock while you told me it was my own fault. I wasn't trying hard enough. I wasn't strong enough. Nights spent scratching my skin until I bled, days spent planning escapes from the misogyny of bikini contests and cocaine bender weekends with the boys.

I never fit there. When you finally told your boss we were leaving, he said that if it didn't work out with us you were always welcome back, and that this town was historically hard on women He missed the association of two statements.

It's all water under the bridge now. You wanted me to be more supportive of your career. I needed you to be kinder and more understanding. I suppose neither of us were getting what we needed and now we're free to go find it elsewhere. Eventually, I'll stop wishing we had been able to work it out.

Love,
Grace

▲

All the pieces of myself I gave up along our journey are slowly surfacing and my mind is wrestling them back into their places. I am trying to assemble the puzzle, to see the picture as a whole. I pick them up and analyze their details, just to set them down again, no closer to finding their place in the photograph.

I know that there is a logic here. All of my education screams back at me that there is sense in the mess and misery somewhere, if I just study it long enough, I will be able to understand. And if I can understand it, then I can control it, and prevent it from ever happening again. The memories come and go like bread crumbs that never lead me home again.

I chase these dreams around until I board a plane home and find myself back int the monotony of a partially rebuilt life.

▲

Dear Hank,   Feb 10

Your neighbor, sent me a message about the broken-down car out front his house. He asked me if I knew whose it was and if they could move it this weekend. I sent him your number and told him that we were no longer together.

Your neighbor is a sweetheart. He offered to meet me for a drink and talk me through the process of getting a divorce. He told me that he and his ex-wife were still on good terms after their divorce in June and that he was happy to lend a listening ear. I told him that I hope they both continue to heal and that I am glad they had such an amicable split, but that ours was not that way. I told him that you were abusive to me and that because of this we did not sign paperwork at the wedding and couldn't be around each other anymore. I can't stand the cute little lie that "it just didn't work out."

I always debate using this word. There is so much stigma around it. "Abuse." Even as a trauma therapist, I find myself questioning its use. There is lingering skepticism in my assumption that it is overused.

I am familiar with the ways that some people will respond to this word. I know that some of them will hear, "Drama, Drama, Drama" and turn away. I know that some of them will wonder what I did to deserve it. I know that some people will simply not believe me and think I'm seeking attention. I am familiar with the negative responses to this statement and because of that I've wondered if it's worth it to say it.

I keep saying it though. I keep saying it because I don't want to be around the kinds of people who believe these things. I want to surround myself with people who can hold my story. I want to have friends who can see me without cringing or blaming, who are afraid it might be contagious.

Truth is contagious and I want to be the host. I don't want to tacitly comply with a culture that tells women they have to lie about their experiences to protect someone's reputation, their own or yours.

This is a small town, and I know that I won't always win this battle, but I hope that my persistence will win the war. I want to pass on a world where my daughters don't have to hide the truth to protect themselves.

Grace

▲

Dear Hank,   Feb 13

Tomorrow is Valentine's Day. I hate this holiday. I always have. I hated it in high school with my boyfriend, I hated it in my twenties while I was single or coupled, and I hated it while I was with you. I hate it all the time, although not getting any attention doesn't make it any better.

I've been crying every night this week. It's my first week back to work since Hawaii and usually I feel so refreshed when I return from a trip. I love coming back and picking up my life again, but not this time. This time, I have been crying every night.

It could be the 8 client days. Although my suspicions are that it's more about you than the 5 intakes I did this week. I can't stop thinking about you.

I miss you terribly. The longing is so acute I almost called you today. I went across the hall to Kerri's office when I had this thought. I needed someone to remind me why that is a terrible idea, or maybe just to hold space for me to remind myself.

It's my clients lately too. They are all in relationships with dysfunctional, abusive, or alcoholic men that don't treat them well, but somehow this week they're all fine. Their partners are shaping up and their quiet perseverance seems to be paying off. Which makes me think that maybe everyone else was right. Maybe if I hadn't been as "hysterical" we could have worked it out. Except that I am not quiet or patient. I am bold and honest. I am strong and independent. I am even sometimes bossy and demanding, but this is who I am.

More than anything else, I know that I gave you chance after chance and you would not change. I know that I begged, pleaded, waited, and you still could not be kind to me. I know that I'll never be demure and quiet like these women who borrow my strength one hour of one day each week, and though I am happy to lend it, sometimes I wish I was not the strong woman. Sometimes, I wish I was the quiet, gentle one instead.

I also know the cycle. That things can be really good for a little while. We hold our breath waiting for it to collapse again, but I prefer to breathe all the time. That is why I left. I guess I just needed to remember that.

Love,
Grace

▲

Dear Hank,   Feb 15

I had weird dreams about you last night. First, I dreamt we had kids and you were a horrid parent. Then, I dreamt that I was fishing with another man and catching so many huge trout. Last, I dreamt about having sex with you again.

I miss you. I miss your body and our familiar sex life. I miss your kisses.
You were always a generous lover. It was the only part of our relationship
where you really seemed invested in my happiness. Previously, I had
always been uncomfortable with partners that focused on my pleasure.
I felt guilty asking for what I wanted, but with you it felt alright to relax
and enjoy, because you enjoyed giving. I know I am remembering this all
through rose colored glasses because I've been sad these last few weeks.
That trip to Hawaii was more triggering than I had anticipated.

I have other memories of our sex life, painful ones. When we started
dating, you were often critical of my body for what I did or did not do
with my body hair, the way I smelled, or how frequently we were having
sex. It was never enough for you and I felt more insecure about my
body than ever before. I spent hours explaining how women get yeast
infections and are sore if they have too much sex. That some women can't
wax everything because their skin is sensitive and they shouldn't have to
because they may just not like it. I felt like I had to explain every choice I
made under the microscope of your gaze and critique.

In the end you decided that you liked my smell. You washed your sheets
when I left to avoid the pain of remembering. You told me you would
rather have not-enough sex with me than as much sex as you wanted for
the rest of your life with someone else. You eventually gave up on what
I did with my body hair and began to understood some of the double
standards placed on women.

Later today, I went to the grocery store. The girl scouts were selling
cookies and I stared at them longingly for a moment, then remembered
my belly on the beach in Hawaii. When one of them asked me if I'd like
to buy any, I told them I really wanted to, but couldn't because I'm on a
diet. The mothers gave me a disapproving look. I would have done the
same.

I think I might be losing my mind. Is it possible to go mad from grief?

Love,
Grace

The letters that I write start to sound manic, like I'm grasping at the straws of my reality between the memories that come back unanticipated and unsolicited. The dreams and memories are so real, so visceral. They contain smells and tastes, feelings and sensations, and when I wake up from them it takes a whole day to shake off the intensity.

Sometimes it feels like I can't tell the difference between dreams and waking. I can't tell what is present and what Is past. My body keeps remembering things I've told it to forget and I'm afraid it will consume me.

I know this is post-trauma. My education allows me the privilege of some self-reflection, and my social circle compensates for my mental health when I can't so it for myself. The despair is knowing the truth and still being unable to escape the experience.

Dear Hank,   Feb 16

I want to be kissed again, but I'm weird about it. It has always felt like the most intimate part of sex to me, someone that close to my face. It's hard to describe. Like eye contact, it just feels so vulnerable, as if I will give away all my private thoughts and feelings with a glance.

Do you remember the first time we kissed? We danced and talked and flirted and when I tried to leave, you followed me. You looked offended that I would leave without saying goodbye. I had assumed you were indifferent with your cold demeanor, and was surprised when you asked to walk with me to my car.

We kissed in the parking lot for a long time. You are a great kisser. I gave you my number and didn't hear from you. Three weeks I waited. I should have known then. You had been too drunk to remember that I had given it to you. I just didn't want to see it.

How many of our other firsts were punctuated by your drinking? The
first night I spent with you. The first time we slept together. Our first
flight. Our first fight. Our birthdays. Our first Christmas. Our first New
Years. And all of the ones after those. There was never a moment that did
not contain a beer or cocktail.

Why didn't I see it? Maybe because I was drinking too. I do a lot less of
that now.

I hope I get kissed again soon, ideally by someone who will remember it
the next day.

Grace

▲

I've read that your body remembers things that don't always feel like
memories. Some things come back as a feeling without the story of
the past to let you know where it came from. They feel like they are
happening in this moment instead. They say this is because they are
stored in a part of our brain that doesn't understand time, the part of our
brain that is the same as my dog or other animals.

The part that makes us human, understands that these things are past and
can change. It is a newer part of the brain. Trauma isn't stored there, its
stored is this animal part that doesn't know that it's over. So, the trauma
gets trapped in a forever repeating cycle of re-experiencing: love and hate
and destruction and fear.

Sometimes I'm angry with myself for this cycle. I miss you and remember
the love. Then I recall the fear of your moods and the destruction of my
self-esteem. Then I recall our dreams together and the adventures we had
together. Then, I begin to hate myself for the choices that I made; how I
allowed all of this to escalate and for missing you even now.

The cruel truth of therapy is that we all went to school hoping that we

could understand away our intolerably painful feelings. When we all
graduated and started practicing, we slowly realized that no amount
of education can excuse you from the human condition and we would
forever be trapped with the knowledge of what is happening with no
escape from the experience.

▲

Dear Hank,   Feb 18

Do you know what makes me crazy about people saying that I was bad
for you? It is the assumption that I brought this nastiness out in you.

You and I both know that's not true!

You told Ben on the phone after the wedding that you recognized your
alcoholism had been progressively escalating for the last five years. That
was long before I met you.

In fact, that was about a year before you ended your last relationship.
That might be why it worked with her for so many years. I believe you
were once a good partner to her. That hurts to think about. She got the
best of you and I'm getting blamed.

Grace

▲

Dear Hank,   Feb 25

Yesterday I had my IUD removed at the doctor's office. We were
supposed to be trying to get pregnant right about now. That was our plan:
pull the plug in October and be trying in the spring.

I want a baby so badly. There have been other times in my life when I
didn't want one, and I went back and forth several times. But it has never
felt as urgently as it does now. I'm going to be 34 in April. I thought I

would be pregnant or have an infant by now. Maybe even working on number two.

Letting go of the idea of having a family has been one of the hardest parts of leaving you. I think I believed that if we had children, you would see the seriousness of your issues and maybe really invest in some life changes. You know, have a baby to save the marriage. You had confessed that you were deeply afraid of being a bad father, but in the end, I just could not take that risk. I could not risk the possibility that you wouldn't change and I would be trapped without resources, and with a child.

My mother keeps telling me, "You don't need a man to have a baby, Grace."

After my last two sexual experiences, I find myself growing more and more angry with men. Angry that when they are angry, they are dangerous. Angry that I have to explain to them why they should provide their own condoms, as if I haven't already invested thousands of dollars in pregnancy prevention and in my own reproductive health. Angry that it doesn't seem to matter what I want with my body, they will have what they want, and have it their way. All the years of the misuse of my body and heart have collected into a veritable well of seething repulsion directed at any man who looks my way.

I haven't wanted to be on birth control for years. This last IUD I had put in 3 years ago, shortly before I began dating you, because I had an accidental pregnancy. I decided to give my body a break from all the hormones over the previous ten years and had my IUD removed after my last long-term relationship ended. I decided that I would just use condoms for pregnancy prevention.

Despite my insistence on their use, every single man I slept with decided, at some point, that he didn't like them anymore and would pull it off before he finished. Maybe justifying it by pulling out, maybe not. Without surprise, I got pregnant. I was furious with myself because I didn't object the first few times, I had just been too shocked. When I finally did object, it didn't matter anyway. So, I went back on birth control to protect myself.

Since then, it's caused weight gain, skin issues, and my body just doesn't seem to tolerate it the way it did in my 20's. I was really looking forward to being comfortable enough with the idea of being pregnant that I was willing to risk being birth control free.

Now, I'm not ready to have a baby. I know that I want one in the next couple of years, with or without a new partner. But until then, because I've realized that men just can't be trusted to respect my boundaries, I guess I just have to practice celibacy. I seem to detest any man that I am intimate with as soon as the orgasm is over anyway, so maybe it's for the best.

My therapist says I'm just not ready yet. Perhaps she's right. Casual sex isn't fun the way it was in my 20's anymore. What I want is a partner with whom I can have meaningful, connective sex or to be left the fuck alone.

Love,
Grace

▲

My anger seems to increase as this month draws to an end. My mind is exhausted by trying to find reason in the madness of our story. The pieces still don't seem to fit together and I am growing frustrated by the puzzle. I just want it to be over, like a neurotic dog without a job, I feel like I am chewing on my own flesh.

I find my way to a yoga class in between moments of self-destruction, grasping for the few things I know I can rely on for self-care. When I arrived to my regular class, I find that the last-woman-you-fucked-before-me is the sub-teacher today.

My brain explodes a little. It's enough to spend every waking moment fighting to avoid memories of you, but to be trapped in a room for 75 minutes with the same face I saw at the bar that day I first left you, is too much.

After 15 minutes of trying to keep my shit together, I leave mid-class.

Embarrassing as it is, I just can't do it. I rush home to write this letter.

▲

Dear Hank,   Feb 27

It's a beautiful spring day here, albeit too early, but I woke up missing you like mad. I cried on the way to work today and was really triggered in my second session. So much that I thought about calling you again. I got through the third and ran out to yoga on my lunch break and, wouldn't you know, that woman was there. You know, the one who was with you at the bar the night I left you. The one you called your stalker.

You used to mock her to me, your co-workers, and friends. I wondered how any woman could tolerate this kind of derision, but that was before I knew about how different your face was from one place to the next.

I don't want to hate her. I know that it's not her fault. I know you just needed a woman's attention because we were arguing and you can't tolerate not being doted on. I want to let this go. It's just another barb in my soul.

Fuck you.

March 2020

Dear Hank,   Mar 3

I saw Rebecca at the old mill trail today. She told me she's been following my travels on Instagram and she is happy that I'm happy.

I'm not. I am not happy. I'm anxious and tired of being afraid, and my heart is broken.

I hate men for looking at me. I hate them for not looking. I am afraid I'll be alone forever, so I keep dating. I am self-conscious and insecure. I don't feel beautiful anymore. I am constantly critiquing my own body to the tune of your voice in my head. I have social anxiety now and feel like everyone is either annoyed with me or hates me already. I cry too much, talk too much, feel too much, and just am too much.

Everyone asks me how I'm doing and I say "fine" because there is nothing new to talk about. There is nothing to do but wait. Wait for the feelings to pass, as they always do. I understand this and I have analyzed it endlessly, but it brings no relief.

Then I hear that some client's abusive marriage that has turned around and is starting to be sweet again, and I am plunged back into doubt that I gave you enough time to get better.

Did I? Did I give you enough warning? Enough time? Enough help? Did I do enough? Was I kind enough? Patient enough? Firm enough? Soft enough? Was I enough?

I know that cycle of harm and sweetness in abusive relationships all too well. I know how loving a partner can be after he's thrown his worst tantrum. I know how sweet he can be after he locks you out of the house or tears at you with his words or hands. What I know most is how easy it is to fall for the sweetness, the little taste of hope that keeps you clinging on in the midst of the storms.

I think of you every day and I can't wait until the day comes when I don't anymore. I don't want to miss you. I don't want to think about you. I want to be free from you.

The biggest mind-fuck about it is that I like my new life. I spend more time laughing, more time adventuring, more time being happy than I did when I was with you. So, it feels insane to miss you this much, to hurt this much. I feel crazy all the time because the facts don't change my feelings.

The abuse, the alcoholism, the cruelty doesn't make me love you less. It doesn't turn off the attachment, the thousands of tiny strings that tie my heart to yours. They are snapping one by one, slowly, but each one sends a shock through my body that ripples into tears and self-doubt. If I could snap them all at once I would, like ripping the band-off suddenly.

I know that if I can make it through this first year, it will be better. I just have to get through this year.

Love,
Grace

▲

My anger grows because the pain gets bigger each day and I feel like I might lose myself in it. I am so angry with you and the more angry I am with you, the more I hate myself. I hate myself for the choices and my lack of foresight. I believe that because of my profession, I should have known better. The unrelenting standards of the burden of my education work against my self-compassion and sink me further in an impossible expectation.

▲

Dear Hank,   Mar 5

I want to be one of those magnanimous ex-girlfriends. The kind that never has anything bad to say. The kind that understands that we just weren't a good fit and wishes you well with the next lady. I want to be kind and sweet and forgiving, but I'm still just so angry and hurt.

Why didn't you go to treatment? Why didn't you just tell me when you were upset instead of punishing me? Why couldn't you be secure in my love, instead of being so suspicious? I didn't want anyone else. I still don't. I just want you. I just want your lips, your kisses, and your long arms around me. I want to hear you tell me I'm the most beautiful woman you've ever seen. I want to breathe in your sweet whiskey smell while we sleep, nose pressed into your back. I want to laugh about our crazy mothers and plan all these summer trips with you.

I just needed you to be kind to me.

Love,
Grace

▲

Dear Hank,   Mar 6

I've decided to make a list. I often have my clients make lists about things
when they are having difficulty making choices: lists of what they do and
do not like about a job, item, relationship. I'm going to make a list of what
would have to change for this to have been a relationship that worked for
me, because I need to remember the fundamental cracks that ended us.

1) I would need you to make an effort to be friendly with my friends.
    I don't know how many times I have introduced you to Ted and
    Jackie, and you could never remember their names. That's so
    rude! I know you used your bad memory as an excuse, but I know
    now that was just the alcohol. You never wanted to have people
    over to visit and I love to entertain. You didn't take the time to
    build a relationship with anyone who was important to me. You
    actually threw a tantrum every time I had a friend visit from the
    city, getting drunk and storming off when you could no longer
    monopolize my attention.

2) Speaking of which, you would have to stop drinking. I would
    have even been ok with some simple limits, like a 3 drink
    maximum, don't drink until after 6, only twice a week, etc, but
    only after you had been sober long enough to recognize the
    lies that you used to keep yourself from the truth. Even though
    I know that you could never keep these limits and that's what
    defines you as an alcoholic: your inability to maintain boundaries
    with your drinking.

3) You would have to call my family and apologize for the wedding;

my mother especially. While we're on it, all of my friends; Jess and Jon, Michael, all the people who I leaned on during this slow train wreck.

4) You would have to stop lying. Stop lying about the boundaries you set with other women, about why you came home bleeding, about me to other people, about why you lost your job, about everything.

5) You would have to support me with your friends. No more talking shit about them to me and me to them in order to keep us separate. I need you to see my perspective and be on my team when we disagree, or at least just allow me to have a different opinion without seeing any dissent as a problem for the group.

There are only 5 things on this list, but these 5 things were everything. The only times that we were ok together were when we were alone. You would never fit with my people and I never fit with yours. Your value system was so different from mine. Our lives were fundamentally incompatible, and I just didn't want to see it.

Grace

▲

I know that this list is just record of my bargaining. I spent all three years of our relationship bargaining with you, trying to make this work. What compromises could I make? What could I offer up to make it possible to stay? I know that are useless ideas. You would never walk towards the middle, but I had to try.

▲

Dear Hank,   Mar 8

You know that we had everything and you fucked it up right?

Grace

Dear Hank,   Mar 10

I don't know what happened, but I just couldn't take the yucky energy
between her and I anymore. I've been hating her, and despite my never
saying anything, I know she can feel that energy whenever we interact. I
just didn't want to carry that around anymore and I don't want to be that
person. So, I went to her class on purpose. I couldn't keep avoiding her.

During class as I seethed and sweated, I thought maybe it was never
about her at all. Maybe you had been lying to me about what you had said
to her and also lying to her about what you had said to me. Like a breeze
on a stagnant day, the realization of your rampant lies dawned on me.
Perhaps this whole thing is a giant misunderstanding orchestrated by you
to retain both of our attention. It was as if a light came on in a dark and
musty room in my heart and I didn't hate her anymore.

I didn't really have time to think through what I'd say or how I'd start.
It was an impulsive decision, and I only debated how much to tell her.
I suddenly didn't want to hurt her. If someone told me that one of my
friends was saying the kinds of things about me that you had said about
her, I would be both mortified and deeply hurt. I honestly didn't know
if I should tell her or not. In the end, I felt compelled to, whether to
vindicate myself or to warn her about you, I don't know. I just know that
as suddenly as the truth appeared to me, I could not hide it anymore.

I am not a jealous woman. I am not insecure in relationship. I am
generally warm and trusting. I do not have difficulties with my partner's
previous lovers or female friendships. I had never felt these things, until I
was with you.

You on the other hand, have always been jealous. You are insecure as a
rule, and you wanted to make me feel the same way. I let you win and I
can't so that anymore.

So, I told her everything. I told her how you had represented her to me.

I told her how you had called her your stalker to the point of expressing concern that she might "show up at our house sometime." I told her how I had asked if you had been clear about your boundaries with her and you told me you had been. I told her how I had grown to hate her for what I believed to be a flagrant dismissal of our boundaries and of me. Finally, I told her how I had chosen to believe you, even when I suspected the lies, because I wasn't ready to face the truth about your character.

Then I apologized. I apologized for hating her, for blaming her, for assuming your truthfulness at her expense. I also apologized for the burden of sharing this all with her now.

She was very kind to me. She was shocked and hurt as I had suspected, but she thanked me for being honest with her. She told me about the new guy she was seeing and gave me a hug. She wished me recovery from you and assured me I had done the right thing by telling her.

I still don't know if it was the right thing or not, but I have been feeling so suffocated by all these lies. The weight of confusion around who knows and believes what, has made me quiet and reserved. It made me feel trapped and avoidant.

I miss the freedom of knowing that how someone responds to me is because of who I am, and not some manufactured version, for better or worse. I don't need everyone to like me, but I do need to know that the judgements passed are based on an accurate representation. I can live with the results.

You used us both. To keep me pacified, you painted her as your stalker, a woman without conscience and character. To keep her attention, on the side, for whenever you might need it, you sacrificed me, by painting me as the jealous, crazy girlfriend. That's so fucked up, Hank.

Disappointedly,
Grace

▲

After this first truth telling experience I have less to say to you. I don't feel inclined to write to you. I don't find myself thinking of you. I feel less angry and less burdened, as I a small part of my soul came back into my body. I can breathe more easily now, having shaken off one small lie.

Then, several things in the world change all at once.

▲

Dear Hank,   Mar 23

The whole world has lost its mind. I never realized how much a therapist depends on the transiency of feelings. Only a few clients are in crisis each week usually, but in a global pandemic, they all are. I am exhausted. I have been compulsively shopping, not because I'm worried about the world ending, but because I'm afraid of not being able to buy toilet paper next week due to panic hoarders. It's crazy making.

Not to mention that being an empathic person at this time is like breathing in the panic like the dense smoky summer air. There is no escape. I can taste the fear every time I walk into a room and I'm starting to choke.

Rob has had 4 ex-girlfriends text him this week saying they miss him. Everyone is saying that is a thing in a global pandemic. I'm not sure if it's the pandemic or just my broken heart that still wants to call you. I keep thinking that we could be laughing at the world in cynical arrogance with our health and age to support the statistics that say this can't touch us. Instead, I'm here wishing that we had met ten years ago when we were really young and maybe just a bit more stupid. Maybe then we would have fought, drank, and cried ourselves into some kind of fiery timeless end in a romantic tragedy.

I loved you. I loved you so much I think it might have killed me if I stayed. That's what all my friends thought, that you would eventually have killed me. I'm not sure those things are that different. There was certainly some time in Costa Rica where I thought I might hurt myself because of how trapped I felt. Maybe that's what I wanted, someone who would drive me straight into the grave with passion. I wanted to be in love with my partner like I can't breathe without knowing that he loves me back, I suppose that's what I got.

Have you started to forget about me yet? Because I think of you less now. The weekends are still hard but my regular daily life is mostly free of you. Dating is still overwhelming or maybe I am overwhelmed and therefore, date. I am constantly in a state of existential crisis about dying alone. It's like I have to find someone to fill the space you left or I'll wake up one day with 12 cats.

I have to go phone a friend to remind me why I shouldn't call you right now. I hope you're thinking of me too.

Love,
Grace

▲

The COVID-19 global pandemic began demanding the attention of everyone, whatever political orientation they held. The polarizing fighting that had defined the Trump administration reached proportions that were threatening to alter the everyday American life in a way that no other political term had ever accomplished before. It highlighted feelings and fears that we all harbored in secret and manages out of sheer grit, causing our carefully constructed coping scaffoldings to crumple. For those that were already struggling in my office weekly, it underscored the work we were doing with deeper urgency.

I waited for it to pass. Everything is temporary I reminded myself and everyone else.

▲

Dear Hank,   Mar 26

Last night Kerri told me something that's stuck in my brain this morning. When I started this job, you told me you were good friends with my co-worker Katie and her husband. I have been trying to get this collective group of counselors to come over for a backyard BBQ since I started working here and no one would ever respond to my messages or invites. I felt so lonely, and assumed that, just like everyone else I'd met in this town (mostly your friends) they just didn't like me.

Last night it was like someone turned the light on in another dark room curtained in your lies. It wasn't me. It was you. Katie knew who you were and she didn't want to come over because she didn't want to be around you.

I'm so embarrassed and so relieved. Katie never said anything about you until after the little-wedding-that-couldn't. Kerri told her that it had been cancelled and Katie asked her if I was OK. Finally Katie volunteered the secret she had been holding onto for years since we first met. She told Kerri that she'd known all along how volatile you were and that being with you would be a "full time job." All the times I felt like she was avoiding me in the office, they were because she didn't want to have anything to do with you.

Over the last few years, you have made me feel like the isolation and rejection I was experiencing was because I was defective in some way: annoying, offensive, rude, too loud, too abrasive, talked too much or any number of other critiques you gave so helpfully. Now I am discovering that I people pulled away from me because of you, and the potential friends I might have made were bridges you already burnt.

Maybe that means that I never was those things. Maybe, I wasn't too loud, or too abrasive. Maybe you were. You were rude and careless with people and I lost connections by choosing to be connected with you. It was terrifying and isolating. I have been so ashamed and lonely. I have let you convince me that I am unlikable and uninteresting, that I'm overwhelming and offensive. Maybe all of these things were just your projections, a way to off load your own shame about all the bridges you have burnt along the way.

I wish I could forget you,
Grace

▲

The pandemic gifts me the space to reflect. Alone on my couch I can't avoid my grief and anger. I can't bury myself in work and activities. I also can't critique my atrophied social life, because we are all isolated together and separately.

This space and time allows me to think about the friends I used to have and the feedback I have received over the years about my social presence. I reflect on both the compliments and critiques. I am old enough to be familiar with both my gifts and failings. Through their eyes, I have learned enough to recognize what is true and what is projection and over the last few years I had lost sight of these things.

I had allowed the constant criticism to shake what I know to be true over decades of similar stories form people that love me. I fell prey to your lies about my social presence due to the isolation from other voices and your projection.

Despite this, the loneliness creeps in at the end of the month bringing with it a slide back into familiar grief.

▲

Dear Hank,   Mar 30

No one watches me get dressed in the mornings anymore. I stand in front of the mirror in the bathroom diffusing my hair and no one sits on the end of the bed to watch. You used to come in from the kitchen when I walked from the shower to the bedroom just to watch me standing in the bedroom naked. You would grab me and throw me onto the bed and I'd push you off saying I was going to be late for work, like a cheesy RomCom. Now I get dressed and put on my make-up, blow-dry my hair, and pick out my clothes, completely un-harassed.

I have a weird relationship with being pretty. I didn't know for most of my life that I was pretty. When I did feel attractive it was a mixed emotion. Women's bodies are so taboo in the culture I grew up in. Wanting to be pretty was vain, and actually being beautiful was worse, because that would mean that you were a danger to the men around you. I can count on one hand the number of times my father has complimented my appearance, and there are countless more examples of being shamed for wearing the wrong bathing suit or dress.

I knew that my mother was beautiful and I watched the way men treated her because of it. I often wondered if that was why my dad hated my beauty, because of hers. I know that I reminded him of her. He told me when that I was 25, and still didn't know the power of my own body.

Sometime after I began to realize I was beautiful, I had so much fun. I dated and flirted and slept with so many men. I finally felt free from the taboos of my conservative upbringing. After a while it started to become scary how easy it was to find someone to take home. It started to scare me because I didn't care about them, and it was hard to believe that they cared about me. I started to be afraid that I would never be truly seen.

I used to tell you that I didn't believe that you were really in love with me, that I thought you were just infatuated with me, the same way all those other men had been. Other men I had been with would try to get me to be a better behaved, less outspoken, and more socially acceptable version of myself. They wanted me to be quiet and gracious and to keep my outlandish thoughts to myself, but I developed this personality long before anyone was looking at me. I tried to soften it now that people look, but it won't seem to dislodge.

You are similar in so many ways. You were happy to ruffle feathers in your own abrasive way, but were very upset when I did. When people asked you "why her?" You would tell them it was because I was the most beautiful woman you had ever seen, but this never made me very happy. I loved the way you looked at me when we were alone, but I wanted you to answer with something more substantive. I wanted you to love my soul. I wanted you to see me as all the best things that I am.

I think that you did eventually come to love these things about me.
You would sometimes tell me that you believed that I was helping you
become a better person, more kind. I think there were things in me that
you wanted to love because you knew they were good, but they were so
terrifying to you that you hated me for them instead. It scared me when
you called me your moral compass and told me I was changing you for
the better. It was too much pressure and I didn't want to be on a pedestal
any more than I wanted to be objectified.

I think you really wanted to love me the way I wanted to be loved and
I stayed longer than I should have in hopes of that love, the classic
"potential" excuse. I knew that somewhere buried under your alcoholism
and anger was the same softness and kindness that lived in me, it was just
shamed out of you by toxic masculinity. I wanted so badly to set it free. I
think you really did too.

You once told me that you were excited to have a daughter with me,
because you wanted your girls to be strong like I was strong. I held that
hope in my heart to keep me afloat in the sea of fears that I had about you
raising my children.

Now when I go on dates and men tell me they like my hair or my eyes or
my tattoos, I have even more complicated feelings. I feel anxious and like
I need to make sure not to get too close in case they make a pass at me
before I'm ready. I distrust these compliments like they are the root of all
the objectification that has ever happened in the world.

Dad used to tell me that the only men in the world with my best interest
in mind are himself and grandpa, and all the rest of them just want to
get laid. I wish I could say that I have found this to be untrue. Maybe it's
confirmation bias, but that seems to be a prophecy of my experience. You
would make any promise I required if it meant you could keep me.

Maybe you did love me in your own tormented way. It breaks my heart to
think of you that way. Loving me and losing me.

Love,
Grace

Dear Hank,   Apr 4

I went for a motorcycle ride today and realized that I left my helmet
at your house. It's a nice, expensive, modular one. So, unblocked your
number and called you. You answered the phone immediately to
my surprise. We only spoke for 3 minutes and you were shockingly
reasonable. You said you would leave everything on the front porch for
me in the next day or so. I really appreciated it.

You asked about the money for the car and I tried to avoid the discussion,
but you said you would not fight with me about it. So, I told you I would
not pay you anything anymore. You didn't argue but I heard the veiled
rage underneath the tone change to curtness.

You wanted me to know that you would probably need another surgery
and that you would not be at home tonight. I felt myself slipping into old
patterns of concern and jealousy and make grounding attempts to notice
the manipulation, but they still work.

I start to wonder who you've moved on with so quickly. I wonder if
you met her while we were together. I know you want me to wonder. I
know you're hoping I'll ask, so you can tell me it's none of my business,
but know that I still care. I know that you want me to worry about your
surgery, because you want a mother more than you want a partner.

The feelings that come up seem more like habit than truth now. They
don't mean anything. They're just chemical repetition. I feel like I miss
you, but I don't want you anymore. I wish things were different, but
they're not. I lost myself and became something I despised. I believe you
did too.

I just want my body to forget the fear and the struggle. I don't want to be
afraid to run into you at a bar downtown, but I still am. I always loved

you when you were reasonable. You just weren't that way very often.

Be well,
Grace

▲

I spent the next few weeks unraveling and trying to pick up the pieces, struggling to remember where I lost my grip. I was hungover and falling apart under the weight of my relapse. It took weeks to organize what had led to that phone call and to understand how far I had fallen. I needed several sessions to find my way back to the path. I was so frightened that I could not even approach Hank's memory in my mind.

▲

Dear Kim,   Apr 17

I'm writing to you this week instead of Hank because I still can't think of what I would say to him or if I want to say anything at all. Somehow it seems unsafe to approach him even inside my own mind. It's been more than two weeks and I still feel the frenetic urge to run away as fast as I can. Things escalated so quickly inside my tired, reactive little brain. I suppose that everything in hindsight is laughable. The way I freaked out. The ways I tried to keep myself from feeling the panic and pain. The drinking, the guy, the new motorcycle. I can laugh about it all in your office, but I know it's not funny. I know that I'm lucky I didn't hurt anyone or myself.

I still feel a little fuzzy about what happened. Like it's all still happening to someone else. As if this is the story of someone else's life. I suppose it started with that client that I swear transformed into Hank in my office right in front of me. I noticed that he had some similar thinking errors and entitlement when I first took him on, but I had always been able to manage, to compartmentalize and remain professionally objective. I thought I had it under control. I talked to you and to Kerri about it. I consulted and received affirmation that I had handled it with proficiency, but the moment haunted my personal life.

When he got angry at me and stormed out of my office, I felt confused. I was surprised and had a hard time keeping hold of reality for the rest of the day. I wanted to be the attentive therapist with the rest of my clients as usual, but he kept popping back into my mind and interrupting my thoughts. I was frightened, but I didn't know why.

That must have been the night that I unraveled. When I went home that night, Rob was having a group happy hour and I joined. I worked my way through a whole bottle of wine, but at bed time, I knew I wouldn't sleep. So, I called that guy, the easiest and most toxic one, the one I was so proud of myself for turning down.

I drove to his town, drunk, late at night. I snuck out like a high school student avoiding their parent's watchful eye. I didn't want to hear Rob's opinions. I didn't want to be judged for my obviously bad choices. He had been drinking too and after we had disappointing sex, I drove home again at 2AM, frustrated and even more alone.

Rob said nothing the next morning or later that afternoon when I went back again. We had better sex the next day and I stayed for a moto ride and that's when I remembered Hank. I remembered the motorcycle gear I had left in his garage. The nice new helmet I had bought before Costa Rica and how I'd been missing my own motorcycle since I got home last July. So, I called him.

I asked for the things from the list I'd been compiling. Things that I had not called him about because they were not significant enough, but the moto gear tipped the scale. I was surprised when he answered the phone. He was working and we didn't talk long. He was cordial and easy. He said he'd put it all on the porch for me and that he knew I had blocked his number. I told him I would unblock him so he could let me know when he was ready. When the conversation ended, I texted something from the list that I had forgotten. That's when he reverted, accusing me of communicating with this friends and family and withholding the money I owe him, telling me he would not be home.

As usual, he couldn't stay away. He will have any of my attention, even if it's bad attention. I don't blame him. I want his attention too. I keep replaying scenes of our summers together and wishing we had another chance. He called the next morning to specify which helmet was mine. He said he'd put it on the porch that evening, but that evening came and went. The next morning, I woke up in a panic attack. I texted him and picked up the gear before I had showered or eaten, because I knew I couldn't function until it was over.

Then I reached out to you. You set aside some time to talk with me that afternoon. I had been crying all morning and continued to cry the rest of the day. You helped me see how triggered I had been all weekend. You pointed out that the relationship I had with this client would have to end for both our sakes because it got too close. I called a few friends and asked them to remind me, if ever I needed something from Hank again, that nothing could possibly be worth this experience.

I bought my motorcycle back from the guy who bought it from me before Costa Rica and then I made another mistake. I asked Mike, if he would mind servicing it for me from time to time. Six hours later Hank sent me a nasty text about leaving his friends alone and what a piece of shit I am for not paying him for the car when I obviously have the money. I re-blocked his number, kicking myself for not having done it before. I was surprised that Mike had told him. Mike had always been able to see Hank as he was and his girlfriend, Leena, was the first person to point out to me that Hank was abusive. Hank hated her. I guess I'm still surprised by how much more important loyalty is than truth to those people.

I went back to that guy's house on Monday night. I just needed someone to hold me and be kind. He did and I felt better. I am so hurt and have so far to go before I can move past this. I want it to be over so that I can move on with my life. I have goals and dreams that didn't die at that wedding and I am still charging ahead like they don't have to be altered. It seems like it's all that I can do. It's the only thing I have control over. I can only keep limping down the trail hoping to find that the future I'm holding onto is still a possibility.

I'm so scared and so sad.

Thank you, for making time for me on Monday, I'm afraid this is still far from over.

Grace

▲

Dear Universe,   Apr 19

I still can't write to Hank. I feel like I've said all the things over and over again and there is nothing left to say.

"I miss you."
"I hate you"
"I love you"
"I was wrong."
"You were wrong."

Maybe I'm still afraid. I can't reach out for him anymore. It's too frightening. Until now, I think I've kept the illusion alive that if I had a weak moment, I could still have him back. That was accurate the last time I saw him, but after that exchange, I can see that any love he had for me has been replaced with hatred and I'm afraid of him. It was always a precarious line anyway.

I don't know if it's right or wrong, but when I want to reach for him now, I reach for someone else. I've been seeing that guy off and on since that first terrible weekend. I haven't been a very good date to him. Last weekend he said to me, "You need to stop pretending that you know exactly how this is going to work out." I was surprised by his insight and direct feedback, but he was right. I am looking for the ways that every man will eventually fail me, because the grief of losing Hank, the pain of misunderstanding, and the fear of his wrath is so overwhelming. I fly out of control so quickly that it frightens me. I'm so afraid to feel this way and what I do when it becomes too much. I don't want to be alone, but it still seems preferable to the way that I felt around Hank.

Thank you for listening,
Grace

▲

The month of April brings beautiful sunny spring days punctuated by fear and loneliness. My grip on myself feels tenuous and I still don't know how far I am from relapse. I am overwhelmed and lost in a global pandemic alone. I spend weekends sunbathing on the sunny law and roll over to find tears on my face that I didn't know had accumulated.

As my 34th birthday approaches I feel the urgency of all my dreams pressing in on me. I am trying to hide the train-wreck of my internal reality from everyone, unsuccessfully. I laugh and make jokes as a secondary defense, but I can read the concern on the faces of the people that love me.

▲

Dear Hank,   Apr 21

I can't decide which is worse in this situation, if you actually forgot my birthday or if you doing this regardless of it. Either way, you're the biggest ass on the planet. You know that, right?

I thought you might reach out today. It crossed my mind last night. It's so like you to be mean and ruin things that you know matter to me. I am so angry with you. How could you? And why, again, am I surprised?

I am actually physically nauseous when I interact with you now. I responded to your contact just so that it would be over and I could go back to having a lovely day. Otherwise, I would have felt sick until it was over. I should have blocked you again after the moto equipment exchange.

Do you remember our first Christmas together? You acted like it wasn't important to you and then ruined all our plans. Or that first New Years,

you were so high you picked a fight with a random girl at the bar and
we had to leave so you got into it with her boyfriend? Anytime we had a
house party, you would storm out and get angry about having people over
right beforehand. The stories of you ruining special moments are endless.

You have ruined my holidays, left me in bars and foreign countries, and
humiliated me in front of my friends and family. From our first Christmas
together to the Little Wedding that Couldn't, you have been creating
drama and destroying moments that could have been our anchors in
stormy times. Even now after I've blocked your number, you find ways to
interrupt my special moments.

Today when I pulled up in front of your house you laughed and said, "I
don't know why you're so angry. I told you it could wait for another day."
Gaslighting me as usual. It's so inconceivable that your unwelcome text
on my birthday about your car title would be upsetting. Further proof
that you have no soul or empathy in you.

"You make me sick, Hank." I spat back.

Of all of the angry things I wanted to shout at you about forgetting my
birthday or interrupting the silence I had requested, never caring about
what mattered to me, all I choked out was, "You make me sick."

You can still get at me.

I Hate You,
Grace

▲

Dear Hank,   Apr 22

It's 3:15 in the morning and I woke up thinking of that Conga line we
started in Bocas del Toro, Panama. The worst part about hating you, is
that I don't hate you at all. I miss you terribly. That is why you have to
leave me alone.

For every terrifying moment in our relationship, there is an equally magical one. The memories that we made together are moments that I don't get to remake with someone else. Experiences I'll never share with my next partner: the Gloria Estaphan song in Selinas of Bocas del Toro and the conga line, jumping naked off that dock at the end of the evening; dancing at Havana Club in Cartagena, Columbia while trying to avoid being abducted by a prostitute as a third; watching the neighboring peak spew lava for hours from the top of Acatenangua in Guatemala, remembering with the locals the eruption that killed 300 people the year before; the Cooper Spur summit of Mount Hood and making new friends who went on to climb several other peaks with me. These are things I can't get back from you. I can't have these experiences with someone else for the first time. The grief of it still wakes me up in the middle of the night and shakes my body with sobs that feel like they might shatter my ribcage.

I want to go back to Havana Club and hold you in my arms again. I want to re-meet the woman dancing on the boat from Ecuador, or hear Pat Za play in Cafe No Se again for the first time. I want to see you smile at me and for that moment feel like everything is alright, that we're doing it right, just like your dad said.

But that will never happen again. I will never hold you again. I will never mix you another secret airplane cocktail, or toss my legs across your lap in those cramped seats. You will never drag me out of another night club wet, half naked, and laughing. We will never drive across another border, or board another plane together. The days of traveling the world with you as my partner are over and we can't have those moments back.

Somehow, I thought these memories would go on forever. I thought I had found my person. The person I would start and end all my adventures with forever. I thought that coming home and getting married and having a baby was just the next wild thing we would do, but there will be no more wild nights with you.

It's early and if I go back to sleep now, there's a chance that I could still be an acceptable human tomorrow at work. Maybe I'll dream of warm tropical nights and the sounds of Latin music and your laughter.

I still love you,
Grace

▲

Dear Hank,   Apr 23

There was no one in the world that I wanted more than you, no other
lips I wanted to kiss. No other body that I wanted to touch. No other
person I wanted to talk to. I was 100% into you. Meanwhile you are still
pretending you can't remember my birthday and concocting ways to hurt
me, when I only ever wanted to love you.

Whenever I hurt you, and I know that I did, at least I can claim that
it was on accident. Common ignorance from a common woman. Your
entitlement taught you to strike back harder than you were hit. All the
times you pulled me close just to push me away again. Well, you won.
You pushed hard enough eventually to send me away forever and now
we've both lost.

This is why we failed. This is also why we can't be friends now, because
when you are hurting, you hurt back intentionally. You are a dangerous
man even without the gun, careless with the people that try to love you.

Love,
Grace

▲

The hurt and anger that surfaced with the birthday betrayal reminded me
of the harsh ways that Hank lashed out when he was sad. It reminded me,
while I was drowning in confusion, of why I had left.

Maybe for that reason it was good for me. My anger revived at the lack of
kindness he held in his heart. It screamed out at me that the line of human
decency cannot be taken for granted in any person, even one espousing
love. There was something twisted justifications for personal gains and if I
had forgotten when I missed him, I was now reminded.

This man is justified in his cruelty and could give you a thousand reasons why each time.

My anger dried up any remnants of grief and returned me, feet on solid ground, back to the road of healing and focusing on myself.

THEN SPRING BROKE

April 2020

I had been living in this little tin can for about six months when I met you. The winter of 2016 was one of the coldest with the most recorded snow of the last 30 years. I had been frozen into, and out of, my little Airstream home on numerous occasions. Sometimes I had to kick the door open because the seal around the edges had frozen, shutting me in like a refrigerator door. One time I had to crawl out of the window above the sink because despite my kicking I couldn't get the door open. I would come home from work and smack the sides of the trailer with a broomstick to get the ice layer on top to shluff off the sides, allowing it to thaw from the inside out.

That winter was a long dark night of the soul. It taught me things about myself that I don't think I could have learned otherwise. It taught me the ways that I am strong and the ways that I am not. It taught me about the things that I am good at and the ones that I am not. It also taught me what I wanted and what I did not.

When we began dating, winter was thawing. Green shoots were springing up out of the ground and the trees had edges of brighter green. My dad had come to fix the plumbing in my little shelter so that I could move off grid and into the woods. I, too, was thawing from that long winter, with hopes of a glorious, simple life summer.

I loved my little tin can, airstream life. It taught me to have courage and know my limitations, but now it is such a tremendous relief to think of selling it.

I had been trying to make this life work for years. I tried to make it work even though it did not suit me. I tried to make it work with you, too. We dressed it up in the backyard and rented it as a cute alternate hotel option. We stored it when we could no longer do that, keeping it as back-up plan in case we came home from Costa Rica before the renters' lease was up. We had even used it as our honeymoon suite at The Little Wedding that Couldn't.

The Airstream, as well as a great teacher, has been a burden to me for many years. I have tried to sell it numerous times only to change my mind because I wasn't ready to let it go. A few months ago, when I left you, it became obvious that it was time. I have been waiting for spring when trailers are in demand to begin marking the price down periodically in order to increase interest. It is now April and I need this burden gone. I can no longer afford it in numerous ways.

So many people have asked about it, but no one has come to look, until today. I am holding my breath that I will see it towed away from me for the last time. This precious time capsule of a season in my life that needs to end. A refrigerator door closing on a long cold chapter for the last time.

▲

As I begin to pack out the storage items that litter the floor of my former tiny home, I am transported back to a time where we spent sunny mornings buried under mounds of down blankets, snuggled up together, because even in summer, it was chilly in our mountains at night. Your smooth skin was warm and soft, and I traced my fingers across your back giving you goose bumps. I ran my fingers through your silky, wavy brown hair, kept long at my request. I loved your body like it was my own, cared for it like it was mine, gave it all the gentleness and tenderness that I had.

Eventually we would wonder outside to sunbath under the clear summer

sky while experimenting with the perfect Bloody Mary recipe. We would
let the dogs run wild in the woods, forever chasing chipmunks to their
hearts' content. The wild dirty beasts had no restraints and grew to resent
their leashes when we returned to town. We all learned to resent our
leashed lives in different ways. You were the sun to my moon in this tiny
silver palace.

While I can taste the dreams of summers past, I know that letting go,
is more than just an act of releasing an inconvenient item that I must
remove from my list of responsibilities. This is letting go of those dreams.
I had retained it for years in hope of the wedding suite it would become
for us, but that dream is gone now too. I glance across the paintings I
lovingly brushed across various surfaces in the airstream. The beautiful
memories that bubble up in context of this sacred place threaten my
resolve to be rid of it. They threaten to overshadow the wise choices that
I pulled from my shattered sense of self and drive me back into your arms
in hopes of finding these moments again.

I kept these memories from my mind because recalling them is more
dangerous to me than any other thought. Sometimes it takes great effort.
Other times I fail and fall into the despair of regret. I shake my head to
clear them now, and continue with my packing.

▲

As I see the large truck pull in, carrying the couple who is eager to view
my vintage treasure, I have only a tattered hope in my pocket. They go
through and test the electricity and then the water system. I have had so
much trouble with the plumbing in this trailer, that I am afraid of what
we might find.

Sure enough, I stand by helplessly by and watch as all of my fears become
reality yet again. The plumbing explodes in a wave of water and I am now
certain that I will be stuck with this burden forever. My fragile hope falls
to the floor and lands in the puddle under my feet.

They ask for some time to think over their purchase and go to find coffee before they head back over the mountain. They have driven all this way to be as disappointed as I am in this moment. I pack up the rest of my things from the inside of the airstream and take them home pondering with resentment what I will do to sell this thing that was once so precious and has become such a curse.

I pull into my driveway certain that I will never hear from them again and begin to unload my boxes onto the shelves where I am store the very few items that I still own. I left behind most everything with you in our home, nine bins are all that I have now. I do not even own the sheets I sleep on at night. I have kept these nine bins in the airstream, but now that I hope to show it more regularly, I need a new storage solution. Rob cleaned some shelves for me in the garage to make space for my tote bins and I push them up on the shelves while I fight the tears of having lost this sale. I didn't realize until now just how burdened I feel by this giant antique liability.

As I lift the last box onto the shelf in front of me, I receive a message from the couple.

They'll take it!

I am startled and relieved. Jumping back in my car, I race back to the RV storage barely able to believe what is about to happen. There is an exchange of money, and a moment where I realize I have never held that much cash in my hands before, and then the signing of multiple papers. I help them hitch the airstream to their truck and I ask them to take one last picture of me standing next to the Airstream Dream that I have to let die in order to be free.

It is the end of a chapter; my chapter in this tin can, and my chapter with you. As they drive away, I feel hot tears stinging my eyes, and a weight falling from my chest. It lands more delicately, like a feather, when it comes to rest and a vapor of joy seems to take its place. I feel like I can breathe again.

It was not possible for me to know before this moment how much this item wearied me. It was as if it were a little chain on my ankle, so delicate

at first, but so heavy in the end. When I look back at what it has meant
to me, I find my own incompetence staring back at me from that chapter.
Since the moment I towed it back and made it my home, I have felt more
incompetent than ever before. It turned me into the damsel in distress
that I never wanted to become.

As I watch it pulling away, I become deeply conscious of the ways that
it drove me to seek a savior. One that I found in you. I am relieved at my
freedom, but at the same time heartbroken that I did this to you, to me,
and to us. I can't help but wonder if I had lived in a different place, if I
had needed you less, would we have been different together?

For the first time since I left you, I can breathe lighter. My chest feels
less constricted and I feel in control of my own tiny reality. I don't need
someone to help me fix this anymore. I have all that I need within myself.
This day marks another layer of the slow unfurling of my stiff and sore
soul. I realize that perhaps I created the very thing I hated in us. You
needed someone to dominate and I needed someone to take responsibility
for the things in my life that made me feel incompetent. We created the
perfect storm, made to sink one another.

▲

Dear Hank,   Apr 25

I wanted to call you yesterday to tell you that I sold the airstream. I cried
while I watched them drive away, tears of sorrow and relief. Sorrow
because it means this chapter has closed. The chapter that started before I
even met you and opened the door for our toxic relationship.

When I bought the airstream almost three and half years ago, I felt so lost.
I had just turned thirty and there were so many things I hadn't done that
I wanted. I wanted to live nomadically, I wanted to live abroad, I wanted
the minimalist, tiny house, lifestyle. I tried on so many things in those
three and half years only to find myself disappointed and unhappy. None
of them suited me.

I have learned so much in that time about what I want and what I need.
I met you and tried you on too. I tried to think the way you thought and
live the way you lived and it made me unhappy too.

I have never been a fast learner or content to learn from everyone else's
mistakes, so I charge ahead to find out for myself. I can't say that it is the
best way to go about self-discovery, but it is my way. At least, no one can
say that I did not live.

Seeing the airstream roll away and thinking of all the beautiful wild
moments we shared inside it, all the tears and frustrations we had because
of it, all the lessons that it brought me, made me miss you. It also feels
like a burden has been lifted. This chapter between us has really closed.
Seeing it roll away felt final. I am one large step closer to letting you go,
to letting our life together go. I may even have caught a glimpse of what it
looks like to start the next chapter, which has been so covered in fog and
uncertainty. I'm still not sure what is coming, but yesterday for the first
time, underneath the grief, I felt excitement.

Love,
Grace

▲

Dear Hank,   Apr 28

I keep opening my laptop to write to you and then closing it again. I'm
finding that I just don't really have anything to say. I'm not distracting
myself either. Something feels different. I haven't thought about you not
because I'm thinking about someone else, but because I'm thinking about
me. I'm thinking about the mountains I want to climb and the trails I
want to walk.

I'm thinking about how I want to invest that money from the sale. I'm
thinking about my 2 and 5 year life goals. I called my bank and made an
appointment with their financial advisor. The Airstream sale showed me
that there are other areas where I need to begin to take responsibility.
Other places in my life that I didn't want to understand, places where I

thought it would be easier to depend on someone else than to learn how to manage them myself. I can see how I created my own chaos; this is where I gave up my power in exchange for something I thought would be easier. I did it because I was scared, but I am not afraid now.

I also deleted my Tinder profile. The frantic feelings of loneliness that drove me to begin dating shortly after leaving are evaporating into a desire to focus on caring for my own fractured heart.

I have spent a lot of time reflecting on my powerlessness and how this came from my desire to avoid responsibility. I can say it now, without shame, owning the things I hope to avoid in the future, taking power back from my own learned helplessness.

I do not have anything new to say to you. I am not having conversations with you in my head as I drive to work. I do not miss you right now. I no longer think of you when I think about my life. I do not want to call you or see you. I went to drop off something I found in the airstream on your porch, hoping you wouldn't be there. You rushed out to meet me, but I felt fine afterwards. What would have been a week-long spiral last month, doesn't seem to hurt at all today.

It's scary to trust this new grounded sense of calm. I know that emotions can be fickle and I am sure that I will have bad days again, but I feel different this time, less frantic, less caged, more hopeful and empowered.

I don't really understand why selling the airstream did that for me, but God, it feels good to be OK.

Love,
Grace

May 2020

Dear Hank,   May 3

I was having a conversation with a friend yesterday about us. He asked me if I had been reflecting on the ways that I had been seeking dependence. I was surprised by his question. It's taboo to ask an abuse victim how they have created their own chaos and if he had asked me a month ago, I could not have answered him.

Abuse is such an ugly cycle. It takes so long to recover from it, and even when you do, sometimes it's so damaging to our souls that we still can't look at the ways we subjugate ourselves and call into our lives someone who will enact this cycle with us. I know that I called you to my life.

I have often reflected on what is wrong with me that I would tolerate, accept, and even co-create the chaotic, ugly kind of love that we had. I am not blind to my contributions, but the shame is so deep that some healing had to happen before I could say them out loud.

I was so small when we met. I was so scared; afraid of my future, afraid to be alone, afraid of the choices that I had made. I felt incompetent about the Airstream, about my finances and I wasn't practicing my career.

I love my job. It's a deep part of my identity. I felt lost while I was taking a break and that incompetence seeped into all the other parts of my life. I didn't trust my choices or my abilities. That's when I went looking for you. I was looking for someone who could do those things for me.

I wanted someone who would mow the lawn, balance the finances, and fix the airstream so that I didn't have to learn to do it. I was willing to accept all of the other things if it meant that I didn't have to learn these things that felt so foreign to me. I would cook and clean and nurture and manage emotions in classic feminine fashion, if it just meant that I did not have to face those fears. The patriarchal model was familiar and secure and I was willing to sacrifice my freedom in the same manner as my grandmothers had been forced to do before me.

I'm sorry. I am sorry that I could not own that pattern before I loved you.
Maybe if I had, I could have loved you better. I am sorry that when you
wanted me to be strong I couldn't. That was unfair of me and I know I
tilted the scales in a way that contributed to our headlong fall into the
co-dependent spiral that killed us. I know it's not all my fault, but I also
know it's not all yours.
Love,
Grace

▲

Dear Hank,   May 9

You're in my dreams again, every night recently. I wake up in the middle
of the night, remember the plot and think, "That's poignant. I should
remember it in the morning." But then I can't. I grasp for the meaning,
but can't reach it in the recesses of my mind. I only remember that it
starts with holding you and ends with chaos.

I was talking with my therapist last week about us and how good I feel
these days, she wanted me to scan through my mind and notice any
place in our story where I still felt distressed. The only feeling I had
when I thought about our story was sadness, particularly when I thought
about the gun. At that time, I was holding onto the notion that we
could split up; You would work on you, I would work on me; and then
maybe we'd give it another go, as our better selves. The moment that
you walked up to that gate with a revolver in your pocket, you made an
irrevocable decision. No one in my life will ever forgive you. You carved
an impassable gulf between you and all the people that I love and I can
never be with you without losing all of them. You finally did something
that no one would ever be able to forgive.

What makes it so sad to me, is that I don't think you knew you were
making that choice. You were so drunk and angry. You weren't thinking
that you were sabotaging the very thing you wanted: to be with me.
There were so many times in our relationship that you did this in small
ways, but that was the big one. The rips in the fabric of us that you made
by accident were frequent, dramatic, and unconscious.

This is why we can't be together. I have to remind myself. Even though
the ache is duller and I think of you less. I still need to remember that if I
called you up for coffee it would not be benign. I can't ever see the tulips
that I planted in the backyard bloom, because it would be a long slide
back into chaos starting with my hope.
Love,
Grace

▲

Dear Hank,   May 17

Every morning while I'm slowly waking up, I daydream of you coming
back to me in a year or so. In my fantasy, you've gone to therapy or AA
and are on step 9, where you have to make amends. Sometimes you
hand me a letter, sometimes we run into each other at a bar, but every
time, you're sorry. You understand, and you've gotten better. This is still
my dream. That we can be together one day when you are no longer an
addict.

I shared this with Michael, because he always says the truth when I need
to hear it, even if it hurts. The truth is that this is not reality. In some
other world, where other choices were made, maybe this could have
been the way it happened. But I live in THIS reality; and in THIS world,
you did NOT choose to get better. You did NOT choose to get help.
You may have stopped drinking, but only to become a dry drunk, just as
manipulative and self-deceived as ever. The world that I day dream about
is not real. That is not the path that we have taken and I have to let it go. I
have to let you go.

Because of these dreams, I have been thinking of contacting you. I miss
you again. I also wonder if seeing you and remembering what it feels
like to be around you might be good for my resolve. It might help me
remember that being near you does not feel good. On the other hand, it
would be hard to see if you had begun to change. So, now I am practicing
the AA mantra, "one day at time" and each night that I lay down to sleep
and I haven't called you seems like one inch closer to the end of this grief.

Good night,
Grace

▲

May came and went quietly, without incident. Despite the periodic
danger of relapse, a strange and steady calm settled into my grief process.
It is something that seems fragile and I am always afraid that I will wake
up one morning to find it gone again, but I so desperately need this
reprieve that I lean into it anyway.

I rest into the coming months by preparing to build a life that is uniquely
mine. I begin to look for housing where I can live alone. I want to
decorate and create a space that feels like mine again.

I am surprised when I find something affordable almost instantly and am
grateful to Rob again for his flexibility with our living arrangements.

SUMMER RETURNED TO ME

June 2020

Dear Hank,   Jun 7

I moved last weekend into my own place on the west-side. The Black
Lives Matter movement has taken over the northwest. The whole world
seems to have lost its mind between global pandemics and racism. I want
to call you, because I still expect that you might comfort me. That is what
partners do right? They hold each other while the sky falls down and it
really seems like the sky is falling right now.

I dreamt about you again last night. In my dream we were somewhere
tropical and I had a friend. You were out somewhere and she told me
where you were, exposing the lie you told. I was surprised but tired of
the lies, so I told you I was leaving. I told you without hysterics or a scene
that I was booking a flight home for the next day. Then I told my new
friend. She and I cried together and said our goodbyes. Then I looked
around to kiss you goodbye and couldn't find you. After looking for some
time, I found you on the beach drinking.

It's hard to tell if this is a dream or a memory, it's so similar to all the times
I tried to leave while we were in Costa Rica.

I love you and I miss you, but I don't miss the lies. So, I'll keep dreaming in my new life, alone.

Love,
Grace

▲

Dear Hank,   Jun 12

Today makes six months since I left you. Yesterday was hard. My body
remembers, even when my mind doesn't notice the date. I wrote this
poem.

The thing that you loved has died.
You can pick it up,
And dance with the corpse,
But that will only leave you smelling,
And covered in rotten flesh.

Or you can bury it in the ground,
And hold only your desperate heart.

Someday there may come someone
New to dance with
Someone with life and sweet breath.

Can you tolerate your empty arms
Long enough to receive?

I still miss you,
Grace

▲

Dear Hank,   Jun 17

It's finally summer! We've all been waiting through the gloomy, overcast spring to see these bright sunny days again. I'm glad I spent the first three weekends of June moving, because it has given me a project. It wasn't even until last weekend that I started to feel restless, like I need to get out into the wilderness again. So, I planned a climbing trip for the weekend and I'm looking forward to it.

This move has consumed all my free time lately. Creating a unique and lovely space is so cathartic to me. It might seem silly to some, but I feels like I am creating a private work of art, designed solely to help me and anyone else who crosses my threshold to relax and feel warm. Until It's completed, I am more than a little obsessive.

It made me remember when I moved in with you. God what a nightmare that was. That whole stupid argument with Bo about the spice rack and how you punished and shamed me for it. I should have known at that time that you weren't ready for the kind of compromise that a relationship requires.

I bought a spice rack for my kitchen this week and painted it teal. I don't even have enough spices to fill it, but I refuse to line the countertop with them. There is something therapeutic about creating this space where there is no one to criticize or punish me for it.

Grace

▲

As I worked hard to create a special place for myself, a place that could be my own home. So many memories of living with you came back to me. From the arguments we had about putting nails in the walls, to the arguments we had about how to relate to roommates.

As I hang each item on the wall with satisfaction, I am thinking about the various adventures from which they were collected. I order more art from my favorite artist in Baja, Mexico and have them framed. I paint everything with bright colors to mimic the things that I miss about Latin America. Part of me starts to yearn for it again, in a way I cannot yet place. Something is stirring in me, longing for new adventures.

▲

Dear Hank,   Jun 25

Thursdays are the worst. I work late on Thursdays, and I see seven clients
instead of my usual six. Today I also spent my lunch break at my new part
time job of giving psych evals to potential hires for the first responders
departments in town. That includes deputies, corrections offices, and
anyone in law enforcement. I am really enjoying that work.

Tonight, I am tired and lonely though. A prime time for my demons to
come haunt me.

I don't really miss you. I just feel lonely. I was trying to recall what I
missed about spending an evening like this with you and honestly, there is
nothing. I would want to come home and snuggle in your arms to remind
me that everything in the world is going to be ok, but you weren't very
comforting and that usually ended in disappointment or an argument.
So, I know that I don't really miss you, I simply miss the idea of being
partnered and the expectation of being comforted.

This is how I feel most of the time now. I miss laughing at partnership
woes with other women, relating over silly household dramas. I miss the
idea that you might be there for me in dark times, but you weren't really.
So, it's not you I miss, but the hope.

You were like a cancer in my life. You had to be cut out or you would
have sucked all the life from me. Despite this knowledge, I still miss the
pound of flesh that was taken out during the surgery. I still get phantom
pains where that tissue used to be and have grief for the change in my
body. I suppose life with parts missing is better than slowly dying, but I
don't really know. I have never had cancer.

Goodnight,
Grace

▲

Dear Hank,   Jun 30

My therapist says that saying "I'm fine" is the same as saying "fuck you."
So, I've started saying, "I'm pretty ok." It gets truer every week.

Sometimes when I'm super lonely it's hard to choke out, but even in those
moments, when I think back to six months ago, or even nine when I was
still in your house, I know it's true. I am pretty OK right now.

Maybe that's all recovery is, hoping you'll be ok, wanting to be ok,
pretending to be ok, until you eventually wake up one day to find that
you really are pretty OK.

Love,
Grace

July 2020

Dear Hank,   Jul 5

I have been losing weight.

It started from my butt
Little bubble of joy
You loved to squeeze when
No one was looking
My best asset
We had joked

Then it was from my breasts

"More than a handful
Is a waste"
My mother used to say.
"Not quite a handful"
You quipped
But that didn't stop you from
Holding them while we fell asleep
Each night

Then from my waist
Which had grown to resemble
Thick with curves
To match the voluptuousness of the land
In that tropical nightmare
That picked apart my skin and
Left us both bleeding
Large red droplets that
Never seemed to dry
In the suffocating humidity

From my head
In handfuls of hair
In the shower
Where my thick curls
Were reduced to
Lifeless drapes over
Scalp and bone
Becoming light again
In the arid desert of
My freedom

From my heart
Where I carried the weight of you
And thousands of your choices
And mine
To stay
Instead of going
To let it slide instead of

fighting

And then from my mind
That has grown quiet
And allowed sleep to return
With its stillness in
The darkness
That used to hold
Only fear

From my face finally
I noticed this last
Where my smile had faded
Into something somber and
Tired
A little softness has returned
Around my eyes

▲

Dear Hank,   Jul 12

Last night I dreamt about your dad. He was returning some things of
mine that he had been using. We were both sad.

Your dad was a horrible enabler, but he was kind and I think we would
have made good in-laws. When we didn't get married, he still called later
that month to discuss the changes to your will. He wanted to ensure that I
would inherent all your property but none of your debt in the event that
something happened to you. He wanted me to have your house while he
inherited your mortgage. What a generous and thoughtful way to handle
your assets.

I told you not to change anything, because I still wasn't sure I could stay
after that event, but I recall being surprised at his kindness towards me
after all he had seen. He was always kind to me, until the end.

I loved your family. You told me once that your sister had never liked any of your girlfriends before me, but she and I laughed and talked and even seemed like friends. I miss her too.

You really were a beautiful man, warm brown eyes, mischievous smile that reveled perfect teeth, thick wavy brown hair. I called you baby face because you could only grow a small amount of stubble around your goatee. You had a perfect set of strong broad shoulders and smooth skin that bronzed in the tropical sunshine. You were tall enough that your long arms could wrap around me twice.

These dreams are hard because my anger at the bad times and the injustice of your alcoholism are what keep me motivated to stay away from you. These memories draw me back. I might continue to miss these things until I find something beautiful with someone new.

Love,
Grace

▲

Dear Hank,   Jul 24

I dreamt about you again last night. I was with your mother and our child. I was waiting for your plane to land and you to arrive. I was anxious, because you were late. I was pacing and upset. When you arrived, you apologized and said you had met someone new.

You had met her on the flight and talked the whole way. She was smart and beautiful and easier than me. You told this to your mother while I sat in the room, instead of saying it directly to me. She encouraged you to choose her despite me sitting there with our baby. "Don't you think you've worked hard enough?" She said. I was too much work, we weren't the right fit, you deserved to be happy with someone who was better for you, she encouraged.

I was devastated. "I have been waiting for you for hours!" I shouted, "For years!" I cried and ran out into the rain.

Grace

▲

Dear Hank,Jul 29

This morning I woke up with an enormous cold sore on my face. I cancelled my morning appointments because it's so huge and hideous.

I made a decision on Monday to meet with an old acquaintance from Costa Rica. Back in February when she first moved to town, I knew you and I were the only people that she knew here, and I assumed that she had come here on your invitation and moved into your house, our house. I blocked her on social media and deleted her number and hoped that I would never see her. I felt the old jealousy rise inside me in ways that I didn't want to remember. Why had you been so close to her that month while I was gone? What kind of relationship did you two really have? I still want to believe that you never cheated on me, but with all the other lies, it's really impossible to know for certain.

Last month, I ran into her at my usual Monday happy hour and she greeted me in a way that quieted my suspicions of cheating. She wanted to get together, but I was still apprehensive in other avenues. I know she must still be in contact with you and I don't trust that whatever I tell her won't find its way back to your ears.

The next week I saw her again, and my mind began to gnaw on itself. Chewing. Wondering. How are you? Who do you spend your time with? Are you sober? So, this week I asked for her new number and we began to plan to get together.

Kerri came over last night and I told her exactly how it will go. "She will ask me what happened between you and I and I will tell her I'm hesitant to talk for fear of gossip. She will say she doesn't have much contact with you because you are isolating from everyone. She will tell me how you helped her move here, but she doesn't live with you anymore or even see you around." I recited knowingly.

"Then, I will tell her about the wedding and the gun. She will be shocked and concerned. She'll probably tell me some snippets of how you tell the story differently. Then, I will tell her it was good to catch up but we won't need to get together again. She'll know this too despite us both promising to stay in touch."

She'll go back and tell you what I said but you won't be able to send me hate mail because I blocked your number again. I will cry for a few days, but my mind will be able to rest again because nothing will have changed.

Kerri responds, wondering if it safe for me to go. "Will you be OK?" She asks me with concern and a little bit of painful understanding in her face. I know it's foolish, but there still some questions that need answers.

Like a dog returning to its vomit, I prepare to play out the scenario but this revolution feels slightly less destabilizing. I tell Michael over the phone that I feel far enough along on my journey to feel the hurt and continue on my path of recovery. I am convincing myself and readying my support team for the aftermath.

I am sad for you. I am sad that you have pulled apart your dreams with your own hands, shredding everything that you loved, left alone with this truth. Your friends tell you things that you can almost believe while sitting around their fires, but when you walk up next to the creek alone with only your rod and your thoughts, you know the truth and it weighs heavy in your heart, pulling at your soul. It brings me no joy to know that you are just smart enough to know and just cowardly enough to continue to run from it.

This morning, I began to think about September. It's getting so close and I still haven't visited our desert again. I know that I need to go back to that place. I have been afraid to go, unsure if I should go alone. Today, I know the answer to at least this question for myself. I set the date: September 21st. I'll stand on that desert and remember everything. Letting it wash over me like the wind. I'll spend the night with a fire, burning away everything left of us, staring at the sky.

I might even reach out to you with one final letter, the last letter I ever write to you, one I can finally send. Maybe, you'll be glad to hear from me and we'll exchange longing sentiments and kind words, agreeing never to speak again; or maybe you'll yell at me and tell me how you hate me. You were never someone I could predict.

I love you,
Grace

▲

Dear Hank,   Jul 30

I did it. I met her yesterday and it went almost exactly as I had expected, except one thing. I did not feel sad afterwards. I felt angry. It wasn't the rage monster that used to well up inside threatening to destroy everything within arm's reach, but it was there, the familiar angst at your lies.

She told me that she moved to town and lived on your couch for two months until you were annoyed enough to finally tell her she needed to find her own place. I imagined you feeling frustrated and being unable to be assertive, I witnessed this countless times before.

She told me that she doesn't talk with you anymore, but that she had dated a guy in Portland who didn't trust your relationship with her. She told me that he broke up with her because he was worried that you wanted to sleep with her, but that she always viewed you as a brother. I know why she needed to tell me this. It's as if she knew that I wondered about you together. Sadly, her reassurances did nothing to soothe me. If anything, they validated my concerns that there was always some sexual tension. I would be offended, except that this pattern is all too familiar: your need to maintain the attention of any woman as a potential partner, even if you did not reciprocate her feelings for you.

She told me that you omitted all the parts of our story that explained why I left and claimed victim like ignorance about my leaving. You were still in love with me and just couldn't understand why I would leave you. She said that she could tell there were parts missing, because your stories just didn't line up. She had suspected that there was more than what you were saying.

I want to call you more than ever, not to soothe you, but to start up the old arguments. I want to call and calmly explain to you exactly why I left, to remind you of what you already know and lurks in the recesses of your mind. You work so hard to keep it there, in denial, to avoid responsibility. It makes me sick.

But I better. I know that in order to preserve your denial, voices would escalate in desperation. Mine raising in pitch to convince you and yours in volume, fighting to keep your ignorance. It would no longer matter if you believe it, because you to keep this circular dance winding and wrapping in the endless rises and falls of chaos. It is the only way to keep my attention anymore.

This is how you hook me, with feigned innocence and martyrdom. I know the games you play to hide the truth from yourself and I will not give in to the temptation and crazymaking of trying to convince you otherwise. You haunt me in my dreams and the depth of your self-deceit has driven me mad on days that seem not long enough ago.

Other men who hear these stories have trivialized these tiny lies, saying that we were not a good fit because your behaviors so similar to their own. They can see the tactics they used themselves with their own lovers, too fragile to admit the ways that they harmed them to protect their egos. It is easier to dismiss me than it is to wrestle with their demons, the demons they recognize in you.

Why is it that men use this tool to convince women that what they know they are seeing is not real? I have chased this idea through my career and through literature. I have heard stories and validated hundreds of women wrestling with their own sense of crazy when they know what they see and cannot continue to deny it despite the denials of a culture around them.

And still, I am here, with the impulse to pick up the phone and ask you to make amends for the three years that you stole from my life and to give me back the hope that you can be an honest man. In the end that is the knife that cuts the deepest, all of the lies; the years of questioning my own perception because it was more painful to identify your dishonesty than it was to lose myself.

I am still fighting to be free of you. I love you and I hate you and I don't know if I will ever be free.

Love,
Grace

▲

In the end, I am glad, I saw her. I did not fall apart again, even if my body revealed my stress with a cold-sore. I felt the anger of the thousands of gas-lit women I have worked with throughout the years. I felt the rage of years of misrepresentation and bullying, but I did not call you. I did not seek you out and I did not buy the lie that you could ever be anything but exactly what you had shown yourself to be time and time again.

And so, another month of summer came and went. I climbed mountains and backpacked deep into the woods. I slept in tents and cabins and chased my longing for freedom all over the pacific wonderland. I had more moments of happiness in this one month than I had in the last 7 months since leaving you.

I continue to unfold and own this new chapter, building friendships, and creating community.

August 2020

Dear Hank,   Aug 4

It finally happened. I finally ran into you somewhere unexpected. I have been trying to prepare myself for this moment since I left. In such a small

town it was inevitable, but never did I imagine this would be the place.
This place is mine. It's too classy for you. Every time I walked into a dive
bar, I would steal myself for the possibility that you might be standing
there. I often avoided these places, saying you had won them in the
divorce, but this place was mine.

You walked out of the building past my patio table after we had already
been there for 2 hours. I could not breathe. I was not ready for the
wave of nausea, thinking that you might have seen me that whole time.
I grabbed Gary's arm in a panic, unable to bring my breathing back to
normal.

I don't know the girls who were with you. One petite blonde, and another
couple. I didn't know you had started seeing someone else. I had not
asked, because I know I am not ready to hear the answer. Seeing it now
feels like my insides got rearranged. I want to vomit and then sleep away
the last three years. I feel sick.

I want to contact you with such a force that I am still not sure I can beat
the impulse. The only reason I haven't already is because I can't think
of anything to say. If I ask you to let me have that place, you won't. Or
maybe you will, but you'll know I'm a regular. If I ask you about her, then
you'll know I still love you, and I don't want to be vulnerable to you. I
want to say something that will hurt you, but that isn't who I am either.

Silence has always been the most productive reaction, but it feels like
giving in to the stuckness of this feeling and I want to vomit it out, or
scream it out, anything to get it out of my body.

I'm actually just devastated. Do you still think of me? Do you still miss
me? Are you as tormented as I am about what happened between us or
have you been able to set it all aside while I spent the last year unhooking
the barbs from my soul? When will I ever be rid of you?

Grace

▲

The happy hour is ended abruptly after I see you. I can't breathe or calm down. I ask the waiter for my check quickly and despite the soothing statements of my four companions, I leave as quickly as I can.

I know that the pretty blonde is your girl. You weren't touching her or sitting close to her, but I could tell by your cold indifference and the way she leaned towards you with openness, that in the privacy of your house, she is yours, but in public you still use shame to distance yourself from her. The scene is frighteningly familiar and the nausea is overwhelming as I process these thoughts.

I flee the restaurant with a panic and am disappointed to find that for all my progress, I am still not done with this.

Dear Hank,   Aug 5- 2 AM

The impulse to wipe your memory from my mind woke me up at 2AM. I started going through our photos with the intention of deleting your face from all of my memories from the last three years but failed because I began by working backwards.

One look at the wedding photos and I deflated like a sad balloon after the party. So, I turned from that to this letter. I hoped I would find something to say, but we both know there is nothing to say. No more begging, no more crying, no more convincing or cajoling. You have made your choices and I have made mine.

The humiliating story is drawing to a close. I can feel it coming like a last piece of shrapnel removed by magnet, ripping its way out my body.

Hank,   Aug 5- noon

There is no reason why I should be surprised at anything. No reason that a new girlfriend should unseat me. If you couldn't go without adoration for a week while we were together, why would I believe that you would go for almost a year after I was gone? I know that the presence of a new partner does not have any bearing on me. It does not mean that you did not love me or that I did not matter. I know that my feelings about it are just pain. They have already done their job and I have already responded to them. They are just talking now because that is what they are used to doing.

I have so much shame about them. I am so ashamed that I still feel this way from time to time. Less intense and with less frequency, but still lingering. I feel this urgency to defend them with "but I loved him". Then I recall your words. "No one gives a fuck about your feelings, Grace" and the urgency of these excuses fall flat.

The reasons that I let this go on for so long does not matter to anyone but me. No one else cares that the scab has been ripped open once more and is hemorrhaging. I am not special or unique. Thousands of women have felt these things before and all have made their choices and lived with those outcomes, just as I made a choice. I made the choice that you were not what I wanted anymore. The cost benefit analysis came up wanting. Our dreams were not worth the trouble anymore, so I left. The happiness was not worth the suffering. The scale tilted and I left.

I decided that my love for you did not matter before anyone else could say it. Walking around shouting it from day to day is only invalidating my choice to move away from you towards this new life I created, quiet and secure. It doesn't matter that I loved you to anyone but me.

Grace

▲

Dear Hank,   Aug 8

There's something personally violent about starving yourself. I have been
starving myself since I saw you. I do not struggle with eating disorders
typically, but since I was young, my appetite dies when I am anxious.
I often call it my anxiety diet and I spent many years consuming just
enough calories to function but not enough to nourish while in periods
of high stress. I never disliked my body or the way it looked, I just didn't
like food anymore. The same things is true now, I'm not hungry and food
makes me feel nauseous.

But this time, I hate myself too. I hate that I betrayed what I knew was
right for so many years and I don't know how to stop hating me. I hear
your voice in my head telling me that people do not like me, that I am not
funny, or I am too much. I hate that I still believe you.

My self-loathing feels so deeply in the pit of my stomach that I wish I
could vomit it out. I don't want to look at myself or touch my own skin. I
am disgusted with me.

▲

Dear Hank,   Aug 13

I am not OK since I saw you last week. I was able to hold it together for
the work week, but around Thursday I started to fall apart in the familiar
self-destructive ways. It was interesting to observe at first. I tried to map
the patterns and notice the feelings without letting them envelope me.

On Saturday, the despair won, and I spent the whole day in bed crying.
I lost two pounds last week from starving myself on the anxiety diet and
finally reached out to an acupuncturist. Yesterday, I started to feel normal
again.

The ferocity of my own self-loathing was frightening to me. I am so
angry at myself. I am so embarrassed. You did some truly terrible things,
but I was too weak to leave you. I was too scared, too disenfranchised,

and too hopeful. I hate myself for not walking away from you at the wedding, or before it, when you called me a cunt. It was a betrayal of myself, by myself, and I am still not sure how to forgive me. I have never hated myself so much for any other decision than to play into that farce between us. I know that the anxiety diet that makes me nauseous is a form of self-flagellation. I can punish my body by depriving it of the things it needs and I have been hating it so much that I wanted to punish it.

Today, I started eating again and the nausea has subsided. I try to remember how my body was slowly falling apart when I loved you. I finally had a solid shit and slept through last night. I look at my hair and eyelashes and notice their fullness. I look at my body and see how strong it's been growing again.

I try to remember how I had no resources after we moved to Costa Rica, and for a while after we came back. I try to remember how I wanted to leave, but couldn't because I didn't have the money and was so isolated from anyone who could help me. I try to remember that my treachery was grief and fear and that it is ok that I am human. I try not to cringe when I think about what others think of me. I try to block out the sound of your voice telling me the ways that everyone is judging me. In the end, you were the only one thinking those things.

It is strange and mind-bending to love someone who is destroying you. I have been contemplating sending you a letter on our wedding anniversary. It might take me a few tries to write that one or to understand what I am hoping to accomplish with it, but I think it is time to begin.

▲

Dear Hank,   Aug 21

It's your birthday, and even though the days are still hot and long they are starting to get shorter and cooler. The autumn breeze has started to blow and mess my curls into the wild jungle hair we used to know.

I thought about sending you a happy birthday message, but I can't quite decide why I would be sending it. I want you to know that I am still thinking about you, but is it out of spite? Or because part of me wants to know if you are still thinking about me? And what good would either of those things do for either of us?

I know that I don't get to decide to be done with grief. It is not linear, but I would like to decide that I am done being angry with you. I would like to be done punishing you, or demanding that you change. I would like to be ready to let go of this toxic thing that happened between us, to stop slinging blame, and to genuinely wish you well. I am not sure I can yet, but I do feel closer today than I did last week, or last month, or last year.

Would it hurt you to hear from me? Would it hurt me to hear back? Or to not hear back? It seems we can't do anything but injure one another. Maybe it's best to just continue in silence.

Happy birthday Hank.

Love,
Grace

▲

Dear Hank,   Aug 28

I woke up early this morning thinking of you. The thinking of you has lightened again. It's less heavy, less hollow, and does not ache. The cool evenings have had a cleansing effect. I have sold all the items that tie me down, just as I ran from the people who held me back. I can move freely, breath lightly, and dance again. I have walked into the woods and climbed mountains this summer. I have reacclimatized to the land that I belong to. The movement of my own free body has shaken my fear loose and now I am threatening to grow all the way back into the full woman that I was before we met. I can see her some days standing inside my eyes. She is waiting for me to be ready make space for her inside my skin again. She has been so patient.

I know I am not done. I don't believe we are ever done with our grief. We build on it and it becomes part of the knotted and sturdy tree of our soul, strengthening us against the next storm.

I thought I had been broken, but I am only just becoming.

FALL BRINGS ALL THINGS TO REST

September 2020

Dear Hank,   Sept 1

In yoga yesterday, I was practicing shoulder stands. After the first set, at my request, the instructor suggested pressing the backs of my thighs and butt into the wall to push my chest towards the center of the room. This would create a chest opener while upside down. As I contorted my body into the shape of an upside-down question mark, I reflected on how easy it is for me to assume these back-bending positions while forward folds are always so challenging.

I heard my mother's voice echoing in the recesses of my mind, "You have to stop bending over backwards to accommodate everyone else at the expense of yourself, Grace." I thought of how hard you used to kiss me and how my body would assume this same position in order to make room for the ferocity of your affection. I thought about how I would often seek a wall or something hard to hold my head in place to avoid the discomfort that came from this contortion. It was how I knew that you loved me despite your inability to be kind to me. Anyone who kisses you like that must love you.

I reflected on the years of my life that I have spent in this position both figuratively and physically. I recalled all the boundaries that I never set. How it would have been easier to have left you the night you came knocking on the Airstream door, rather than waiting to be publicly humiliated last September. I recalled folding over backwards from my knees onto the ground after leading my first therapy group in a circle with my peers at university. The position melted away the stress of the moments before.

Bending and bending and bending, until there was no further to go. I was already on the ground, pressed into a contorted version of myself, flat against the floor, bearing little resemblance to the woman that walks upright.

I have written you a letter, one final letter. I plan to visit the playa on the 21st and send it to you from that place.

Love,
Grace

▲

I'm sitting at my favorite patio downtown on a Wednesday afternoon with Nellie and a fresh squeezed greyhound. I am reading a book and enjoying the end of the season's warm weather, watching the leaves slowly change from green to brown. There are two middle school aged students playing violin poorly on the street corner next to me and I am eating the same fried green beans and I smile at the same waitress that I see here each week. I am enjoying a new book, and reflecting on my book club meeting last night.

How did I get so lucky? Lucky enough to have a beautiful life, in a beautiful place, with beautiful friends, and a full heart. If someone had told me a year ago, that today I would feel this full, I would have laughed in their face and then cried for the hope of it.

It's been a long, hard year; a dark night of the soul. Darkness so thick that I could not see my own hands outstretched in front of me. The darkness seeped into my cracks and separated me from myself. Finding my way back was a long painful process while losing me seemed so easy and happened so fast.

Last March I got a small tattoo on the ring finger of my left hand. To remind me that when I lay my head down on my pillow at night, the only person I cannot escape from is myself. So, I had better like the landscape inside my own mind. To remind me that I am married to myself, first and foremost. When I got the tattoo, it was reminder, a reach for hope. A way to draw me back from the paths that I knew I would wander in my grief. I was so far from myself that I had to actively grope in the dark towards the something that I knew was there.

Today, I need to see it less. I need fewer reminders to check in with my body, to breathe, to stay grounded in my values. I can laugh and remember that I'm funny and deserve to be treated with kindness and respect. I've made new friends and learned so many things. I am calmer, more kind, and have more capacity for all the tiny inconveniences of everyday life and the people around me. I am not perfect, but I am back inside my own skin again.

On Tuesday evening at my regular monthly book club meeting, I announce that I am leaving for Mexico in two weeks and ask the girls to set up the next month's meeting without me.

"We can't have book club without you! You're our founder!" They insist and I'm flattered.

"What're you doing in Mexico for a month anyway?" They ask.

"I'm planning to finish that book I've been writing this last year." I reply. They're all familiar with the book I've been working on, saying one day we'll make it a book club reading. I don't know if I could allow that, but I'm honored that they'd be interested.

"Did you finally figure out the ending?"

"Hmmm, I'm still not entirely sure. Maybe it's just this." I respond. "Being pretty ok after all of it."

"I thought it would be you falling in love again, with a partner who treats you well." Jess says.

"I thought it would end with a baby!" Kylie chimes in.

"Haha. Sorry to disappoint gals, but I think it just ends like this, knowing that I'll be alright. That I have my life back and I'm ok."

We all chuckle and they continue to debate the various preferable endings to my story. I wonder if any of them will eventually come true. I know that either way I will be just fine, because I have me again.

RETURNING TO THE SCENE

September 2020

I have never been so far out in the ocean that I cannot see the land, but I imagine that it would feel similar to this place. There is so much open space here that despite miles and miles of empty Playa people instinctively seem to clump together. It is as if being in this place highlights our existential crisis and causes us to need to be close to one another so we don't feel so alone in the world. Even though that is what we came her to do, be alone.

I understand this need. As my wheels hit the playa and I began to drive as far and as fast as I can to get away from civilization, I also feel the subtle quickening of my heart and shortening of my breath that makes me wonder, "how far away do I really want to go?"

I went further than the others, marking the edge of what could be seen, but as evening rolls in so do other campers. They quietly arrive and set up in places that are not quite far enough away from me and I understanding the feeling that causes them to stop so close to me here at the edge of all things.

Today I came here to be alone. I came here to remember.

I build a small fire and begin burning the photos of us that used to hang

on our walls, photos of our adventures because my therapist suggested
I burn something. Photo paper is interesting to watch while it burns.
The chemical film on the front melts like plastic and bubbles in strange
constellations before the paper turns black and finally to ash. I see your
face melt away before the paper turns to dust.

I brought the last drops of the toasting mezcal we bought from our
wedding, remembering the well wishes that were written and sealed in a
box hand made by one of your friends. I wonder if you've broken it open
yet and enjoyed that bottle of tequila. I drink the mexcal straight from the
bottle. It burns my mouth and throat and I am hopeful that it will bring
you to me in my dreams tonight. I let myself miss your baby face and your
warm arms. There are so many things I would give up to have you again,
just not myself. This is the last time I will let myself miss you, the last time
I will nurture this longing. It is time to say goodbye.

▲

One year ago, today I stood in this spot in a bathrobe and sun hat with
last-night's red lipstick still on my mouth. Your arm was draped over my
shoulders and you had yet to discover that we were not married. A gift I
would get to share with you the next day.

We waved goodbye to our guests and I looked around at the shattered
remnants of my dreams. They littered the playa like confetti after a party
and we had just had a very expensive playa kegger. That's what your dad
called it.

My heart was broken, and it wasn't done breaking. For the next month,
I would cry every Tuesday morning. I would wake up unable to console
myself, weeping and wondering if there would be anyway to undo what
had been done here. The answer was no. There would be no way back
from this place to where we had previously been.

Now it feels right to be here. I am not sure what I thought would happen,
what I thought I would feel, or what I thought I would find, but I know
that I need to be standing here today, remembering.

In this state, I send you the last letter I will ever write to you.

▲

Dear Hank,

I am standing on the desert. I'm not sure what I expected to find here: explanation, apology, closure?

One year ago today, our lives together ended, but you didn't know it yet. Somehow Calen failed to mention to you that he had called off the wedding. Something I was not brave enough to do myself and he was not brave enough to tell you.

But I am not writing this now to rehash old wounds. I know that would be useless because it's over for us. There is nothing that you could do that would amend you to my friends and family and I am sure that yours feel the same way about me. Two warring tribes that could never see across the aisle.

I am not sure if I should send this to you or not, but despite my agonizing about it, it feels symbolic and necessary. Maybe I am just looking for closure to a chapter that will never quite make sense to either one of us.

There are memories that I have with you that I can't create with someone else. There are things that I shared with you that I will never have back in order to give to someone else. And when I look back on us, it wasn't all bad. There were beautiful moments in the mountains together, when it was just us two with no one else around to have an opinion. Mornings before you started drinking that were kind and loving. I think about the way that you would walk into a room and it felt like there were no other men on the planet. I still feel pulled to you like a magnet. It was these moments that I held in my heart during all the ugly times. These were the things that kept me from leaving for so long.

I wish you could have trusted me to dance in Latin America. I wish you could have loved the ways that I was unique in the world instead of trying to get me to behave the way you thought I should. Most of all I wish that you had been able to control your drinking. All the jealousy, anger, and anxiety that you kept inside was so much worse when you were drunk. I wish I had seen it earlier and we could have gotten help before it was too late to salvage us.

I am also so very sorry. I am so sorry that I lost my way. I am sorry I yelled and cried, not just because it made me look crazy to everyone around you, but also because it was not the kindness that I wanted to give you. I got so lost in my anger and fear that I stopped asking you to change with a compassionate heart. I wish you could have heard my pleas before I was "hysterical" and I am sorry that I went that far to get you to notice. I should have left you before it escalated and got ugly. It would have been better for both of us. I am sorry that I clung so tightly to you that we both drowned. Maybe we each would have been able to swim if I had just let go earlier. I loved you so much it was hard to imagine a life without you.

I guess I just wanted to tell you that I will always love you and that I forgive you. I so badly wanted to be the kind of woman that would draw you towards your better self. He was the man that I loved: the generous lover, the wise environmentalist, the thoughtful pursuer of knowledge, a man with depth. Mostly, I just hope that you get better and can be happy, because I love you and I only ever wanted to be good for you.

Goodbye,
Grace

EPILOGUE

I bought a plane ticket to Mexico, in anticipation of the desert anniversary. I have a friend near Cancun and that's a part of Mexico we missed on our wild adventure. I planned to board the plan the day after visiting the desert, because despite feeling OK these days, I am unsure what I might feel when I go back there.

When I land in Mexico, I smell the spices in air and feel the heat and moisture on my skin. I hear the sounds of the language we lived in and I am reminded of us. My mind has the tendency to romanticize the things that are past. I rationalize that this makes me happier in the present, but I am also aware that it clouds my ability to stick to the hard choices I need to make.

Now I am transported to Howler monkey wake up calls and you making me breakfast tacos. I am not thinking of the nights where you didn't come home and I had to drive to Rum Bar in my bathrobe to find you, high and indifferent to my tears. Those memories come back more slowly and with effort. I have been using this effort to ground myself to keep me from going back to you for some time now, so the motion of grasping for it is familiar and practiced. I shake my head to scatter the thoughts.

I'm not sure what I plan to do here, other than write. After my week of vacation, I'll have to work also, but how will I pass my evening hours? I know my friends are not always available, so I will need to find something to occupy myself. I am still a little afraid of my own loneliness.

I meet my friends for ceviche because I have been craving it since I purchased this plane ticket. Such a funny dish to explain, cold fish in lime juice with salt, onion, and bell peppers, eaten with tortilla chips. It sounds awful but might it be my favorite Latin American food. After we eat our fill, they are tired. They head back to their homes, but I am not ready yet. I am antsy and lost in my own mind. I feel the pull to explore, again, searching for something that I don't know that I need, a distraction, to move. I'm not sure, but I need to go.

I walk down the main avenue of restaurantes y vendadores, Latin men calling to me in my language and their own, inviting me into their shops. I smile coyly and keep walking, finally halting outside a place where everyone is dancing. I linger in the walkway, my eyes fixed on the dancers. They are smiling and their movement reminds me of something I used to know in my own body, something I can't quite recall. I envy their freedom, and a culture where everyone grows up learning to move, a place where women's bodies are worshiped for the art that they are in all their forms. This world is so different from my own stiffness that slowly knit itself into my bones in the years since you.

The restaurant manager calls to me from the host stand, "Quiere Bailar?"

"Oh no gracias. No se como!" I call back.

Quickly he grabs one of his waiters and instructs him to give me an impromptu salsa lesson. We are laughing at me, with my two left feet, stumbling over one another. I feel my smile widen until it becomes my whole face. When the song ends, I reach to gather my things from the table where the waiter had set them. There are three of the most beautiful women I have ever seen sitting there. They see the longing in my eyes as I glance back at the rest of the dancers and ask me to stay in Spanish. After 5 minutes of conversation, when I reach the end of my vocabulary, one says, "Wait are you an American? So are we!"

We dance all night, me and these strangers. None of us can stay in a seat, and I don't find my way home around 1AM. I have danced with almost every man in the room, all generous with instructions as I fumble my way through the steps and the Spanish. The woman at the table let me know who not to dance with, when one of them becomes to direct with his attentions. Everyone is inviting and warm, and most of all patient. I am mesmerized by them; their casual movements, their sexy confidence.

▲

Three weeks later, I am nearing the end of my planned trip. I have spent every night learning to dance. I remembered that I have hips that I once loved to move and the dancers are generous with their compliments. So, I learn to accept them while laughing.

I have met lovers and friends here. They are all shocked at how much I have improved with my Salsa and Bachata steps. I practice 4 hours a night until my feet are so sore that I spend the days elevating them in order to be able to dance again when night comes. I have lost myself and found myself on this dance floor and I feel beautiful again.

So, I decide to stay and my new adventure begins.